About the

Brian Thomas-Peter is Canadian but came to live in the UK as a teenager. Although he majored in economics at university, he trained as a clinical psychologist. As a young psychologist, he worked with children in care, adults with mental health difficulties and the families of elderly mentally infirm. In 1982, he joined a high-security forensic psychiatry service, where he completed a PhD.

Helping those with damaging backgrounds and mental disorders became his life's work. He trained others in Australia and the UK, provided expert psychological evidence in major criminal trials, and advised parole boards and inquiries. Subsequently, he was invited to advise internationally on how institutions care for mentally disordered offenders and on caring for those with severe personality disorders.

He has held many honorary academic posts, including three international fellowships and an 11-year tenure as Professor of Psychology at Birmingham University. He moved to Oxford as Director of the Regional Forensic Psychiatry service, before returning to Canada in 2010 as Provincial Executive Director of Forensic Psychiatry for British Columbia. Later, he turned his attention to education again, as dean of a faculty of human services.

He currently lives on an island on the west coast of Canada, runs a small consultancy and spends most of his time writing.

THE LAST TRUTH

THE LAST TRUTH

BRIAN THOMAS-PETER

This edition first published in 2016

Unbound

6th Floor Mutual House, 70 Conduit Street, London W1S 2GF

www.unbound.com

ISBN (eBook): 978-1-78352-974-2

ISBN (Paperback): 978-1-911586-23-4

Design by Mark Ecob

Cover photographs:
© iStockphoto.com / Juanmonino
© iStockphoto.com / princessdlaf
© iStockphoto.com / Mlenny
© Shutterstock.com / Milan M
© Shutterstock.com / pokki77

This book was produced using Pressbooks.com, and PDF rendering was done by PrinceXML.

For Kate

Dear Reader,

The book you are holding came about in a rather different way to most others. It was funded directly by readers through a new website: Unbound.

Unbound is the creation of three writers. We started the company because we believed there had to be a better deal for both writers and readers. On the Unbound website, authors share the ideas for the books they want to write directly with readers. If enough of you support the book by pledging for it in advance, we produce a beautifully bound special subscribers' edition and distribute a regular edition and e-book wherever books are sold, in shops and online.

This new way of publishing is actually a very old idea (Samuel Johnson funded his dictionary this way). We're just using the internet to build each writer a network of patrons. Here, at the back of this book, you'll find the names of all the people who made it happen.

Publishing in this way means readers are no longer just passive consumers of the books they buy, and authors are free to write the books they really want. They get a much fairer return too – half the profits their books generate, rather than a tiny percentage of the cover price.

If you're not yet a subscriber, we hope that you'll want to join our publishing revolution and have your name listed in one of our books in the future. To get you started, here is a £5 discount on your first pledge. Just visit unbound.com, make your pledge and type TLTRUTH in the promo code box when you check out.

Thank you for your support,

Dan, Justin and John
Founders, Unbound

Super Patrons

Carla Alexander
Nick Baldwin
Rebecca & Jonny Bates
Angie Batham
Nick Berry
Peter Brook
Graham Butler
Grant Charles
Judy Christensen
Ellen Coburn
Kate Coffey
Mike Cormack
Andy Cottrill
Leonie Coxon
James Cutler
Lori d'Agincourt-Canning
Alexandra Da Cunha
Caroline Dobell
Dan Donnelly
Kevin Epps
Heather Fairs
Mike Fardon
James Feeney
Judith Gedye
Chris Gibson
Justinian Habner
Brean Hammond
Janette Hammond
Ruth Hammond
Donald Heth
John Higenbottam

Rona Higgins
Gina Hillis
Lekkie Hopkins
Carol Ireland
Jim Johnston
Dan Kieran
Jessica King
Judy Lawrence
Emilie Lemons
Osmaan Malik
Mary McMurran
Steve Minett
John Mitchinson
Adam Morton
Stephen Murgatroyd
Tina Nielsen
Kathleen OConnell
Allard Ockeloen
Jan & Femi Oyebode
Caroline Parker
Adrienne Plunkett
Justin Pollard
Clare Rees
Colleen Reid
Deirdre Ryan
George Scott-Welsh
Duncan Smith
Emily Smith Ewing
Victoria Smye
Patricia Swain
Gary Tennant
Chris & Sue Thomas-Peter
Nick Thomas-Peter
Kathryn Thomas-Peter
Malcolm Thomson

Jacki Walker
Hannah Walsh
Martin Willmott

With grateful thanks to Hannah Walsh

Contents

Book Three

Book One

Ending

This was justice, not the exhilarating slaughter he had practised until sweat sprayed from him. There was no thrill now, and there would be no catharsis to soothe him when it was over. Even so, it waited to be done. He pushed closer, leaning over her with the knife held low and behind him, as if to surprise her. With his free hand he pulled her upright by the hair. There was no resistance remaining and she fell back into the chair. Gravity took her as far from him as it could. It was not far enough to save her from the ending he intended.

Twenty-Two Years Earlier: Stepping Out

Jenny watched her mother from the shadow of the hallway outside the bathroom. She had dragged her duvet from her bedroom and secured her thumb in her mouth. Angela sipped from the glass of wine by the sink and began the ritual of make-up: moving forward, getting ever closer to the image of herself applying the detail, and then back to admire the full effect. Each forward motion brought with it a contortion of the face, arms held at angles and an instrument dabbing close to her eyes or a brush fluttering on her cheek. It was a lengthy process, which drew Jenny. She looked forward to the time when she could prepare herself this way. Final adjustments to her mother's hair would be next, then lipstick would be applied, and then the top layer of something tight and pretty.

Angela asked, *What are you doing up, Jenny? Shouldn't you be dreaming?* She turned to the mirror.

Where are you going? Jenny asked with her thumb still in her mouth.

I remember asking the same question of my mum. Her eyebrows lifted ready for the lids to be painted. *That was a long time ago.*

Did she wear make-up? asked Jenny.

No. It wasn't like that when I was your age, said Angela. Something desperate flickered in Angela's eyes. Jenny saw the discomfort of a sudden memory passing through her mother.

I'm going into town with a friend tonight. Maybe I'll find someone nice, to come and stay with us. We could be a family again. What do you think? Would you like that? Angela said.

Men had stayed in the house before, always with the promise of how much better it would be. Jenny understood how important it was to her mother. A sloppy thumb was removed long enough for Jenny to ask, *Are you going to find a new daddy for me?*

Angela reddened. *No, Jenny. It's not like that.* Her mother was looking in the mirror. The disappointment of being less beautiful than before was obvious.

Am I pretty too?

Angela looked at her daughter. *Very pretty. So much prettier than me.* They both smiled.

Can I have a story?

Go on now, said Angela. *Get back to your bed and I'll be there in a moment.* Jenny reached with the duvet and sticky thumb to be hugged away to bed, as was the custom. Angela bent down, craning her neck to avoid her make-up being wiped with the quilt or smudged with the thumb. Jenny turned and went off to her room, like the good little girl she wanted to be. It was always hard to sleep when her mum was unhappy.

The bright light in the bathroom was, Angela thought, unforgiving of motherhood and disparaging of her youth. It was getting harder to achieve what was needed for going out. She dragged the brush through her hair and thought she was still pretty, but not as she had been. Still young, but not like the carefree girls out at night. Something had been lost and her desperation was starting to show. She worried that a man would not take her as a partner with Jenny in tow. Angela reminded herself not to drink too much, or too quickly mould herself to some young man on the dance floor.

Her neck flushed scarlet with how pathetic it seemed and then she looked to snap off the stare of anyone watching. She was at home and there was no one, but she resented the judgement of her own thoughts. The lipstick twisted out; she pursed her lips and began to smear. Sex was such an effective means of inviting men into her life, and there might be one who would stay. *Why shouldn't I?* she muttered to her image through barely animated lips. Everyone had a weakness. For men, it was lust: the urgent, distressing need that preoccupied them from time to time and for which she could offer sordid diversion and panting tonic, just by tolerating what they wanted. It was simply bartering her body for companionship as women have always done. At least she was honest about it.

Angela looked at her watch. She might find time for another glass of wine before the babysitter arrived.

The two women giggled into the street from the taxi parked outside the club. The glass of wine at her friend's apartment had set the tone for the outing and now they emerged onto the evening stage ready to be players. Alcohol fuelled the guffawing and confident young men, walking past, eyeing the pair with cartoon interest. Angela and her friend slipped in front of them and walked past the doorman and into the pulsing noise emanating from down the stairs. The doormen stepped forward to stop the boys.

Pointing to the women, two young men protested, *We're with them.* Angela looked back and caught the eye of one. The doorman nodded and on they went. It had started.

Late into the evening loud music and thumping rhythm dominated their senses. The circling young men and sparkling women had settled on their luck, and those without moved off, up the stairs into the cool air and garish light of the town centre.

Angela's friend inserted her head between Angela and a young man and shouted. *Don't wait for me. I'll make my own way home.* The two women grinned at each other. Over her shoulder, a young man waited. *What time do you have to be back? Will you be okay?*

I've just been bought some vodka and… cranberry, Angela said, inspecting the red bottle. *I think I'll be fine.* Her grin conveyed the alcohol consumed and salacious intent. Her friend smiled back and bounced off.

It was quiet when she woke. In another room music played and people could be heard. She was sitting in a small room, leaning back, uncomfortable and stiff. Opening her eyes, Angela knew it was a toilet cubicle and felt an unpleasant surge of adrenaline at not knowing where it was or how she had arrived there. She wondered what she must look like and cursed herself for letting this happen; but there was nothing to do but take stock. Her clothes had been unsettled and everything was out of place: skirt up, underclothes twisted. From entering the club only fragments remained in memory. She could recall feeling hot and perspiring, and then feeling dizzy. Angela began adjusting her clothing back into position and remembered her friend leaving. She reached between her legs to ease a sudden discomfort, and then inspected the sticky moisture on her hand. She knew what it was and a sudden alarm rushed through her.

The babysitter came to mind. Angela looked at her watch and remembered Jenny would now be home alone. Jenny would be upstairs asleep. She recalled what a good girl she was. She would be okay. Angela stood on wobbly legs, quickly organising herself to get out of the cubicle.

Home

From her bedroom window at the front of the house, Jenny watched the street until a taxi arrived, and felt the disappointment of seeing it did not bring her mother home. Instead she heard the front door of the house open and close, and saw the babysitter walk into the dark street to the taxi before it drove off. It was not difficult to be home alone, but it was difficult to sleep. She worried about her mum being unhappy and somewhere else.

Finally a second taxi arrived, with her mother. Jenny listened to Angela coming in; the door closed, a tap ran, footsteps made their way up the stairs. The toilet flushed, her bedroom door opened wide enough for her mother to look in and then Angela opened her own bedroom door. Jenny waited long enough for her mother to undress and lie down before leaving her own bed. To arrive in her mother's bedroom when she was still up risked being brought back to a lonely bed. She waited until it was quiet before crossing the landing and getting into her mother's bed and snuggling in. Her mother smelled of something sweet, and of cigarettes, but she was home and warm. Jenny found the crevice between her mother's arm and bosom, and allowed sleep to come.

Jenny woke alone in her mother's bed. The sun was up. The house was still quiet save for the radio. It was Saturday and it meant there was no school or rush to get out of the house. Angela was down-stairs. It was not like her mother to be up so soon on Saturday. She wondered if her mother was all right, and then slipped out of bed to find her.

School

It was important to be good for her mum today. There was something wrong this morning and Jenny was anxious about her mother, and going to school. At the school gate, Jenny turned to her mother, who made the final checks of her kit and apparel, as did all the mums. She reached up for a hug and a kiss and turned to launch herself into the schoolyard. She walked quickly, with purpose, feeling her mother's gaze. Jenny was gradually being engulfed by children and noise. She offered her mum a final smile and wave, and allowed herself to be swallowed by the red-brick school building. Like all the other Victorian school buildings dotted around the city, this one had seen more than a hundred classes of new starters and endured countless modifications. Prefabricated grey classrooms squatted between school and playing field. Jenny watched Angela turn away and make her way towards the bus stop, and wondered how her mother would be when she got home.

The bus arrived and Angela heaved herself up the step, showed her card to the driver and sat heavily in the first available seat. The waistband of her jeans was becoming harder to close and she was feeling bloated. In fleeting and terrified moments, she knew the cause of the changing arch of her abdomen, but hoped that it was something else. At first she thought it was wind. A week later it might have been constipation, so she had filled her shopping bag with remedies from the chemist. Finally, as the pressure on her clothing became inescapable, she considered the possibility that she might have a tapeworm or even a tumour of some kind. In any case, her doctor was sure to help. She had phoned earlier to make an appointment, apologising for the one she had forgotten, and was grateful to the receptionist for fitting her in quickly.

The bus rumbled along. Angela felt her temperature rise. More and more people squeezed on. Getting off and going home was on her mind, but the crowd hemmed her in, overcoming the half-hearted commitment to changing her mind, and it was too late to forget the appointment.

Angela walked briskly to the door of her family doctor's surgery, a large detached house in a suburban street, indistinguishable from the other houses save for the brass plate by the door announcing that it was the surgery of Dr Burrows, Family Physician. She entered the hallway leading to the receptionist. Every step caused the floorboards to creak and moan. *I am sorry I missed my last appointment, but I'm here to see Dr Burrows. I usually see him.*

The receptionist hardly looked up from her desk. *Take a seat, please*, she said, pointing to the waiting area beside her, with four others sitting in it. Angela knew well where the waiting area was and scanned each of the occupants keenly. None of them looked to be in pain or to be struggling very much. Her sense of deserving established firmly in her mind, she sat on the nearest chair, feeling reasonably satisfied that she should be there, at least as deserving as them. There was silence and coughing, while she concerned herself with what they were thinking about her. Minutes passed. Several patients came and went, and gradually Angela relaxed enough to believe no one was minding her business very much.

The receptionist spoke. *Angela, would you like to go through now?* Angela leapt up. With a raise of the eyebrows and tilt of the head the receptionist directed her out of the waiting room back into the corridor. She knew where to go and set off down the hall to the doctor's consulting room on the left. Straight ahead, at the end of the corridor, the bathroom door was open. A wild-eyed woman stared at Angela from over the sink. It was a moment before she dismissed her own image and turned into the consulting room.

Angela sat down beside the doctor's desk. Dr Burrows smiled at her and said, *Hello, Angela. What can I do for you today?* Angela began talking to the doctor, knowing he would help her. All the possibilities tumbled out.

Angela fixed her gaze on Dr Burrows as intently as the doctor looked at her. Gradually, she could see that the doctor was no longer listening. It was what professional people sometimes did when they did not understand or did not want to hear an explanation. With his practised gaze, Dr Burrows maintained eye contact, but Angela knew that behind the eyes he was thinking, judging, and it was pointless speaking more with professionals when they got into that state of believing they knew everything before you told them.

Dr Burrows began, *Angela, I'm trying to make sense of this.* He smiled. *It isn't uncommon that a woman arrives here complaining of stomach problems, only to be told that they are pregnant. It does not happen very often when it has become obvious. I'm happy to do some tests and tick off all the other possibilities until we find out for certain, but I think you're likely to be pregnant. Do you think you could be pregnant?*

I can't be pregnant.

Dr Burrows waited a moment and started again: *Some people struggle to come to terms with it, but we can help.*

How can you help? Angela looked up.

Well, we can refer you to the local hospital for counselling or you could see the practice nurse here. Dr Burrows smiled again and looked at her carefully.

I can't wait.

All right. Just wait in the waiting room for now and I'll get the practice nurse to see you this morning, while you're here. I'll arrange for some tests to be done. The two walked out of the doctor's office. Angela returned to the waiting area and Dr Burrows crossed the corridor to speak to the practice nurse.

Angela waited, in turmoil, now oblivious to those around her. It was not possible for her to disentangle the feelings and thoughts that rushed past her, each pushed on by the one following. It was as if she was lost forever in a world of being endlessly responsible for others. Jenny was almost six years old now and it had been hard. She had been a lovely, smiling child who had loved her mother, but the burden had taken its toll. It had been lonely and difficult to establish friendships.

There was no one to help look after the house, the money, the shopping or Jenny. Angela had been to social workers and doctors and friends, but there was no help that she could rely on. It was always on her. Now, just as Jenny was starting school and Angela would get some relief in time and support, it was starting again. It was not even her fault that she was in this situation, but mostly she did not want the blame for all that would go wrong with the child and everything she did as a parent and mother.

She tried to imagine having a different life and finding a partner, but her prospects became entangled in the implications of a new child. It might be possible, Angela thought, to establish a relationship before telling them that she had children, by which time they might be willing to stay with her. A series of agitated loops played around and around for the 30 minutes she waited for the practice nurse. When the nurse arrived, Angela was in a swirling mist of anxiety and despair. She would never find a partner.

Hello, said the nurse cheerfully. *I'm the practice nurse. Call me Jordan.* Angela looked up and saw the grinning woman, who was bulging and straining from every button and pocket. *Come in and sit down.* Angela was motioned in and directed to a plain wooden chair in an examination room that served all the nurse's practice needs, from taking blood to bereavement counselling and offering birth control advice. The nurse sat down, overwhelming a small chair. *Dr Burrows has asked me to speak with you. He said that you seemed upset when you spoke to him.* Angela was silent. Nurse Jordan opened a set of fresh case notes on the table beside them and became poised to record the conversation. *I know you're having some tests but we understand you're going to have a baby*, she said with a grin. Angela looked carefully at Nurse Jordan and realised she was without the first idea of the impact such a thing would have on her. *It can come as quite a shock, can't it?* There was a long silence. *Would you like to talk about it?*

Angela had been occupying an internal world of denial until encountering Dr Burrows; it was only that which held back the wild emotion, and since then the terror had not been manageable.

Suddenly the conversation with Nurse Jordan had captured her attention. She was like every professional Angela had ever met and contempt gurgled suddenly, converting the anxiety to anger in an instant. There was no other reason for her to be in the room than to talk about it, but just asking the question landed Angela with the problem. The responsibility was already being pushed onto her.

I want you to help me. I want you to take it away! I have to get rid of it.

Angela stared defiantly at Nurse Jordan.

Angela… Dr Burrows has told me that you're probably more than five months pregnant. I know we can't be sure because you're not sure of your dates, so we'll have to wait until the scan is done…

Angela knew the exact date on which she had become pregnant and could recall enough about the event to flush again with embarrassment without it being spoken. The criticism of her apparent uncertainty about dates was unbearable. It implied that she was randomly and frequently engaging in sex and had no idea which encounter had left her pregnant. Even if that was true, whose business was it other than hers?

Why do you need the dates? All I want is an abortion. That word thickened the air.

Well, Angela, said Nurse Jordan in a voice nearly whispering with classroom sincerity, *there may be a difficulty with that. Had you come to the doctor sooner, it might have been possible, but we think you're past the point of having a termination.*

There it was again. Angela was reeling with fear and now anger that she would not be helped. It was never their fault. All they needed to do was say it was not their fault and it became hers. It was always this way.

Nurse Jordan no longer mattered. She would not help. Hot, molten tears reddened her cheeks. Desperation rumbled in her chest. She squeezed her face with her fists, clamped her arms to her sides to prevent her chest from erupting and rocked back and forth.

Oh no, oh no, oh no. I can't have a baby. I can't have another baby. It's not my fault; it's not my fault. Just help me.

Six Years Later: Early Days

The summer heat made inside and out unbearable. Only one corner of the small English garden escaped burning sun in the afternoon. Angela sat in the shade, closing her eyes against the glare of the sky, and cast away the noise of her two children. Jenny listened to music on the radio and all over the garden Tad kicked a football. The hum of the traffic seemed far away.

Angela said, *Jenny, get me a drink, would you please? Thanks, darling. Some of that cordial with some ice would be nice.* She let her head fall back and fanned her neck with the local paper.

Why don't you play inside? Jenny said to her little brother.

You play inside! Tad was defiant.

Jenny stood and walked stiffly through the back door into the kitchen. She plucked a cherry candy from the paper bag on the windowsill. It was something to relish that Tad did not have. She loved being in the kitchen.

Cubes of ice from the white tray were tipped into the sink. Jenny held a pair in her fist and drew broad strokes on her forehead. She lifted a glass from the drainer and dropped the cubes into it, and did it again with a second glass. Elderflower cordial was lifted from the fridge. Each glass took a glug from the bottle. She turned the tap on over the sink, which chased the cubes to all four corners. The white tray, filled to the brim, was stowed away in the freezer. Each glass was swooped under the tap. Through the kitchen window she saw that Tad was no longer playing with the ball, but had taken her seat in the shade and was holding the radio.

With a glass in each hand she stepped out into the garden, making her way towards Angela and Tad. Tad looked up and saw the drinks coming. Turning to his mother, he said, *Mum, can I have a drink?* She opened her eyes to see Jenny on the tightrope walking towards them.

You can have some of mine, said Angela. Tad's face crumpled. *I want my own. Jenny has one!* His whining voice seemed to push tears out.

Jenny arrived beside her mother and placed the two glasses on the grass at the side of her chair. She waited a moment while Tad pleaded.

Tad, said Jenny, pushing the ball of sweet candy into her cheek. *Don't be upset – you can have my drink. I've even put ice in it.* The crying stopped. Tad eased himself off the chair, rounded his mother and headed for the glass of cold juice.

Angela said, without opening her eyes, *Say 'thank you', Timmy Tadpole. You are a treasure, Jenny Jen Jen.* Her arm extended and made contact with Jenny's. Jenny always liked being called by the nickname devised by her mother. Jenny moved to the chair and picked up the radio.

Tad gulped at his glass and gasped aloud, set it down on the grass, then realised he had been dispossessed of the chair beside his mother. *I was sitting there. Mum! I was sitting there.* The whine in his voice returned. He pushed at Jenny's knees and scrabbled to claim a corner of the chair. She did not move. He dug his hands under her leg and trapped her flesh against the chair.

Ow! Mum, he's pinching me. Stop it, stop it. Jenny allowed her shrill voice to fill the hot air.

Stop it, Tad! Angela stirred from her summer torpor. *Go inside.*

It's my chair.

Tad! Go inside this minute, said Angela, rocking forward with menace. Tad ran to the house with a single continuous wail.

At the kitchen door he looked back. His face was hot with the day and sticky with sweat, juice and tears. Mum had already settled back down and closed her eyes. Jenny swung her legs. She had tricked him and Mum was indifferent. Jenny could always say things better, or knew what he did not know, and now she sat beside Mum in the shade. She was never in trouble.

Tad turned from the door and headed upstairs. At least there was no one in the house to tell him what to do. He liked going into Mum's room and went straight there. The bed was bigger than his room. Climbing onto the mattress, the silky quilt pressed against his arms and legs. He laid his cheek on the quilt. It was cool and absorbed him. He could just stay there and be happy, but his mum and sister were talking in the garden and he began longing to be with them, and to hear what they were talking about. He slid off the bed, crossed the hallway from his mother's room to his own and went to the window overlooking the garden. The window had been fixed to open only six inches and he looked through the narrow opening. They were still in the shade. Their voices drifted through the open window with the radio.

Jenny asked her mother, *Why does he have to be with us all the time?*

He's just a boy, said Angela. *Try not to let it bother you. All boys are like that.*

No, they're not. Not like him. He just won't leave me alone.

Angela let her head roll from one shoulder to the other towards Jenny. *You'd better get used to it, Jen. You're too pretty to be left alone. They'll always be at you.* Jenny understood the faint warning in her mother's voice, and recognised the other theme: she was not interested in Jenny's anger.

Jenny asked, *Why is he called 'Tad' when his name's Timothy?*

Angela seemed wistful. *He was born earlier than he should have been, and was just so small he needed me all the time. It was a nurse that first called him 'Tadpole'. She visited me for months after he was born, to make sure I was all right with him.* Angela opened her eyes and smiled. *She saved me. She would come into the house and ask where her 'little Tadpole' was. It made us smile, so I started calling him 'Timmy Tadpole', and then he was called 'Tad'. It suited him, but I don't think he knows that other children are bigger.* They both laughed. *I don't think he knows what a tadpole is.* They laughed again. *Poor little thing.*

Poor little monster! said Jenny.

Don't say that, Jenny, said Angela mournfully. *You have to look after him. He's your brother.*

Angela closed her eyes. Talking had stopped and just the tinny sound of the little radio rose from the garden. Tad liked to hear Mum call him 'Timmy Tadpole', which she did sometimes when he hurt himself.

Tad left the window for the box of toys. On his knees, he pulled the box from under the bed. The bang of something striking the window caused him to turn quickly and see a shadow fall. His heart pounded with the fright of it and he shouted *Mum!*, more loudly than ever before, and then ran for the stairs.

In the garden Angela and Jenny heard the shout but waited for something more. Tad emerged, running, from the back door. *Mum, Mum. A bird hit my window. I saw it!* His eyes were wide.

Angela leaned forward to steady him. *What happened? Tell me again, and just calm yourself.*

Mum! Really, a bird hit the window in my bedroom. He pointed as if his mother did not know where his bedroom was.

Then what happened? Is the window broken?

It fell. I saw it. The boy was excited and Angela wondered if he was making it up.

She said, *Birds sometimes do that. They do bump into windows and then fly off. Don't worry about a little bird. They are quite clever and look after themselves, even the small ones.*

It fell, Mum. I saw it fall.

Well, perhaps you had better go find it. Angela pointed towards the house. *It might be in the garden, under the kitchen window.*

Tad turned to Jenny, who dropped off her chair and started walking with him towards the kitchen window. They stood at the edge of the small kitchen garden and looked for the bird. Angela watched them hesitate at the edge of the flowerbed, hoping to find it and not to find it in equal measure. The small bird, head up, wings spread, lay by the wall of the house. Tad went to it and gathered it up in his hands. It was warm, soft and offered no resistance. Jenny ran her finger over the head.

The two children stared in amazement at it, neither child having ever touched a bird before. It was more than something that flew in the garden or in the park. To have one in your hands, its feet scratching your palms, the eye looking at you, and to see the colours shimmer in the sun, made it magical. In a moment the bird tried to flap its wings as Tad held it, panicking slightly. Jenny cupped her hands around his and then it was still. The head dangled from their fingers.

Let's show Mum, said Jenny.

What's wrong? asked Tad.

You did nothing wrong, said Jenny. *It flew into the window and was hurt. Now it's gone. It's okay.* Fear and sadness bubbled up in her brother's face. The pair walked solemnly towards their mother, holding the dead bird between them.

Angela said, *Oh dear, you found it. Is it dead?* Jenny nodded. *Put it in the garden and the worms can have it*, Angela said. Tad looked at the bird. It was still warm and beautiful.

I don't want the worms to have it. Tears began running down his red cheeks.

Angela pulled Tad towards her and embraced him. *Okay, Timmy Tadpole, we won't put it in the garden*, said Angela, hugging his little body. *Perhaps he has just gone to sleep.* She squeezed Tad and put her head near his ear. *I bet he has such a headache from flying into the window. Imagine, flying into a window! We would all need a sleep, wouldn't we?*

He could not find words but tried to squeeze his head into his mother's bosom, still cupping the bird in his hands. *I'll take care of the bird, don't you worry, Timmy Tadpole.* She lifted the bird from his hands and looked at Jenny. *You take him inside, Jenny, and both of you wash your hands.* Angela pulled herself away from Tad as Jenny took her brother's hand and led him away.

At the back door Jenny heard the sound of the rubbish bin lid being removed and returned. *When we've washed our hands, we can go into my bedroom and play.* Jenny smiled at the tragic face of her young brother, who said nothing. *Don't you want to play in my room?* Silence. *Well, poop to you!* Tad looked at his sister in surprise, only to see her poke out the tip of her tongue at him. He stuck out his, all the way, and then she stuck out the longest, most livid tongue, painted crimson by the cherry candy, that he had ever seen. He burst into laughter. She did it again in a great, mocking gesture. With a squeal of delight, he turned to escape the red-tongued monster giving chase to him up the stairs and into Jenny's bedroom.

Rescue

Tad padded towards the crack of light coming into his room from the landing. The bark of a child and the rocking of furniture, like the creaking of a sailing ship, had woken him. He opened his door, rubbing his sleepy eyes. Someone was crying, but more than crying, in his mother's room, from where the light emerged. The boy moved to his mother's door and slowly pushed it open just enough to see down the wall of the room to the head of his mother's bed. He had heard noises from this room before, when Mum's friends had stayed, but nothing like this. At first he could not make out who the person on the bed was; then he drew back with surprise as the unfamiliar parts came together. His sister's face was wet, its features crunched together and her hair stuck to it like wet ribbon. It was the noise she made that was something he had never heard; not pain, fear, frustration or the insistent demand of a spoilt child. The boy would have known those, but he had never before seen or heard a life being extinguished. The desperate urgency of the struggle was foreign to him.

It came to him with a clarity that could not be mistaken. Even at five years of age there are primal things that are known without instruction or words. He knew that his sister was dying at that moment and would be dead soon if someone did not help her. That terrible image writhed before him and he could not move or speak for fear. Tears came uncontrollably as he stood outside the room, looking in at his sister dying. He did not want her to die and be put in the rubbish. She was kind to him. Jenny was seven years older but knew the world he lived in and he did not want to be left without her.

Thick and hairy arms stretched over his sister's head, pinning her by the wrists, face down on the bed. She struggled to be free of it, like the flapping bird he once held in his hand, but a man's body came into view, falling over her like a tree, causing everything to shudder. Her voice changed as the breath was squeezed from her. How could she live with him on her? His sister would be dead if he did not stop it. Still he could not move for fear and trembling.

Suddenly, there was a moment of near quiet. His sister must be dead. There was movement inside the room. Footsteps approached the door. The boy turned without thinking and made for his room in quick little steps. His breath squeaked in and out of his body. More footsteps came from across the landing and before he could hide, the light opened up the room. Mum stood in the doorway. His sister, who was now quiet, was squeezed against her. His mum reached down and stroked his head and he looked back at her, his black eyes swimming. *Shhhh, Timmy Tadpole, everything is all right,* she said. *Jenny was upset but she's okay now. Pop back into bed and I'll come up and tuck you in in a minute.*

Tad scrambled onto his bed and turned before Jenny was out the door. *Jenny.* He pushed the tip of his tongue out at her and waited for a reply. It was their special sign. It meant anything and everything. I understand, I am sorry, you are forgiven, it will be fine, don't worry, I don't care, I don't mind, we can talk later, are we still friends? It was shorthand messaging that said it all and made Tad feel like he and his sister were special together and each of them was okay. He waited, but it did not come.

He got off the bed again, opened the door and watched his mum lead Jenny towards her own bedroom. He was glad she was alive and that his mum had saved her, but he was worried about his sister. Jenny hesitated at her bedroom door and looked back into the near darkness from where he watched, sticking her tongue out so quickly only he would have noticed.

It would be easier to sleep now. Mum would come and tuck him in soon.

The House

The house had changed. It had been normal, before, for Mum's friends to visit the house overnight or for a few days. His mother would shuffle Tad from one room to another, to be out of the way, and would ask Jenny to look after him. Then the friend would go and the house and his mum would return to normal. He would belong there again. Although never liking it, he was used to this routine with Mum's friends, but this one was different. This friend was always there, soaking up the space and comfort from the house. He always wanted Mum to himself, finding ways to get her alone. He sat in the middle of the sofa, or in the space between the door of the kitchen and the table. You could not get in or out without asking him to move or squeezing by and touching him seemed inevitable. Tad had found a way of diving under his chair and emerging on the other side of the table. It pleased him to move around without being obstructed by the new friend, but everyone else was trapped either in or out of the kitchen when the friend was there.

He knew that Jenny did not like it, although she did not say it. Tad watched her whenever she was around but these days she was in her room most of the time and seemed fed up with being asked to look after him. At first she was 'as always' with the new friend, but after the night she almost died, she was in her room nearly all the time. He had tried to go in, but she wanted him out. She avoided being seen by Mum's new friend and would never be in a room with him. Tad had watched her fly up the stairs as he came to the door and stay there until everyone was watching the television, when she would sneak downstairs and whisper into the kitchen to find food.

He would often hear voices and footsteps across the landing but could never quite make out what was going on. It had become busy some nights on the upstairs landing outside his room. Occa-

25

sionally someone would close his door from the outside. Low-volume conversations muttered annoyingly outside the grasp of hearing, but it was never clear whom they were between or what they were about. It was a secret for someone else. Normally, he stayed in his bed, but sometimes he took his quilt and sat behind the door to listen. He could never hear things properly, but he liked being close to what was going on. Although Mum was there to make sure Jenny was okay, he could not help but be worried all of the time.

He waited for the noise to settle. As quietly as he could, he turned the handle of the door and looked out. There was not much light. Only the L-shaped light etching the outline of his mum's door could be seen clearly. It was enough to guide him. Noises grew as he pushed the door open an inch and then two. He peered down the wall and was able to see the head of his mother's bed, just as he had done months before, and just as before he could see Jenny facing him. She was not struggling or flapping like the dying bird. She lay on the bed like a damp towel would drape into the folds and crevices. Her eyes were open and she must have seen him looking in, but there was no expression on her face, no recognition. At least she was not dead, but was she going to be dead soon? He tilted his head to one side to get a better look. Jenny blinked slowly. Her eyelids, in slow motion, cleared the moisture from her eye and onto her cheek. It was as if she had stretched back from a daydream and had become aware of the world around her. There was a commotion in the room and before he could escape the door swinging open, he heard the desperate shout, *No, no, you can't see.* For a brief moment he could see into the room past the onrushing limbs of Mum's friend, but then he was travelling backwards, off his feet.

The large man clamped his arms to his sides. *You nosey...* The thick fingers pinched the skin on his little arms. Tad shouted in pain. *Just be quiet.* Through his bedroom door they travelled, Tad bounced against a sweating belly before being planted on the floor beside his bed. The man's face came close. It carried the smell of lotion he always used. A thumb pushed into his mouth and pressed his tongue down. *Stay in your room and keep this tongue still.* It tasted bitter.

The door closed loudly and the friend was gone. Only the smell lingered. His arms hurt and he held his tongue out against the bitter taste of the finger. He could not understand what he had seen. It simply did not make sense to him. He heard Jenny struggling to say something but she was being prevented. Mum was telling her to be quiet, but she was not to be made quiet.

The man shouted at both of them: *Shut her up. Get her out.* There was more movement on the landing. Tad could tell from the footsteps that two people had gone into Jenny's room.

A few minutes passed and one person walked from Jenny's room to Mum's. There was an argument in Mum's room. The man's voice was loudest. Tad could make out phrases that he did not understand but, all the same, he did not like hearing them. It was his mother's voice that troubled him. He tried to hear her words. She was crying and he heard her saying *sorry* again and again. She was promising something. What had she done? She was sobbing now, pleading with him about something. Tad wanted to know what was being said and shuffled towards the door to listen. The man had gripped his upper arms and pinched the skin together. It stung. He folded his arms and rubbed them, and rested his head on the door. The man's words came back to Tad as he tried to hear. Was he hurting Mum too? Was that why Mum was crying and saying sorry? If only he could hear what was being said.

Mum arrived in his bedroom before sleep. She sat on the edge of the bed and seemed cross with him. Her face was red and eyes puffy. *Tad, you must not come into my bedroom, ever. Richard was very angry with you. When you come to bed, you must stay in your room.*

What if I need you? Tad replied. Tears came again and his voice turned from normal to high squelch in a single phrase.

You must not upset Richard! We need him to stay and he won't stay if we upset him. There was insistence in her voice and desperation in her eyes as she spoke. It did not matter to Tad and he blurted out his protest.

I don't want him to stay. I don't like him and Jenny doesn't like him. Jenny will be dead if he stays. I don't want Jenny to be dead.

Mother's voice was lowered like the times when he or Jenny had done something very bad. *You be quiet about Jenny. Nothing has happened to Jenny. Don't you dare say anything about her; she won't be dead. Do you understand? Jenny will be fine and Richard is staying. Now go to sleep.* With that she stood up. There was no tucking in and no gentle teasing. He was crying but she did not call him Timmy Tadpole. She had just gone. The door closed, the footsteps thumped unusually hard over the landing and down the stairs. Rasping whispers were now in the kitchen.

There was no sleep to be had in his dark room. It was quiet now, and there was nothing to do but wrestle with what could not be understood. The struggle ended suddenly with the creak of his bedroom door opening. It was dark on the landing so he could not make out who it was, but the company was welcome. The door closed with hardly a sound and the lightest of footsteps made their way to the bed. *Move over*, said Jenny. The quilt corner was lifted and in she slipped beside him. She draped her arm over her younger brother. *Don't worry about Mum. We will be all right.* Tad felt the comfort of Jenny's warm body beside him and her soothing voice; whatever she meant by those words, it only mattered that they were kind. A few moments of blissful relief of tension passed.

Can you sleep in my bed every night? asked Tad. Jenny raced to find something to say but nothing came to her. It was too complicated and she was too troubled. It was a long pause. *You won't die, will you?*

The question did not make sense to her. *No. I won't die. Don't worry. Just sleep now.*

Sacrifice

She heard the voices from her mother's bedroom, muffled by the distance, two wooden doors and harsh whispering. Jenny, sitting in the middle of her bed half-listening to the stereo, waited for her mother to arrive at the door and plead with her. There was a heavy lump in her stomach to accompany the twisting cramp. There was nothing else to do but wait and decide if there was time to go again to the bathroom. The whispering stopped. Down the corridor a door handle rattled and a door opened. Jenny listened to her mother's footfall across the landing. She looked at the inside of her door in anticipation of the furtive knock and quiet intrusion. The knock did not come. The steps continued past her door and down the stairs, with moist snuffling sounds. The cramp left her as she swung her legs off the bed and bounced to the door. The far door opened again and heavier footsteps thudded into the hallway. She stepped back from her door and waited for his arrival. It would be unannounced and already she was indignant. This had never happened before. Despite everything her room was always off-limits to everyone. They all knew that. The toilet flushed and the footsteps approached. She stared at her door, daring him to enter. Instead the footsteps altered course at the last moment and stairs creaked and groaned with his descent. Jenny waited a moment until they were both in the kitchen and then quietly opened the door and followed them down the dark stairs as far as she needed to hear the voices curling around the kitchen doorframe with the light.

She did not need to see inside the kitchen for the scene to be clear to her. Angela sat at the far side of the kitchen table in her dressing gown, face reddened. She would look up at him as he entered and then look away. He would not look at her but would open the fridge like he owned it before taking his position at the door, obstructing access in or out. The silence set his agenda. His dissatisfaction would eventually emerge from the brooding anger that grew until it erupted or he could be appeased.

Don't go, said Angela. There was no response. Jenny was desperate for her mum not to beg.

Angela said, *Are you leaving?* Jenny flinched at her mother's plaintive appeal to this man, Richard.

They remained silent for a few moments. Jenny's stereo sounded far away and she thought about getting back to her room, but the silence kept her there. The unhappiness of her mother was more than could be walked away from. It was not her mother's fear or her pain. It was the shame. Still, Angela could not speak. Jenny's face reddened with a mixture of anger and embarrassment for her. The image of her mum pleading while he sat brooding, reading the paper, was excruciating. The thought came suddenly to her, without form or clarity. Jenny searched for images and the trappings of the character she was about to be. There was time for her now to go upstairs to the bathroom and sort herself out.

A few minutes later, she arrived at the top of the stairs, hair brushed but nervous, ready to pretend to be a woman. She descended the stairs without disguising her steps and the full burst of light from the kitchen greeted her at the doorway. She waited for the small increment of space through which he might allow her to enter. *What now?* Jenny thought.

Jenny. What are you doing up? Angela's question was nothing to respond to. Jenny looked at her quickly, knowing her mother expected an appeal to be made to her, and that she would do as her mother asked of her, that she would drift away and be absent through the sweating, grunting minutes before returning to her bedroom. The pretence of unknowing crystallised a plan as she waited, framed within the kitchen doorway.

He shuffled the chair forward an inch or two. She pressed herself through the gap between the doorframe and his shoulder. Her hand landed on his back, and her hip pressed against his arm. It could have been nothing, but he felt those few ounces of pressure and, looking at her walking away from him into the kitchen, he wondered. The fire had started in him. Angela saw it. Everyone knew.

So you're leaving, said Jenny without looking. He watched her but did not reply. Her hair swayed behind her as she walked between the sink and kettle, arranging something hot to drink. Jenny played out the scene, knowing instinctively that she commanded this audience. Her pyjamas hung loosely and draped against her body as she reached over the counter. The thin cotton revealed all of her form and hinted at the softness of her skin. She stretched further and spent longer than needed in the action, always listening to the silence in which he was now trapped. Another opportunity to extend herself was offered, stretching the silence. She clattered an end to the tension, dropping her spoon into the metal sink, and walked towards the door, stopping to wait for him to move. *You look tired.* He could not look at her, and could not reply, but shuffled himself as close as he could to the table. *Goodnight*, she said to the room. Holding the drink high, she nearly squeezed through the gap without touching him. She wondered how long he would sit there, burning.

Jenny walked up the stairs, passed by her room and across the landing. She hesitated for a moment to look at Tad's door and listen for noises. He often found ways to listen to or watch what he should not. There was no creaking from the floorboards of her brother's room. It was quiet, but she would check that he was asleep. He must never know what she was about to do.

Across the corridor from his mother's room, Jenny's little brother listened and tried to make sense of the comings and goings on the landing and up and down the stairs. He could tell that Jenny did not want to make any more noise than was necessary. The rattle was taken out of the doorknob by pulling gently before turning and the door opened. In the dark, Tad heard his bedroom door open and a gentle light drifted in. The silhouette of Jenny's head was all he could see. She was unmistakable to him. He did not move and she watched briefly in silence for a few moments before closing the door again. He listened to her cross the corridor and go into Mum's room. It was strange; he had been expecting her to come into his bed as she often did, but it did not matter. Jenny was looking out for him. It seemed settled. Mum was still downstairs. He could sleep now. Everyone was safe.

Angela's Temptation

Angela sat on a small plastic seat near the counter, hoping the chemist would not keep her exposed to the world for very long. The store staff, in their crisply ironed white coats, hygienic gloves and tight hair, would know what the prescription was for and would, almost certainly, glance over and judge her. They could not possibly have really known, but they thought that they did. That was enough for them and too much for her.

The visit to the doctor with Jenny had been among the most uncomfortable moments of her life. Angela was paralysed with the recollection. The doctor had undertaken the examination of Jenny with a soberness that made her twitch for the want of something to say. He was a kindly man and was gentle with Jenny. For her part, she was entirely compliant, limp and accessible. *Thank God she didn't put up a fuss.* It was embarrassing to hear that her 12-year-old daughter had acquired a vaginal infection, although she had already known. The smell was apparent to everyone, but nothing was said. The doctor had asked questions of Angela that had been difficult. Was Angela living in the same place as the children? Was anyone else in the house? How were things generally? Was Jenny eating and sleeping normally? How was school going? Angela forced herself to offer bland and encouraging responses, relying on Jenny to remain quiet.

The doctor had asked Jenny about boyfriends and if she was having intercourse. Her surly silence seemed to convince him that she was having sex and the infection was an STD. She recalled how he had said there had been a rash of infections among teenagers that had responded to antibiotics. He advised Angela that she needed to exert more control over her daughter, and offered her the option of arranging birth control for Jenny. In the meantime, he was prepared to offer her a prescription to deal with the infection. All of it reverberated in her body and caused waves of embarrassment.

Now she waited by the chemist's counter for the medicine that was needed and hoped she had enough money in her purse to pay for it. It came to her that she had done all that she should have done. She had taken her daughter to the doctor; now she was getting the medication. It was what was expected of her. When the medication came, Angela stood and reached across the counter, but the chemist held back. *Are you Jenny Tanner?* There was no one else waiting.

I'm her mother. The declaration seemed hollow. It was obvious the prescription was for the only people waiting. There was no need to announce it to the store. Angela's neck and face went hot with anger. She rummaged in her purse, spilling coins on the counter. The chemist ignored the reply and sorted through the thin, round shrapnel. Angela guessed that she had collected enough when the chemist started offering last-minute instructions on how to take the pills. She wanted to grab the little white bag and run, but was frozen by the thought that the chemist knew. She was in turmoil as she swept up the remaining coins into her purse. Angela reached over the counter and took hold of the bag as the chemist reached mid-patter. *Let me have it,* she thought. Angela had not heard anything that had been said. Her mind was elsewhere. *I need these pills before anyone sees.* Finally, the chemist released her control of the medication. Angela folded the white paper bag into her handbag defiantly, refuting the wicked accusation in the chemist's eyes. *She doesn't know. She can't know.*

Comfort

Tad heard the door open and recognised Jenny's footsteps and her way of closing the door behind her. She walked quickly to the side of his bed. In a single motion, she lifted the quilt and tucked herself in the space he had made beside him. It was the greatest thing to have Jenny snuggle up to him each night until he slept. She was never there when he woke, but he looked forward to her coming because lately he worried that he must have done something wrong. Everyone but Jenny seemed mad with him and he had no idea why. Even Jenny was changing. He could normally read her mood from her face and how she moved, but now her hair was in lanky strings that hid her face. She had started wearing floppy sweaters with long arms covering her hands. They were okay together, even if sometimes she did smell of pee.

Book Two: Fifteen Years On

First Day

Jenny could not wait to get through the door. Her head swirled with everything she had learned that day and her feet hurt. She pushed the key into the lock and turned it. The red-brick terraced house had a character that belied its circumstances. Once there had been rows of them, housing workers in factories and mines all over England. Now those remaining in the city had been bought up and renovated. In the bigger cities they had become fashionable, offering an industrial look of old Labour, but inside they were testimony to individual expression and an affluence they could never have imagined. Jenny had been determined to have light and colour in her first home with Mark and their little house was an IKEA model home.

Mark greeted her in the hallway and looked at the shopping bags at her feet. *It must've gone well. You're celebrating already.* He was smiling and she beamed at him.

It did go well. I think I'm going to like it. She shook her hands out of her jacket, hung it, kissed his cheek and reached for the bags, lifting them into the living room.

Mark said, *I'd better put the kettle on. This looks like it will take some time.*

There isn't that much, really. Jenny raised her voice to travel after Mark. *I had to buy a few things for the house and I was running out of knickers anyway. I just wanted to make sure I had some good shoes. There's lots of walking.*

Mark returned from the kitchen and sat among the shopping bags next to Jenny. *I knew your first day would go well, so I brought home some bubbles to celebrate.* He produced two glasses and a bottle of sparkling wine.

Oh, that's nice. She melted towards him and kissed his cheek again. The bottle popped and he poured. *It's a little extravagant*, she said, taking a glass from him.

It is, but then you're economically viable now, and that means we can afford to celebrate. And eat. They both laughed. *Cheers,* Mark said.

Cheers, and thanks for being so enthusiastic for me. Just remember my contract is only for six months to start with.

Six months of celebration, then. So, was there anyone wearing sandals?

Don't mock my new colleagues. They're nice. I didn't know they all came from the university. Well, most of them did. The boss was a full professor there, researching homelessness and what happens to homeless people, but ran into some horrible politics and had to leave to do it.

Politics get horrible everywhere, eventually. Did the politics follow them?

Not sure, really. A few people haven't had their contracts renewed recently. I guess because the money ran out for their project. Someone left just last month. That's how the job came up.

What will you be doing?

Jenny began lifting her shopping from the bags. *Jon, the boss, wants me to join the sampling team. The whole city is divided into sections and we go from location to location to count homeless people. They kept saying it's got to be done accurately and scientifically so the homeless numbers can be calculated; all to do with sampling theory and statistics. That's just one project. There're people looking at movement in and out of the area, hospital closures, policing policy, nutrition and health. It's really interesting. Look, here's my ID.*

It sounds like you might get hooked with a research project for yourself. Mark took the ID and read 'HRG' next to Jenny's picture. *What's it stand for?*

Homelessness Research Group. It's a bit early to know if I'll be allowed to do my own research, but they didn't say 'no' at my interview. Doctor Me, can you imagine?

Jenny was more animated than he had seen her. *It's got you excited. I'm excited for you. Well done.* Mark put his hand on her shoulder and stroked her face. *You're happy. It's a good look. It makes me happy.*

Wanna see my new shoes?

He let his hand fall from her. *Sure. Let's see them.*

How was school? she asked.

Pretty good. It's taken half a term but I think I'm on top of them now. Something came up today. A Child Protection Case Conference has been called for tomorrow, so I might be a little late home.

Oh? Who is it for?

I don't think I've mentioned her to you. She's just one of the gang. I don't know anything about it, but they are coming to the school. There's a school involvement, is what they said. I guess we'll find out tomorrow.

It was a subject close to Jenny, but the fact that she had been taken into care was as much as he knew. This moment, with bubbling wine in her hand and a smile on her face, was not the time to find out more. It did not really affect how he felt about her, but he was interested in what had happened to her. The secrecy marked the importance of it. Maybe later.

Are you hungry?

Mmm, yes. She left the shoes in the box.

Okay, I'll get something started. He got up and headed for the kitchen. *Come and help if you like.*

Jenny finished what was in her glass, lifted the bottle and followed Mark. Nothing would spoil her first day.

In The Long Run, We Are All Dead

The Case Conference was in progress as Mark entered the class-room.

The chairwoman acknowledged his arrival. *I assume you are Kylie's teacher.*

Yes, Mark Warren.

Please take a seat.

Mark looked around at the large classroom with chairs pushed aside, tables butted against each other to make a long formal plat-form for papers and elbows. He headed for a chair on the far side of the table. Proceedings halted as papers and chairs shuffled to allow Mark to make his way.

Mark wondered what Jenny would make of this. He knew the cynicism that burned her and already he understood what she had said about the system overwhelming those new or unfamiliar with it. It was slightly nerve-racking to be among them. The chair had such experience of this, knowing the language, the process and how to control everything. Others sat, waiting obediently to speak.

The chair spoke. *Mr Warren, you've missed all the introductions, but we all know who you are, and we are very pleased to have you come to the meeting. My name is Andrea Morris, and I'm the chair of this meeting on behalf of the Local Authority. You should know that there's a minute–taker with us today who will be making detailed notes of what is said. It also goes without saying that the sensitive matters we're discussing should not be discussed outside this meeting, and the minutes are in strict confidence.*

The meeting had been convened in the school after the chil-dren had gone. It meant that everyone could attend but, most importantly, it meant the Local Authority could report to the court that they had considered all the evidence available before deciding what they would recommend. Jenny had warned him that in all likelihood a decision had already been made on the future of young

Kylie Tay. It was left to the chair of the Child Protection Case Conference to listen to the facts, arrange the arguments in a fair and balanced way, and arrive at the outcome nearly everyone knew to be likely.

That's fine. Sorry I'm late.

Not at all. We know how busy you must be at this point in the term. Let me remind you, as I have everyone else, that we're here to discuss the Tay family, specifically the protection of Kylie, whose possible physical abuse has been brought to our attention. We must decide if what we know satisfies the criteria for 'physical abuse' and determine what action we should be taking to ensure her safety. She turned to the table. *Now, we were just hearing from Ms Lennon, from the Child Protection Team.*

Mark looked at the woman speaking, sitting up straight in her chair. It took a moment to realise who she was. She had always been startling. White skin and curly red hair that would tumble when set free. It was the confidence in her voice, a certainty in her manner that had always been the hook he had bitten on. Now she captivated the table. Everything she said came with authority. The name tag on her chest said 'Siobhan Lennon, Social Worker', but he spotted something new. A tattoo on her neckline, travelling from her left breast towards her shoulder. From under her short blouse sleeve a delicate emerald vine emerged and wound around her arm to her wrist. Small leaves and blue flowers decorated the vine. It was beautiful and he stared unconsciously at the transformed skin he had once caressed. Suddenly she stopped speaking, sat back in her chair and looked at Mark gawping. He had been caught and her smile revealed her pleasure in still being able to charm him.

Thank you, that's very helpful, said Andrea Morris. *Are there any questions for the social worker?* She waited a moment. *Perhaps now we can hear from Mr Warren. Mr Warren, are you ready?*

Yes, I don't think I have very much to contribute. Kylie has been with me only a few months and I have met the parents once.

You mustn't worry about that, said the chair. *There're lots of pieces to put together, and the piece you offer may be very important to the bigger picture.*

Well, Kylie is a very outgoing girl. She is with friends at break time and seems happy. That group of friends are into music and fashion. You can hear them chattering across the playground and the noise before class starts is incredible, but they settle down when I ask them. Sometimes she's a problem in class because she likes her phone, but no more than some of the others. She can disrupt the other children, but she gets disrupted more often. She is not cheeky or regularly in trouble and I have never sent her to the headteacher. I don't think she stands out in that way. Perhaps that's the way to describe her. She just doesn't stand out. Her grades are about average, absenteeism is not excessive, she doesn't ask for help, neither does she appear to need it. Not every child wants attention from the teacher and I don't push this, providing the work is done. I said this to her parents at the parent–teacher night.

How did you find the parents? asked the chair.

Fine. It's unusual for both parents to come but, from what I remember, they both had questions and seemed interested. He paused and the room waited. *Actually, I do remember the father asking me about boys. He was concerned that Kylie was taking an early interest in some boys and wanted to know if I had seen her with any particular boys. I said I hadn't. He seemed satisfied with that.*

Looks were exchanged around the table, and the chair spoke to Mark directly. *You probably don't know some of the detail that has brought us together. Kylie phoned emergency services in the middle of last week, which was the half–term break, claiming that her father had assaulted her. The police investigated and found that there had been quite a disturbance. We can't be sure exactly what happened but the police didn't arrest Mr Tay or seek a place of safety for Kylie, because Mr Tay convinced them he was the victim of an assault rather than the perpetrator.*

How'd he do that? Mark asked.

Well, there are two critical pieces of information. First, Mr Tay had teeth marks on his arms, which he claims were caused by Kylie biting him when he tried to take her phone from her. Apparently, he was concerned that she had sent nude photos of herself to someone. This, it turns out, is true. However, in the struggle for her phone, Mr Tay slapped Kylie across the face, with enough force to knock her over and leave his finger marks on her face. The complication is, as we have heard from our police colleague – she gestured to the uniformed man at the end of the table – *Mr Tay has two previous convictions for violence. Our job is to decide if there is a continuing risk of harm to Kylie.*

Mark understood within a few seconds how hard it would be to conclude anything. It would be a longer meeting than he had been hoping for.

How have you been? Mark asked Siobhan. *You're looking well.* It was probably the wrong decision to spend an hour in the pub with her but, by the end of the meeting, he needed something to relieve the burden of all he had learned of the life of his student. Siobhan's invitation to share a beer was perfectly timed. In any case, he was intrigued to see her.

Well, mixed, if I'm honest. I came off a motorbike a few years ago. I'm okay now, but it has taken a while to get back to work.

What did you do?

Broke my arm, my leg, lost some skin. Her hand swept up and down the tattoo and then she smiled as if it was nothing. *Fortunately, I had a helmet on.*

Mark managed to stop himself commenting on the loss of beautiful skin.

What's the tattoo about?

I saw you looking. She smiled.

Sorry. Didn't mean to be obvious. But it does attract attention.

It's cosmetic, but I like it. Look. She offered her arm across the table between their glasses of beer.

His hand reached for her arm. It was instinctive and in a moment he knew it was a mistake. Holding her forearm, he examined the tattoo. Her skin was as he remembered. Raised scar tissue gave the vine a three-dimensional look. *It's clever, and beautiful.* It was not what he really wanted to say. He let go of the arm and pulled his hands from the table. She lingered, allowing him to see down her cleavage.

I lost lots of skin. You can't see it all.

It's only your arse I can't see now. Was that hurt, too? Siobhan laughed out loud and sat up.

Now it's me being obvious, she said with a chuckle and reached for her glass. *You're the funniest man I've been with. I miss it.*

It was on, if he wanted, and now both of them knew it. He loved her clarity, the direct expression of need. There was never doubt about what she wanted. It was just not what he had wanted to live with; someone who was so certain of what they wanted that what you wanted stopped mattering.

Is there no man in your life?

Not now. There was someone a few years ago, after you and I broke up, but he's gone. She left it hanging.

I'm guessing he was on the motorbike.

He was driving. Bloody idiot killed himself. Nearly killed the both of us.

I'm sorry. It must've made it harder to get over the injuries.

Actually, it helped that he was gone. It made me furious. Stopped me getting sentimental. She took a long swig from the glass. *You can do anything with anger.*

I can't see you again. You understand that, don't you?

Not really.

I'm with someone. This is it for me. She's special. We have a place, trying for a family.

I hope you're enjoying the trying as much as we did.

Mark smiled. *That was very good, but we were never in it for the long run. Well, you were never in it for the long run. Isn't that why you left?*

What was it that politician said? 'In the long run, we're all dead.' I think we're all in it for the long run, whether we like it or not. Right now is the start and the middle of the long run.

I think I might agree with you on that one. You do have to make a choice on some things and stick with it, no matter what.

Is that what I mean? said Siobhan. *Maybe that's why things don't work out for me. Too many starts.*

I'd better go. It's been really nice to see you again. Next time you come to the school, give some warning, would you? He smiled, stood and stepped from the table before a final embrace could be made. *Oh. It was an economist who said it.*

Said what?

'In the long run, we are all dead.' John Maynard Keynes. He was an economist, not a politician.

Siobhan acknowledged the correction with a nod. *No wonder we're all fucked.*

Goodbye, Siobhan. Take care.

Jenny: Domestic

The conversation with Mark about the case conference had reminded her of her mother's house. Drab and tired, it offered nothing of the cheerful colour of her own. But nothing could be as bad as the magnolia and fug of the children's home she had moved to when she was first taken. The social work offices, the waiting rooms at the court buildings and the children's home were all the colour of disappointment. None would be part of any place she lived now.

So… What happened? Mark asked. Jenny looked up at him, returning to the conversation.

Sorry, I was lost for a moment. What did you say? It was a play for time. She had mentioned that she'd been taken into care, as some of the homeless young people she had seen on the street had been taken, and said that she had been lucky. It had opened the door.

Rarely did he pry into her private world. He did not ever seek to open her like a tin and pour out her inner world, as social workers, doctors and so many others had done time after time. There had been times when she knew he had waited for her to say something about being removed from her home, but he would not press the issue or prevent her from diverting him. She had thought he loved her without the need to broach this private place. These questions needed some processing in the few moments before replying.

I was asking what happened. Why did they take you into care?

It had been a difficult time for them, she thought, but they had found time to be together. Their income, until a few days ago, had been meagre, although neither had really cared about money. His job was going well. Jenny looked at him to judge his vulnerability. Not money, not time, not work; it could only be what was left. They had been trying for a baby for six months now, without success. It had caused a strain between them. Sex had become even more perfunctory than usual. It was only the beginning part that she liked, but lately they had forgone most of that in the effort to become pregnant. It was hard for him to know what it was like, but it could not have been great.

It was Jenny's belief that a baby would change everything. Being unsure why this had become the single fulcrum on which her whole life could be articulated did not undermine her confidence in this. The balance of her life would tip into conventional comfort and she would be like others, just normal. Neither could she explain how being a mother would make her fundamentally different, but she was certain that it would. It was simply consuming. She did know that having a baby would be an achievement of sorts and that people would acknowledge her place in the world. The child would be the focus, and she would no longer be centre stage. She yearned to be in the world without leering men and watching women who assumed, implied and accused from nothing other than her presence. It was only her presence that people saw; the pretty physical shell that contained her. She looked out from within that shell. It contained her and all that entered it was filtered through a dead zone, insulating, protecting and comforting. Sometimes it was hard to get into the real world from that place, even when she wanted to. Other people seemed to feel things with such power. Emotion oozed from them: hysterical laughter, tears at the television, joy in gossip, passion in greeting a friend. It was hard to feel anything like that. With her own child she was sure to experience some of it.

Perhaps she had been too contained recently even for Mark's unending tolerance. She needed to let him in a little.

So… What happened? Mark's tone moved in a small increment towards insistence. She had to give up something.

My mother couldn't look after me. Mark looked up and waited for more. *She had a boyfriend. The social workers said they couldn't protect my brother and me, and neither could my mother. So, we were put into care.* He knew that much already but it was a response and he accepted it as being new.

What happened to your brother?

I don't really know. He was six years younger than me. I only saw him a few times after I was taken. I guess he was adopted.

Mark furrowed his brow in his struggle to understand. *It seems odd these days for brother and sister to be separated.* His few years of teaching gave him a rudimentary knowledge of child protection. *There must have been a problem somewhere. They normally do what they can to keep brothers and sisters together.*

I don't really know what happened, she said. *I was first and it happened very quickly. I wasn't allowed to see my mum for a few months and after a year or so, he was gone too.* It was already enough and she sighed heavily. *We haven't been out in ages. Can we go see a film or something tonight?* She looked at his face and saw instantly that the diversion had not worked.

She had given him a chink of light from the rarely opened door, but the morsel he had been offered had implications she did not want him to piece together. That she had been taken first and needed protection from her mother's boyfriend was data that someone could use.

Have you ever thought of looking for your mum?

Not really. I don't really feel the need. She's all right. She doesn't need me. It was an odd response. He would be wondering how she could know that.

You never know, he said. *She might be looking for you.*

I don't think so. She hoped that would end the questions for the day. He would know, surely, that to push for more would put distance between them. At least he might understand something more about her without getting too near. It seemed a very long time without words between them.

I'll see what's on, he said. She heard something in his voice: frustration, exasperation or was it something else? He rose slowly, stretched lazily towards the newspaper, brought it to the kitchen table and sat heavily. He laid the paper down, swept his hand over it and with a snap it uncurled at the edge. The conversation had not been enough for him. She was again relying on his patience without knowing when it would expire. He was the right man to have children with if only she could maintain the connection. The fear of losing Mark bubbled up again.

There had been longing for one or two of the men that she had known, but it was never easy to convince them of her affection or desire. Something stopped her connecting in those times when letting go of herself, feeling joy or ecstasy, should have overwhelmed her. Everything else seemed to work just fine. She had made some friends at college, with whom she had shared nearly everything, although it was mostly a matter of listening to them. She could be supportive of friends in need and worked hard when she needed to. There had never been drugs and only rarely had she had too much to drink. It was a puzzle to her why she should feel so disconnected from the men in her life, even those she thought she loved. Perhaps it was time to do what she could do.

Christ! Did you see this?

She looked over, grateful for the distraction. He stared at the front page. From across the table and upside down, she started fluently reading the article as only prisoners, patients and children in care are capable of doing. It told of a woman trying to snatch a child from outside the local supermarket. Mark consumed the article. *This was at the Safeway playground!* Jenny was still reading too.

Poor woman, she said.

Mark shook his head. *She must have been frantic to get her daughter back.*

No, I meant the other woman. Mark looked at her in amazement. *She must have been desperate to do that.* Mark's confusion caused her to regret saying anything, but she couldn't stop now, an explanation was needed. *The mother has her daughter back, but this woman... she must be even more desperate now. I guess...*

He watched her turning away from him, walking towards the sink. Jenny could understand people in a way that stripped them clean of everything, but it always took him by surprise. She was never encumbered with the impression someone sought to make or by what they said. She could look past the impression, through the status and words that people used to separate themselves and justify their actions, and see them instead for what they wanted. It came without judgement, just an acceptance. When Jenny took notice she seemed to understand everything about him, and would pull his head into her breasts and soothe him. Her understanding was unconditional. But she did not always notice.

Go on. See what's on at the cinema. She had to break the drift of conversation before it spiralled into another conversation about having children that discouraged them from trying. Jenny began, knowing that she only had to wait until he noticed her. It was being deliberate in what she did but doing it without apparent intent. Her walk, a movement, an outline against the window, a hesitation, leaning on the back of a chair, something would arrest him; distract him from doubt and start a fire burning. She need only be patient. Concentrating completely on being observed is what electrified the men she had known. Some were content with the long tantalising encounter, surrendering to the flow of her directions. She liked the pace to continue in that rhythm of restraint even when the outcome had become inevitable. Others found the torment of self-denial too much to bear and would grasp the lead, breaking the spell. It was a relief when that happened. She could then be absent for the duration.

There's a good film on at the Cineplex, he said, looking at the paper. She ignored it. Finally he looked up, allowing her to captivate him in that moment. A flow of seemingly irrelevant actions, all of which could be denied as having intent of any kind, had begun. All of it calculated in every detail to engulf him.

Mark was not quite sure what was happening. At one moment he had thought he had annoyed her, then they were going to the cinema, and at the next moment something else was happening. A switch had been thrown and everything was different. Jenny sallied one way and then the other, arching her back a little more than usual as she stretched to open the window. *So what's on?* she said, arriving at his shoulder and staring at the page on the kitchen table. Neither wasreading. She allowed her hand to rest on his shoulder and gently pressed her body against him. The tension from the undone conversation vanished, and he eased in the reassurance of her touch.

There are a few things on at the Odeon. She said nothing while both looked aimlessly at the newsprint. Her flat hand smoothed the creases of his shirt just as he had spread the paper on the kitchen table, before breaking off and moving in full view of him. She leaned back on the countertop with both arms cocked behind her, ready, poised to hoist herself to a sitting position near the sink. The summer skirt fell across her legs. She felt the coolness from the door into the garden swirl under her.

I'm not sure what I want to see. You decide. I'll get us something to eat.

An open bottle of wine rattled against the milk as she opened the fridge. There was a long inspection of the lower shelves before she retrieved the contents of tonight's salad. They landed on the counter. She held two glasses in one hand and poured the wine into both without asking if he wanted it. It was a long and precarious reach across the table, balancing both glasses at rakish angles in one hand and landing them on the Cineplex ad. A drop or two fell from the lip of his glass, down the stem, bleeding in an arc around the base into the newsprint. She ran her fingers from stem to lip and licked them quickly. *Sorry!* she said, as she placed her own glass on the edge of the counter and turned to the chopping board. Mark watched her from behind. She moved easily, with confidence, as if dancing familiar steps. It was only movement between the sink, the counter and the refrigerator, but it enchanted him. He was drawn to see her slender arms and the curve of her hips. Jenny had done the same movements and actions many times before, without drawing attention to herself, but today something was upon her. Without effort, Jenny transformed an everyday movement, apparently without doing anything differently. It was what had first attracted him to her. Swinging her hair off her shoulder and looking back at Mark. *Pasta and salad okay for you?*

That sounds good. Food and films escaped his mind. She smiled and could see that already he was less troubled. Jenny turned the radio on and lifted her wine glass to her lips as if toasting the new spirit in the kitchen. She wondered if she had done enough to distract him from the doubts and thought it could be time to move. She set about bringing the salad together. Each movement smooth and mischievous. Vegetables waited on their fate, but she broke off and reached for a pot. Filling it with water while turning on the burner seemed impossible and yet it was all done in a single elegant motion. On another day, it would go unnoticed, but she wanted it to be noticed on this day.

She walked behind him and draped her arms over his shoulders, crossed her arms and tucked her hands in his armpits. It could have been a moment of affection, but the softness of her breasts behind him suggested something else. Her arms untangled and she approached the table beside him. Both hands pressed flat on the paper. *We can see a film any time*, she said. His attention was undivided now and intimacy was inevitable. For just a moment, she thought, it was such a pity that the end was known and she reminded herself to stay with him and resist the temptation to let him get on with it. She reached for her skirt and lifted it a few inches; an invitation that he accepted. His hand followed the line of her leg, across the back of the knee and along her thigh. He swept his hand over her underclothes in broad strokes, while she closed her eyes and tried to concentrate on the sensation, blocking out her worry. His hand moved from one thigh to the other. Jenny grasped his hand, turned with it, dragging him off the chair, leading him upstairs. It was important to lead and make the decisions or she would be just be obliging again, allowing herself to drift away. Whatever the variety of sex, it was all that she could do to stay with it. There would be a time, she hoped, when the sensation, the emotion, or something would cause her to stay until the end. In the past, each time she would hope her absence would go unnoticed, but she knew her partners were frequently perplexed by it. Mark would not become angry as some had been, and she could not risk him being so punished by the experience that he would think of leaving. She promised herself, as she had before, to be present until the end. Every step had to be hers to stop from sinking deeply into that comforting private space beneath awareness of what was happening to her body.

Oh no! Jenny sat bolt upright. *I left the burner on.* She was up, still naked on the landing, gathering her dressing gown into some order on the way downstairs. She caught a glimpse of Mark as she left the bed. He was staring at the ceiling. She wondered what he had made of it. She had taken the initiative but lost it. She had tried to be energetic and active, but gradually she had drifted off, leaving him to perform with her. It would have been difficult to make sense of and it worried her that it would drive him away. The conclusion must have loomed large in his mind that she had become bored with proceedings and, sort of... left. As she switched off the burner, she thought the time was coming for her to speak with him about it, if she only understood it well enough to find the words.

Tad: Just Looking

The hostel had been open for more than an hour but he had learned that it was not a good idea to be waiting at the door. There would be others waiting, in the hope of adding to the day's bounty or repairing the frustrations of a long wet day walking the streets. Stretching a meagre allowance, protecting a bottle or hunting the opportunity that would change things was part of the relentless life of a hostel dweller when they closed during the day. Cadging a cigarette, borrowing some money, selling some weed, securing a few tins, taking from someone might put you up on the day. Tad understood it and avoided the sniffing opportunists where they gathered. He would wait for them to settle to their supper before making his way in.

It was evening and the internal world of the houses beyond the fences stood more clearly against the growing darkness. From one house the illumination jabbed through wooden slats and invited him to look along the shafts of light into the lives of others. He hesitated. *Wanker. What's the matter? Just look, you wanker.* Through the upright slats of the fence were views into the home. Lights came on and people could be seen moving. A television and kitchen clatter could be heard through the layers of double-glazing, the space of lawn and rough, wood fence. He peered through them. The TV was on. A man's legs stretched across the room, taking all the space. Nothing was happening but he was drawn into the scene.

A small dog jumped onto the man's legs and was swept off in a single brush. Lights went off in the kitchen and a woman arrived in the room with cups, bent down to place one on a table and then sat down on the sofa next to the legs. The channel changed. There was laughter coming from somewhere. He tried but could not make out their faces. The contrast of light between inside and out was not quite great enough to read the faces.

A girl arrived wearing socks and a long T-shirt, and flopped into a chair. She lifted her legs to her chest. The dog followed, wriggling into the crook of her body. The girl was not a woman yet, but her movement intrigued him. He knew just by her striding into the room, and collapsing on the chair, that she was not shy in this space. He moved sideways along the fence to find an opening that allowed a better angle. She had landed on the chair, allowing her thighs to be exposed. It was not coy like a shy teenager in company, but unconscious and careless like someone who believes they are not being watched. If only he could get the right angle he was sure he could see further along her thighs. He tried getting lower, then standing, pressing closer to the fence, but nothing was quite right. The light was wrong; the angle was wrong. The girl with milky thighs could have sat on the sofa if only her mother had not taken the spot, and he would have seen more clearly. He imagined himself disappearing into the bush like a soldier. There he would remain, silent and waiting for darkness before getting closer.

The temperature fell with the darkness. Standing at the edge of the bush, he stayed close enough to the path to see the lights of the house through the fence. In just a light shirt and jeans, he shivered. The scratches to his arms caused by forcing himself into the bush burned uncomfortably. There was relief and pain in rubbing them. The more he rubbed, the more they burned and the more he rubbed. It was one of life's little traps.

The light was almost gone. He thought he was tall enough to scale the fence and noticed a tree in the corner of the yard that would disguise his descent on the other side. He looked through the cracks in the fence. The family was engrossed. Milky Thighs was fast asleep and unguarded. He would get inside the fence and make his way to within a few feet of the window to get the best view of her and then get away unnoticed with his secret.

Grabbing the top of the fence, he pushed off with his feet and for a moment was suspended near the top, but fell back suddenly. *Wanker.* There was laughter somewhere. He shook it off and tried again. This time he launched and allowed his momentum to take his body over the fence and lean into the yard. The rough edges of the fence pinched his stomach. There was a tug as a button was dragged onto his skin and then scraped from his shirt. The pain was astonishing and every muscle seemed taut in an effort to hold himself upright on the fence. He thought that if he had been a soldier he could do this; he had to control himself and hang on. *You'd never be a soldier. You're an idiot.*

Tad pushed harder and lifted his right knee onto the fence and then slung his leg over until he sat astride it. He looked for a clear landing spot and started reaching with his foot towards the ground, behind the tree. He shifted his weight and slid his bottom off the fence, easing himself towards the ground. The crook of his left knee hooked the top of the fence and for a few moments held his position secure. His left leg opened and allowed his descent. He waited for the pain in his calf muscle trailing across the fence. Progress stopped suddenly.

The heel of his shoe caught fast. All of his weight was suspended from the top edge of the fence and he could move neither up nor down. Fear began to swamp him. *You've done it now.* He reached desperately with a sniffing foot to find the earth but it was not there. Muscles strained to lift him. What would he say to them when he was caught? *Should have thought of something.* His neck twisted to see if there was movement in the room. *Look at you! Look at you! Idiot.*

The pain of his groin distracted him from the fear. His legs stretched akimbo from the top of the fence to near the bottom. The stitches in the crotch of his jeans popped. Then suddenly the ensnared shoe escaped from his foot, springing away from the top of the fence, dropping onto the path outside the yard. His left leg swept in a long uncontrolled arc inside the fence, towards the ground. His body came into contact with the fence in a twisting and whipping action, yanking his hands away, and he fell helplessly backwards into the garden. *Wanker, wanker, wanker!* There was such pleasure in the singing mockery. A fierce hollow knock of cranium on tree and the snapping together of his jaws was all he heard, before the blackness.

Tad awoke to the sound of rushing water and something like screaming in his ears. Surfacing from the noise, the first pulse of pain in his head bulged into his consciousness. Lying on his back, he wondered if he had broken something but the pain and cold occluded everything. Gradually he began feeling the cold earth and smelled wet leaves close to his face. His situation was difficult to make sense of. He had fallen into darkness but there was light even before he allowed his lids to open. Bright light squeezed in through his squint but nothing was very clear. The garden was now brightly lit and he had come to rest in the one part of it that was shaded from the new light by the large tree, except for his head and shoulders, which were bathed in the garish, colour-free light. He looked around to see how exposed he had become and shuffled quickly into the shade.

The back door opened and a dog scampered to the fence. There was nothing he could do but lie still and watch the man he presumed was Legs follow the yapping dog to the fence, open a gate and step out with the dog onto the path. *What could I say to them?* He could say that he had been beaten up and was hiding. They might take him in and he could meet the girl.

Anger snagged at him through the pounding headache and alarm. *There was a gate! A fucking gate and you didn't see it. Tosser.* It was flush with the fence line, so he had missed it. He looked in the house and saw the woman waking Milky Thighs. There was a chance that he could take what he came to take, even if he was to be caught and they would never know what had been taken. He pushed closer to see, through blurry eyes, the girl lying on her side. The long T-shirt had ridden to her hip, gathering at her waist, exposing the white briefs. He watched the woman smooth the T-shirt gently down the girl's leg and then pull her upright. The girl got up and plodded out of the room. Tad inched himself into the shadow. Whatever happened tonight, he had done something.

Legs walked along the path and stood opposite to where he lay, at the foot of the tree, with only the fence between them. He was probably five feet from detection. He could see the man, illuminated by shards of light through the fence, and hear the rustle of the dog in the bushes. After a few seconds the dog was called, more rustling, and the pair returned to the gate. Tad drew in breath. The gate opened, the man stepped into the light and the dog followed. Any moment now the squirming would begin. There was pounding in his head as he tried to rehearse what he would say when caught. The window cleaner story was possible, but being beaten up was better and would give him a chance. Years of creating stories had taught him that any story is better than the truth. You needed to create just a moment of doubt in a person with a conventional life for them to give you the benefit of any doubt. They always wanted to believe you and doubted only afterwards. By then he would be away and gone. There was laughter from the television he could hear through the open back door.

Legs turned and bent down, grabbing something held fast in the jaws of the little dog. There was a tussle and the dog growled without conviction, now playing a game with his man. It was the shoe that had sprung free of Tad's foot. The game was a short bout and ended with Legs lifting the dog into his arms and twisting the shoe out of its mouth. The yapping started immediately, but the dog was in the man's arms and the game was nearly over. Without hesitation the man threw the shoe over the fence and the game was on again. The little beast squirmed and yapped, finally struggled free and leapt towards the fence. Legs followed, scooping it up at the gate. For the dog, the game was nearly over again but for the licking of his man's face. As Legs stood up and turned towards the house the beast made eye contact with Tad in the shadows. There was a moment of suspended animation. An energised struggle started abruptly with all the noise and commotion the little dog could produce, scrabbling and fighting to free itself and investigate the intruder.

In the shadow, his breath still held, Tad was rigid. The note and energy had changed from playful yapping to barking and desperation. It was no longer a game. At this stage, nothing could be worse than being undone by a lapdog, but this time the dog could not escape the clutches of his bemused master, who could not understand the urgency. In the shadow of the tree, he raised his middle finger at the dog. The beast could not be consoled and was still yapping and struggling as the door was closed with Legs and the dog inside the house. He saw the dog's shape through the bottom pane of frosted glass in the door. Yapping, scratching and jumping, but it was hopeless.

Under the tree, in the shadows, breath was released and a long plume of mist rushed into the cold air. The garden light was extinguished. The TV was off. He could hear footsteps on a staircase inside. The kitchen light went off and a softer light emerged upstairs behind curtains. It became quiet. There was no laughter. He closed his eyes and waited in the cool night air for the house to settle, for his heart to slow and the pounding in his head to abate. The prospect of getting back to the hostel without drawing attention to himself was the next challenge. He would have to find his shoe or walk back to the hostel in his socks. *You'll look like a dickhead with just one shoe.* At least he would not have to climb the fence to get out. His head was hurting through the inescapable thumping, but he would be okay. With some luck, he would get back to the hostel without being seen.

Jenny: Work

Jenny left the meeting with the others, each having noted down the instructions for the day and the route to be taken. At her workstation she assembled her bag of papers, pens and information leaflets. She laid the map out and traced the route, while working out the best order to visit all of the sites she had been allocated. She folded it so that just her route was exposed, covered it with a clear plastic bag and slid it into her carrier. From her drawer, she took a counting clicker to make sure all her observations were recorded accurately. Jenny inspected it carefully to see it was working, set at zero, and she was ready. Pulling her jacket from the back of the chair, she started walking to the door, swapping her bags from one arm to the other as her arms were pushed through the sleeves.

Jenny! The voice of her boss caught her from behind before her escape was complete. She turned her head and looked back at Jon without swivelling her body to face him. He ignored her signal and walked towards her. There was little choice but to turn and face him and wait for him to stop before colliding with her. *I meant to say how pleased I've been with your work. Thanks for going the extra mile and for all your ideas. It makes a big difference to the project. Really appreciated.* His smile caused her to cringe momentarily and then she forced herself to look at him, resisting the impulse to step back.

Thanks, she said, acknowledging his words with rising eyebrows and a tight-lipped smile. The pause was awkward almost immediately.

So, are you happy with the plan for the day? You need to let me know if you think we could do the sampling any better.

Sure. I think it's fine. She thought it was a ridiculous question, designed only to prolong the contact with her. They looked towards the noise of her colleagues making their way towards them and to the door. It was obvious what he was up to and he reddened. She softened. *No, I mean, yes. I think it will be fine.* Over Jon's shoulder, Jenny watched her colleague approach. Dee rolled her eyes and mouthed *Creep* as she passed. Jenny locked contact with his eyes and said, *I'll keep a lookout to see if we're capturing the data we need. Perhaps when I finish today, I'll check in with you.*

Good. I'll look forward to that. He smiled again, horribly. It was important that she break the contact off before he did. Otherwise, there was more than a chance of him thinking that a spark had ignited between them that he could turn on at his choosing. It was nothing new to her. She had one of those faces that meant she need only be nice to a man to implant the notion that she wanted fucking. She had to keep control of it, or they would.

Look, she said, *I had better get going.*

Sure. I'll see you when you get back.

She was out and away. Outside, relief, cool air and Dee waited.

Dee smirked as Jenny approached. *Sorry, I should have said something to you. He tries it with everyone, but he's harmless if you don't take him seriously.* Jenny kept walking and Dee tagged onto her stride.

I'd already worked out that I needed to keep my distance, but I did feel sorry for him. So embarrassing!

Don't feel embarrassed for that creep. It has nothing to do with you, said Dee. Jenny thought that it probably did.

No, I thought he might be embarrassed, so I felt sorry for him.

Yeah. I guess he is a pretty sad man.

The two women walked in silence towards their routes.

Jenny distracted them. *I had no idea there were so many homeless people in the city centre until I started with HRG. It's really opened my eyes.*

We've been reporting it getting worse for seven years or so, but it started years before that. The problem is we can't get anyone to give a shit. Every country has done something like care in the community. Dee paused and rummaged in her bag for cigarettes. Jenny felt Dee's contempt growing. *The fuck-up is near universal. No one cares. No votes in it.*

There would be no appeasing Dee. Jenny said, *It didn't help when the psych hospitals closed.*

'Meds not Beds' and all that. They stopped at a corner, waiting to cross the street. Dee took a long drag on a cigarette. *It's the young ones that trouble me. They come out of care, straight onto the streets and have 40-odd years of it. In and out of prison. Hopeless.* Smoke drifted upwards.

Jenny recalled some of those she knew had been in care. *Such a waste. How long have you worked at HRG?*

Since it started, said Dee. *I came from the university with Jon and set up the Homelessness Research Group. You know; wide-eyed liberal postgrad following the idolised professor into the world of social action.* She paused as the sparkle in her voice left her. *We haven't changed the world much, have we?* Another drag. Jenny ignored the question.

When did it become a 'Group'?

That's a game we had to play. Research funders just won't cough up unless you are part of a collaboration of agencies. Jon set up several agencies with his contacts, and we 'collaborate' with them. It's what you have to do. Jon plays the game better than anyone.

You're not still together?

Oh no. That ended when I worked out that he only left the university because there were lots of other wide-eyed liberal postgrads with a crush on the professor. I don't think he had a choice about leaving in the end. By that time, I was committed here. Jenny nodded, now understanding why Jon had been embarrassed when Dee approached them in the office.

That must be awkward for both of you. But you stayed? Jenny knew she had exposed Dee too quickly.

Dee looked away and sucked on the cigarette. *Not sure why, really. I walked away from a PhD, so that was the end of my academic career.* Jenny waited. Dee looked at her as if Jenny might understand. *Sometimes you don't leave, even when you go, so why go?*

Jenny helped her. *Some connections are never broken. I can understand that.* A few moments lingered.

Well, we better get counting our homeless men or the next report will miss the policy round, and they'll ignore us again.

Jenny managed to touch her arm before they parted. *See you later.*

Happy counting!

Jenny quickened her stride towards the railway arches, her first stop of the day. It seemed such a simple task to count those sleeping rough, but there was a strict method they all worked to. Without the actual numbers, counted one by one, the problem remained deniable. Deniability, as she had been taught on the first day of her employment, was the enemy of social action agencies. Their data had to be without challenge if they were to influence the city council or government to develop plans and services for the growing number of homeless men sleeping rough.

The task was simply to count in the right place and in the allotted time period, and then enter the data, but Jenny took pleasure in the contact with the men, some of whom she would recognise on her rounds. Some recognised her. She looked in their faces and saw who they were. The young ones also made her ache, and think of the brother long since lost to her.

Tad: The Hostel

Tad stood outside the hostel and looked up; three storeys, double-fronted, facing the street and all the suspicion of the locals. Rain broke on the concrete steps. On each side were similar buildings in the same state of repair. Lesser hotels, hostels, 'nursing' homes, some faded houses. It was the fate of all neighbourhoods in which successful merchants and industrialists had constructed oversized homes at the turn of the 19th century. Then two world wars and the Great Depression neglected their maintenance, making them desirable only as multi-lets for those who could not afford to live independently.

By now the evening meal would be over and the residents would be settling in to an evening of scavenging and cadging before bedtime. The only peace to be had was in the darkness of the television room where endless DVDs played. On other nights he had waited for the movie to start and the choice of chairs to be established before entering. There was some risk for those entering in the darkness and taking up a remaining place at the back, but less risk than choosing a seat above your status. In any case, it was better than waiting in your room for the opportunists to knock on your door and remind you of a debt to be repaid that you did not actually have, an obligation you could not remember or an indiscretion that placed you in debt. It did not matter that it was not true. There was no less peril if you did not oblige them. The only strategies were to be like them, pay up or not be seen by them. Years of hostel living meant Tad tried not to be seen.

He approached the door and pushed open the letterbox to see if there were people lurking within. The large frame of Benny passed through the hall. Tad guessed that Benny had been waiting for him. Having been reminded by the large young man that they were going to watch tonight's film together, a pang of guilt joined the discomforts. Benny would only watch a film if Tad would go with him but tonight Tad just wanted to be left alone. He took another look through the letterbox. It was clear, so he pushed his key into the lock, turned it and the door opened. He was in, trailing debris and moisture up the stairs and into his room. Damp footprints of one shoe and one sock marked his path. He hoped for a few minutes before he was noticed. The evening still rattled within him and the tension would not leave. It was the worst time to be seen. Staff would ask where he had been and when they saw the state he was in, there would be more questions, always questions to know your business and catch you out. Tonight he was lucky to get up the stairs without being collared by staff or Benny. He quickly undressed and slipped down the corridor and into the shower room with his towel around him.

The cheap soap and hot water from the shower stung the long red lines of scratches on his arms and back. His head had not stopped throbbing. The shoeless foot complained during cleaning. Tad waited for the water to wash away the tension and give him relief, but it would not. *You won't sleep unless you do it. Just pull your little pecker again. Go on, do it.* Tad checked that the door was locked and lifted the soap. The lather whipped up on his chest and as ever his hands quickly found his groin. Before the insults came he reminded himself that he had to clean himself properly and allowed his hands to slide and slurp backside and front. *Little wanker. You fucking little pervert.* Tad thought of Milky Thighs and relief from torment swept over him. With his cock hard in one hand and the soapy fingers of the other digging at his bottom, the tension of the day funnelled into a knot of concentration. The pulsating waves came quickly, occluding all else, and he swayed involuntarily. It did not matter that the pounding in his head worsened momentarily; within seconds there was a settling. It was the only pleasure he could rely on and the best feeling he ever had. Finally at ease, he felt the warm water begin working; easing the headache and soothing the flesh. Then he thought of the evening before him. There would be about 30 minutes of relief from the tension, a couple of hours before bed, and maybe time enough to do it again. Hunger was starting to occupy him.

The grey hostel towel roughed the scratches, even with patting. Specks of blood appeared on the towel, but it did not matter. He would explain to the staff that he had been chased by some people and was scratched as he ran through the bushes, but he must not say that tonight. The staff would pester him to report it to the police. The story was almost true and he would be believed but it was a complication he could avoid. In any case, he might not have to tell the tale. Tomorrow was linen change day. With the towel wrapped around him, Tad opened the door of his shower cubicle and stepped out.

I saved you some dinner. Tad startled upright. Benny was waiting outside the shower room with a covered plate of warm food gone cold. *I was waiting for you.*

Thanks, Benny, said Tad, smiling at him, ignoring the implicit question and grabbing the covered plate. *I'm starved.*

They were closing the kitchen so I couldn't leave it in the oven.

Thanks for keeping it. Sorry I'm late. I had some trouble getting back. Benny swayed like a door swinging open and shut, as he always did. 'Trouble' was something everyone had in the hostel. Everyone understood and allowed it to explain everything. *I'll get dressed and meet you downstairs. We can watch the rest of the film.* Benny smiled and set off downstairs to wait in the open hallway, not far from the night staff, where he could be watched over until Tad arrived.

Even in the dark, Benny was a target. There was always one and, in this hostel, it was Benny. For those at the bottom of the pecking order, it was not just the top of the food chain predators that had to be avoided; it was unpredictable middle-ranking wannabes, skulking around, looking for opportunities. It was even dangerous to be associated with someone at the bottom of the food chain. They were magnets for anyone seeking to repair their mood or wanting to climb the ladder.

Jenny: Wanting

Sitting in the waiting room of the doctor's surgery Jenny mused that despite the modern design and brighter colours, she had spent most of her teens in rooms just like this. It was quiet and people whispered. Even with the changes, there were still well-thumbed magazines, leaflets of promised services, occupants who looked at you furtively. Family doctors, she had come to know, had been gifted huge wealth in the form of income and new premises in return for putting up with new accountability for health targets, and keeping quiet about the selling-off of the NHS to private interests. At least the changes had dispensed with the distinctive smell of leather, disinfectant or decay that had pervaded nearly all of the NHS when Jenny was young. She wondered if there was now some other feature that became welded in the minds of all those who waited helplessly in waiting rooms.

Somewhere nearby in a room of tables and chairs decisions were being made. She remembered her middle teen years waiting and waiting, passively, for something to be taken or excused. She knew nothing of those people except how they treated her. When she was young she had thought those with her, waiting in the quiet rooms, also knew about her. Perhaps this was why people did not look at each other. It was why no one could look anyone in the face. At least today it was different – no decision was to be made today; it was just helping her to have a baby. There was no reason to avoid their eyes. The others waiting could not know what she was there for and there was no reason that they should not see her. Still, it reminded her.

The electronic number over the door counted up until it finally matched the number held in her hand. She followed the corridor to the doctor's office. The door was open, so she knocked quietly and was invited in. He was an experienced man nearing retirement and had known her for nearly ten years. He knew something about her background and had accepted her into his surgery with a welcome. He smiled at her as she sat down.

Now, he said and smiled again, *what can I do for you today?* Her response splashed out before she meant it to.

I want to have a baby and can't get pregnant. She had liked this doctor once she had overcome the suspicion. He seemed to take her seriously even when she was 19 years old. He did not ask difficult questions or examine her on every visit, just when he really needed to. Today, something microscopic altered in his expression as she spilled her problem to him. Even with all his compassion and experience, the doctor could not hide his disapproval from someone so attuned to the expressions of others. She had always been able to detect these changes. As a teenager the lack of enthusiasm and the blank expression she offered belied her understanding of how the people in the rooms of tables and chairs conveyed their intentions. Time after time she had been asked to give her opinion, express her wishes or say what she wanted to, but she always knew, by the use of these expressions, that a decision had already been made. They were always earnest, animated, professionally sincere, and then they would end the meeting with something she did not want. She always saw it coming. From the moment of his altered expression, Jenny began to feel she could not be seen in the quiet room and was already thinking of how she would get out before the occupants knew her secrets. Of course, it was a foolish thought and Jenny knew it to be so, but there it was. They could not possibly know anything, but her knowing of the doctor's disapproval was enough to change her relationship with everyone.

The doctor's brow furrowed despite his kindly smile as she spoke of having a troubled relationship with her partner. Well, it was not that they were having trouble, but tensions over getting pregnant were always present. She heard her own words escape and it was too late to recover them. He seemed reluctant to help her at all. Now he was asking her about their financial situation. Why did that matter to him or to the problem of her getting pregnant? Her mouth opened and Jenny watched her words being soaked up in the doctor's crinkled face. She spoke of having a job that did not pay well, but enjoying it, and of doing some volunteering, hoping that he would see her as being more compassionate and able to care for a child than he would otherwise. As she spoke a memory pushed forward. A social worker had used the term 'depression' in a report more than 15 years ago. Perhaps the doctor knew of it and it had put him off helping her. She realised that he may or may not know how it came to be that the attribution of 'depression' had been made. She had said to her social worker, only once, that her life might not recover from what had happened, and from being taken away from her mother and brother. She was not allowed to go back to her school and said she might as well be dead. For some years following this anguished statement, all the professionals raised it. Social workers, care workers, doctors would ask her. Time after time the same questions, at every meeting, would arise. She knew the sequence better than they did and they floated to the surface with the recollection.

They would ask about any suicidal thoughts and impulses; had she been losing weight; had her mood changed during the day; 'Are you sleeping okay?'; 'Do you wake early and worry about things?' More and more notes being written, about her answers but mostly about the questions being asked. That was what harmed her. The great accumulated wodge of notes and letters, all referring to something she did not have, convinced everyone that she must have it. It made her want to kill them. Sometimes she wondered what would have happened if she had said *yes* to their incessant questions. Saying *no* to them had a paradoxical effect; it seemed so important to them that she agree with the propositions. Why else would they ask so frequently?

The doctor was speaking to her about her medical notes, but she was struggling to concentrate. He was saying that her gynaecological history was complicated, reaching back years, even before he had known her. She tried to hear his words. Something like, *Even women without a history of problems... You may be lucky... You must not get your hopes up.* He had moved on to something else by the time she reconstructed his words. It did not matter. He did not understand the urgency of the problem and how her very being was at stake.

I want to see a specialist gushed from her as she surfaced for breath. The doctor stopped. *Whatever you think, I have a medical problem and I want help. I want to see a specialist.*

He smiled again. *Of course, I could always refer you to a specialist if you wish.* She heard the paternal note in his voice and let it go. *Do you mind if I send your notes to the specialist?* She hated the idea of her notes being shared when she had not seen them herself, but the doctor's capitulation had wrong-footed her. She nodded agreement. *Well, that's what I'll do. Is there anything else I can help you with?*

No, thank you.

Well then, thank you for coming to see me and let's hope we can help you. The doctor stood and offered his hand as if to a colleague at the end of a meeting. It was not usual for him to shake her hand when leaving, but she could see his effort to stay on good terms and played along, prevented steam from building. *You should get a letter with an appointment for the specialist in a few weeks and if you don't, let me know. It has been good seeing you again.* He continued to speak kindly to her as she shook his hand uncomfortably. She had got all that she had wanted but cringed inside. He was such a nice man, but helping her was not what he was thinking and it was obvious to her. They both knew.

Jenny stood up and walked to the door, opened it and started moving quickly down the corridor towards the quiet room where others waited. She could see a few people looking up and then looking away. She kept moving, glancing back over her shoulder at the receptionist, who did not look away. She had forgotten to thank the doctor. Her dash to the street was halted when she felt her balance unsettled by some resistance to her stride, and heard a quiet thump. She stopped and looked down. A little boy sat before her looking up with surprise. Tears arrived with an explosion of noise from the now corrugated face. Everyone looked up. *I'm sorry, I'm sorry,* she said. The boy's mother sprang from the waiting area. Eyes burned into her from everywhere. The child squealed as Jenny reached under his arms to lift him to his feet. *What are you doing?* said his mother. She was wiry and fierce.

I'm sorry. The noise was growing. *I bumped into him and he fell. I'm sorry.* Jenny clung to the child in hope of subduing the rising emotion of the scene. The child turned to his mother and reached. His mother tried to force her arm between Jenny and the boy and, for an instant, Jenny felt the little body slip out of her grasp and gripped him tightly.

Give him to me, the mother demanded. *Give him to me!* The child's squeal grew with the grip of the hands pulling at him. Jenny saw the eyes of the mother. The mother looked at her, not with the anxiety of a mother attending a crying child, but with the anger of a competitor; she had become a righteous saviour squaring up to a brute. Jenny let go of the child and watched the mother pull him away, scrabbling to hold him close to her. The noise faded to nothing and a still moment passed.

I'm sorry. I didn't mean to bump into him. Involuntarily her hand reached out to share in the comforting of the boy. The mother recoiled and held Jenny's gaze. *I'm sorry. It was an accident*, insisted Jenny. There was no response, no acceptance. She headed for the door. The eyes still burned.

Tad: Secret Pleasure

Tad could not sleep for pain and for worry. Even in his soft bed his head pounded on the pillow. The shoe had not been found and he would have to go back to find it before the dog did. He had long been sensitive about his hands and feet. Warts had plagued him at school and he recalled his endless fretting about them being seen. His hands seemed to have thick pads like a quadruped animal that spent its life walking on difficult ground. His peers were quick to spot the feature and had called him 'monkey'. How they laughed. Tad had understood perfectly that he was funny to others because of his hands and because of his small stature. Even those of the class who had turned away in embarrassment had played a part in his humiliation. The worst had been the gaggle of chirping girls who seemed to have greatest pleasure in his torment. Then an older girl approached without laughter. She was pretty and there was kindness in her face. She towered over him and when she took his arm to inspect the pads on his hand there was little point in resistance. He allowed her to see. She inspected the hand carefully.

Does it hurt?

Tad responded to her as if there was no one else there. *No, I can't feel it.*

Well, she said, smiling, *I don't think you're a monster.* Her mouth was full of braces, but she didn't care and neither did he. There was no time for Tad to return the smile.

That's because you're a monster too! The shrill girl's voice sparked a chorus of laughter and screeching.

Aren't they sweet, two monsters together! More laughter.

Tad was already running when the laughter from that insult and the next caught up with him, chasing him out of the school-yard.

He had so wanted a new start and to be welcomed. He was never going to make it among the boys but hoped the girls would allow a connection. The ignominy of their mockery overwhelmed him and he just stopped going to school. There was a foster-mother who had tried to soothe him back, but he was inconsolable and refused. Being alone was infinitely preferable to the emotional tumble of being with others. The pretty girl in the schoolyard had left her mark.

He sat up quickly to shut out the thought. The pillow stuck to his head before pulling away. The scab from last night's injury squelched between his fingers. *You little monkey.* A voice played in his head. *Nobody likes little monkey.* He had only known the charitable scraps on the edge of a social world, and the memories flooded in. Maybe, he wondered, he did not need them to be kind, or to accept him in friendship. Maybe it was enough that they learned not to harm him. He could control the space he occupied, but not if he was a monkey. *But you are a monkey.* The frustration that tormented him for years was the fear of allowing his anger to show. *It makes you look stupid.* The willingness of others to jibe at his every effort to be normal seemed endless. To fight back seemed pointless. He posed no threat. Every challenge was readily accepted. The beatings he had taken did not trouble him as much as the nagging, mocking voice, from which he could not escape. Even denying the accusations of those effortless and cruel words had the impact of making worse the unforgiving contempt in his head. Only in fantasy was there momentary relief.

Now his heel was bruised and some skin from his big toe had been claimed by the sock as he peeled it off when he finally got home. Standing on branches and uneven ground in the bush when looking for his shoe had made the whole foot sore, and somehow amplified the recollection of his near humiliation on the fence. He was covered in additional scratches from the effort of looking for his shoe in the dark, but the most debilitating of his injuries was just below his left buttock where his groin had been stretched almost to snapping as he had descended from the fence into the yard. It had made itself known to him while foraging for the shoe and now it was warning him not to get up too quickly. The shoe was too much to think about. He lifted himself upright, grunting as bruised muscles were deployed for the first time in the day. He should have gone downstairs again last night to be with Benny, but he could not face it. The shower had helped, but by the time he had consumed the food, he just needed to lie down, and then it was over until morning. There was nothing remaining in the reserves of energy. It would be another apology to Benny. Tad hoped he had come to no harm during the night.

Thoughts carried him in and out of the aches and pains. At least he had seen what he had intended to see, without being caught. Legs had failed to detect him, even with the help of a dog. All of the hardship and the cold remained clear to him, but most of all he remembered Milky Thighs. He had seen her walk with the confidence of not being seen, but he had seen her. Her careless flopping onto a sofa was not just in the presence of her parents. He had been there too. He had watched her sleeping and seen her thighs and panties. No one from the outside would have seen this and no one knew but him. The pulse of his heart altered with the memory. There was excitement like he could not recall. Getting inside their world and having got away with a secret was something.

It was getting close to chucking-out time, when the hostel residents spilled into the streets until opening-up time in the late afternoon. He gathered up his towel, bloodied sheets and pillowcase and limped downstairs. It was always a good idea to get out first, or last.

Jenny: Domestic II

I went to the doctor's today, Jenny said to Mark as they cleared the dishes from the table.

Mark looked up and hesitated before he asked, *What's up?*

I asked to see a specialist.

What for? Of course he knew, but some months ago Mark had decided to pretend that the issue was not an issue. If it was an issue for him, it would become more of one to Jenny.

Well, I'm not getting pregnant am I, so I thought it was time to see a specialist.

What did the doc say?

He said he would refer me.

That's good. How long will it take?

Forgot to ask that.

At least the appointment is in the works.

Jenny's sensors bristled. She could see in his face that Mark was disappointed. In the family he had come from, no one really acted independently.

Do you mind? Is there something wrong?

Nothing wrong. Plates clattered on the worktop. The fridge opened and closed. *You could have told me.* Water gushed from the tap. *I guess I think it will be my baby, too, and I should at least know of these things. I'd like to be more than a donor!* A note of irritation had entered his voice. *Sorry, didn't mean that to sound so sharp.*

She appeared at his side. Her head rested on his shoulder and arms lassoed him around his waist. *That's fair. Don't be too cross with me. Sorry.* He let her melt a little longer into his side. They stood together at the sink in an awkward snuggle.

I suppose you want a shag now, said Mark. Jenny smacked his bottom with an open hand.

You'll have to play your cards better than that, she said. It was not what she wanted to do but she contained her reluctance, knowing the reassurance he needed was disguised in the humour. It did not matter; she could entertain him again without hardship. It might even be the time she fell pregnant.

Tad: Evolution

Light faded as Tad made his way to the ridge path to collect secrets from any of the houses offering a chance: a curtain open, a gate unlocked or a fence to climb.

The ridge path was in darkness by the time he arrived. Tad walked along it and almost without hesitation he was at the house of Legs, Milky Thighs and the yapping dog. He knew that he would have to be out of the garden before they went to bed, as the dog would be taken out and he might not be so lucky as to go unnoticed a second time. He looked through the fence slats. The French doors of the living room into the garden were closed, and no curtains could be seen. Inside, the television was on and Legs stretched out as before, but he was alone. Upstairs there was a light showing through frosted glass and steam exiting a small window. It must have been the bathroom. Inside that room, he could see movement. Stepping back from the fence to get a better angle allowed him to see a surreal outline of a person with large head and narrow shoulders like E.T. He guessed it was a woman with a towel around her head. If he could get a little more height, it might be possible to catch a glimpse of the woman through the small window. The best view would be from the large tree in the garden.

The task of getting up that tree was made easier by the gate in the fence, which he undid by inserting his narrow hand between the slats and undoing the latch. He was in the garden, along the fence and in the shadow of the large tree. He listened for sounds of someone walking along the ridge path and then looked to see signs of movement in the house. All was quiet.

Tad started the ascent of the tree. It was an easy tree to get up using the low boughs, and once up he was concealed from every angle and in the darkness. He found a sturdy branch to stand on, turned his head to look at the house and found himself looking directly into a bedroom with no one in it. The light in the bathroom was still on, but there was no view through that window. There was nothing to see. *Idiot. You fucking idiot. Up a tree in someone's yard. It's a fucking joke.* Legs was still in the living room downstairs. Milky Thighs was nowhere to be seen. He wondered how long he had there before the dog would be taken for a walk. Perhaps he should climb down. *You might as well get down before you get caught. Tosser.*

Tad looked down the trunk of the tree to find the first foothold for the descent. The bathroom light switched off and the light in the bedroom came on. He recoiled from the new light and looked into the bedroom. E.T. entered. It was Mrs Legs, in full view, wearing a dressing gown and a towel around her head. She turned a lamp on beside the bed and returned to the door to turn off the main light. It was a soft light now, turning the room reddish brown and adding no new light into the garden. The towel came off her head with an easy tug and her shoulder-length hair fell in dreads in front of the mirror. He could see her back and some of the reflection. The well-practised routine of brushing and drying started with a tilt of the head and easy movements of her long arms. Tad watched without breathing and with trembling limbs. She did not know that these private moments were being stolen and allowed the dressing gown to fall open. He squinted to see some of the reflection. It looked like she was naked under there. He strained to see all that he could, lifting himself up and moving to the side to take all the secrets of her body and these private times.

She walked around the bed towards the window, keeping her robe around her body with one arm as she closed the curtains. There was not a very large gap left between them, but it was enough to keep him suspended in the tree, stretching one way and then the other to see through it. He knew that she was naked now, or at least probably naked. He watched her body pass by the gap once and then a second time, believing on each occasion that he could detect the shape of her breasts. It did not matter that he might not have seen anything because his sight was not good enough, the gap in the curtains was too small or the light in the room was too low.

He believed that he had the secret he had come for and that was enough. The surge of energy overcame the trembling in his legs from balancing in the tree.

The light upstairs went out but Tad whirred and hummed. *Mission accomplished; just deserts; in the bag.* He was triumphant but had to get away now. That would complete the mission. He moved down the tree with a new confidence, hesitating only momentarily behind the tree to check for movement in the house. He looked for Legs in the living room as he walked casually towards the gate. The room was empty but suddenly there were noises near the back door. *Fuck, the dog is coming.* The excitement and confidence were overwhelmed by the panic to get to the gate. *I'll say someone was chasing me.* The little beast was scrabbling behind the door, desperate for its nightly walk along the ridge path. *I'm only hiding from people.* The gate opened and he slipped through it. *I'm not doing anything.* The rehearsal stopped as the gate closed behind him. The kitchen door opened. The dog came out of the trap heading for the gate as if it knew there was quarry there. Through the slats of the fence Tad saw the dog approaching at speed and clattering into the gate. The yapping became urgent and the beast scrabbled frantically at the opening. Legs left the house and followed the yapping dog to the gate and let it out. There was no time to close the latch, but it did not matter. Tad had thwarted the beast again and before turning away and bolting along the path he raised his middle finger in contemptuous triumph. He was away. It was magic.

The adventure of stealing the secrets of that house had been more than exciting. He had achieved more in this night than he had ever before and skipped along like the schoolboy he never was. People on the street walked by without tension. He was among the 'normals' without shame and without avoiding eyes and their mockery. He knew something they did not know. He could learn secrets of these people too if he chose to, and he might. Tad scrutinised the slim teenager hanging on the arm of a boy, walking along in front of him. Her body could be seen under the skirt swaying back and forth as she walked. He thought, *It could be your secrets, if I want it to be.*

The young girl glanced over her shoulder, causing her hair to swish away from her face. *What's wrong?* asked the boyfriend, following her glance to the short young man following behind.

Nothing, she said, without breaking stride. There was nothing she could say, just an uneasiness she could feel. The boyfriend looked back again and inspected the man behind once more. Tad watched him and for a moment felt the need to get away, and then the thought came to him and he held his ground. *It could be you too,* he thought. *I could have your secrets.*

He felt like howling from a tall building and proclaiming his new-found status as a person to reckon with. This night he was part of the world, but it did not prevent him from being ravenous. The anticipation of the evening had meant he was too nervous all day to eat properly and had managed only to nibble biscuits. Adrenaline had overwhelmed his body and his gut gurgled as it left him. Fatigue arrived suddenly, with hunger.

Jenny: Telling

Mark's head lay on the pillow. He listened to his heartbeat rebound off the pillow and waited for the pace to lessen. *I don't think I'm fit enough for this anymore.*

It didn't seem that way to me. Jenny emerged from that distant place in time to respond to his reflection. Her hand landed on his back. She had managed to turn her face to the mattress and squeeze her pillow before he began the urgent pushing to the end. He could not have noticed her absence, surely he could not have. He lay heavily beside her while she moved her hand across his shoulders. She sat up suddenly.

I didn't tell you about a strange thing that happened when I went to the doctor's. He rolled to one side to look at her. *There was a woman as I left who got upset with me. There was a little boy who walked in front of me and I bumped him over. Not hard. He just sat down and started to cry. I tried to pick him up, but his mother came and seemed really upset with me. It was like she thought I was trying to run out the door with him. She was really frightened.*

What did you say to her?

Just that I was sorry, but she snatched the boy from me. I couldn't really explain. She wouldn't let me.

Did she say anything?

Not really. She just looked at me like I was a monster of some kind. Jenny looked away, and Mark closed on her.

It doesn't sound like the boy was harmed at all. Maybe that incident at the supermarket has got mothers a little jumpy. Remember? We read about it. Someone was trying to snatch a child.

Jenny remembered. *Oh yes, I remember.*

Tad: Fish and Chips

A garish light pushed through the drabness of the street on which he walked. It invited him to eat fish and chips and he was drawn to it. Young men and women wandered in and out of the shop carrying bags of chips. Even the laughing swarm of young people seemed benign tonight. Tad's attention narrowed to satisfying the craving.

Endless seconds ticked past in the queue waiting for his turn at the counter. He could hardly see over it to the Chinese server being harassed from all sides to provide small mountains of fried potato doused in vinegar and wrapped in paper. His face was impassive and there was no hint of the stress he was under. Tad tried to ignore the hesitations of customers at the counter, changing their minds, fumbling with change, laughing with friends, but gradually it drew him in. It still did not distract the server. A new group of revellers tumbled into the shop and the noise rose. No impact. At last he looked at the server and asked for his bag of fries, shouting over the noise. He watched the man scoop, salt, splash, wrap and deliver his food with a speed and mechanical certainty that was mesmerising. He handed the man his money and took the bag off the counter.

Before he had moved away, the next order was being prepared. It happened in exactly the same way as his had been delivered. Scooping the fries with the little shovel involved picking it up, sweeping into the fries, dumping them in the brown paper and releasing the shovel, in almost the same motion. As the shovel was released with one hand, the salt was raised with the other. As it was set down the vinegar was in motion and with a violent shake spat the splashes around the fries with a symmetry derived from constant practice. Finally, the package was wrapped with brutish authority and lifted onto the counter, in exactly the same spot as all the others, as if completing the final act of precision assembly. The noise in the little shop continued, but it no longer troubled Tad. He opened the bag and shoved fingers of tart and salty potato into his mouth.

He sighed with relief and leaned against the wall, just away from the jostling crowd, but close enough to watch the server a few more times. It was perfect in its own way. There was never a mistake and it could not be made better. Tad wondered if there was anyone in the world more able to do that and how long it had taken him to be so capable.

The server hesitated in his work for the first time that evening. Despite the frantic activity and noise in the shop, he had become aware of the short young man and wondered what he was doing cluttering up his shop, obstructing others from getting served and staring intently at him. There was time to wait it out, but eventually he concluded that trouble was coming. He looked in silent challenge at the young man, knowing that there might be consequences for standing up to the threat but that there might also be consequences if he did not eventually meet the challenge with equal resolve. There had been a number of drunken men with the need to exorcise their demons at his expense over the years. Nearly all had been surprised by his willingness to stand up to them and most had chosen discretion. Among the locals he was known as someone to leave alone. He knew how to handle these occasional situations. It was part of the skill set those who run shops like this have to develop.

First, he would remain solemn and avoid eye contact for as long as he could. He was to portray humility without inviting the conclusion that he was cowardly. If he got it wrong it would invite the young man to try his luck. Usually, it was enough. It bought time for the drunken young men to become distracted or lose interest, often with the assistance of a friend or a girl offering the prospect of a better adventure elsewhere. Where it was not enough, the server knew there was a moment in every potential confrontation when a bold strategy could be effective. He would stop everything, force himself out of the aching stoop in which he had worked for years, look directly at the adversary, and then wait for the other to see the stare. If the adversary saw the stare and met it squarely, trouble was inevitable. If he looked away, the trick, at this precise moment, was to look away also and return to work quickly as if there had been nothing between them. This was meeting the challenge with equal measure and allowed both parties to exit the conflict without incident. Returning to work quickly was the exit for the server. Having signalled a willingness to go to war and then a willingness to let it go allowed each party to believe it was a mistaken exchange or the other had backed down early. It did not matter.

Holding the stare for longer than was needed increased the risk of conflict. A prolonged stare exceeded the original challenge and could be designed to humble the opponent. Then a new dimension came into play. What had been an encapsulated, deniable rehearsal was now public theatre, the actors thrust into the limelight, and each would play their part; even the reluctant would tread the boards. These rules, learned in schools, backyards, fish and chip shops and sports fields, were effortlessly available to the server, who applied them unconsciously.

Tad had not realised the sequence had been started and was alarmed when it emerged. All the permutations were computed and weighed in divided seconds by the server. It did not matter that he secretly hoped that the young man would go and not add a further burden to his long day, or that Tad's staring was in awe of the efficiency of action rather than intended as a threat. For the server, the next stage was already being contemplated. For Tad, finding himself close to conflict was a surprise and he reacted like a startled deer. Both now knew the sequence of violent engagement among men had been activated and the final calculations had started.

Tad went for the door without hesitation or looking back. He had not meant to provoke the server but immediately knew that he had done so and why. If he did not look away and move quickly, trouble was coming and he was content to avoid it. In any case, he had seen what he needed to see and did not want to spoil this day. Outside he tucked himself into a doorway and held his face close to the bag of fries and ate like a beast. What a night it had been. Mrs Legs had been seen naked and he had got away.

In the backyard of the house on the ridge path, Legs looked at the gate as if it had malfunctioned inexplicably. He had never before left it unlatched, so why was it open on this night? He inspected it from every angle and manipulated it in his fingers to see if the simple latch had broken in some way. The only conclusion was that someone had opened it from the outside, but it seemed unlikely that a normal-sized arm would get through the slats in the fence. He looked around for a stick or wire coat hanger that might have been used to gain entry. Then he walked along the fence to the base of the tree, then to the back of the house to look for signs of entry. There was nothing. It was a mystery. Even so, at the weekend he would change the latch, or the gate, or both. He would be uncomfortable until it was done.

Jenny: The Specialist's Letter

The letter from the specialist inviting her to an appointment lay on the floor inside her door. She knew what it was from the mark on the envelope and cursed the hospital for making it obvious where it was from. It was not something to pick up right away. The letter had brought with it a small electric recall of knocking over the child and having failed to thank her doctor. The doctor's doubts had undermined her confidence that she would ever be a mother. The barely discernible alteration of the doctor's face had told her that she should not be a mother. Anger flashed at the cruel adjustment that had revealed the belief from behind his professional mask. She could put off being angry again by leaving the letter where it was, like a sleeping dog lying. The appointment would not be for several weeks anyway.

Waves of doubt rolled into her consciousness as she left the house to go to work. Maybe he was right. She was barren and each time she looked in the mirror, the curse of being beautiful reflected back to her. She wanted to be a mother, not beautiful, but maybe it was not to be. There was doubt spreading like fungus. Now the hope was focused on new tests to be done to discover if she was capable of having children. She could not drift away and wait for it to end, even though she wanted to. It came to her that there would be little point in doing anything if she were told that she could not have children. She would be beautiful until that was gone, and then she would be nothing at all.

It was an especially difficult journey, with the dreaded letter on the floor and the noise of children in the air. They seemed to be everywhere. Through an iron fence she watched the children in a playground. The noise built as more and more children tumbled into the schoolyard. A four-wheel drive pulled to the kerb in front of her. A military operation ensued, with two young women and three small children disembarking. Bags, boxes, jackets gathered and distributed in one continuous operation. Hugs, kisses, final instructions signalled the time to venture into the separate hurly-burly world of the schoolyard. They scrambled through the gate, with only one looking back. Schoolyard life consumed them and all were oblivious to everything outside the fence. A group of mothers chatted at the school gate. Jenny longed for all of it. There was nothing of it that she had and it was everything she wanted. The bell was a few minutes off yet and her longing could not be broken.

Are you new? A young mother approached her, smiling. *Are your children here?*

No. I'm just hopeful. They exchanged smiles.

The young mother nodded towards the playground. *I have one in there, this little fella*, she said pointing to the buggy. *And another one in here.* She offered a wry smile and a pat on her bulge. *My husband just has to look at me and I'm pregnant.*

You're so lucky. Jenny felt the sting of her friendly words. *I wish it was as easy for me.* She bent down to see the little boy in the pushchair. *Who is this?* The young boy had breakfast across his face and down his front. It might have been part of the apple that was being gnawed at in one hand.

That's Timothy, who is 18 months old. Jenny inspected the boy, who was completely content despite being bundled and bunched in the pushchair. The apple was his world. It was a moment before Jenny made the connection.

I have a brother with that name. Unwanted memories interfered with the moment and she stood up and looked across the playground. *So many children. You would have thought that there would be enough for me to have just one.* It was an idle, wistful remark that grew heavier with the few seconds that passed. *I didn't mean…*

Don't worry, said the young woman. *There are so many children. I guess it doesn't seem fair.* Jenny knew, because it was obvious, that the implications of what she had said were as clear to the young woman as they had become to her, and she had to get away.

I'm sorry. Jenny hesitated. *I'm just desperate.* Tears were going to come if she stayed a moment longer. *Bye then. Good luck with the next one.* Jenny offered a lame smile.

Good luck with your first. The young woman said it brightly, but it did not help.

Jenny walked on. She felt observed; eyes burning into her as she departed. Within a few strides she walked past the mother of the boy she had tripped over in the doctor's surgery. The mother clocked her and turned away. Jenny was too moist in the eyes to see anything clearly and strode quickly past. Sometimes, she thought, the sense of being watched doesn't leave you.

Tad: The Way Home

Half the bag of chips sated the first hunger and Tad moved into the street with the late evening crowd of young people on their way to or from some place of alcohol and fun. It was an easy mood and Tad enjoyed the success of the night and the sense of moving along in the flow. A commotion ahead of him caught the attention of the street. A handful of young women cackled and clacked along the street. Tight black dresses, livid make-up, high heels scuffing the street, long legs and bare arms, cold in the night air. A group of tall men with crisply cut hair and fresh shirts followed them closely.

We don't need to go to the chip shop. He'll give us some, won't you? A chubby black-haired woman clacked towards Tad and looked down at him, smiling through a face slackened by wine. She reached for his chips and Tad recoiled. *Go on*, she said. *Just one.* He had seen that look and heard that appeal before. The garish shamble in front of him was helpless and would soon be overtaken by vomiting or sleep. He opened the bundle of chips and held it up towards her. The woman reached out to the open package, grabbed it in both hands and pulled it towards her. He held it firmly and was pulled forward by her effort. Tad yanked back at her, trying to hold the bag together, until she let go and it exploded. Fries flew into Tad's face and over his head as he fell backwards. There was a screech of delight from the other clackers.

Tad bounced up with the empty paper still in his hands and rushed the drunken woman, without any plan but to obliterate her with the salted paper. He pushed it in her face and she fell off her heels, landing heavily on the street. The laughter stopped. Some of the screeching crows fussed over the woman and others descended on him. In a moment he was overwhelmed with hair and clothes being pulled back and forth, random slaps, punches and kicks, swearing and shouting. All he could do was back up against the wall, hold his arms up to cover his head and keep as low as possible. Through the bodies that surrounded him Tad found a gap through which he could see the young woman lying on the street, legs splayed. From his angle, he could see the full length of her thighs. The women may have been intent on pecking him to death, but they did not know what he could see.

The escorting young men restrained the women. Screaming accusations followed of how he had attacked the drunken woman. Counter-accusations that she had started it came shouting back and anger erupted. They grabbed each other and pulled back and forth with truth in the balance. A young man held Tad safely against the wall. Another young man broke away from the crowd around the prone young woman and walked towards them.

She might get done for assault! What's the matter with you, for fuck's sake! He was just standing here and she tried to steal his chips. He pushed her, that's all. She's drunk. We all saw it. He looked over his shoulder at the girlfriends. *She's always been a mad bitch when she's out. I don't know what they're making a fuss about.* Tad felt the grip of his captor ease. He turned to Tad.

The young man turned and put his face near. *Look, if you're here when the cops come you both might get arrested. If you just fuck off now, everybody goes home tonight.* Tad nodded, the grip was released and he pushed by them to get away. He kept walking briskly away from the sounds. Behind him a shrill voice sounded.

Don't let the little bastard walk off! More shouting came and a few started to follow Tad up the road.

The young man stood his ground. *Just shut up, and leave him alone.* The night turned blue behind Tad.

He was away from it and heading back to the hostel. Tad thought about the night as he walked home. He had taught the fat drunken bitch a lesson, seen up her skirt and got away. Almost never had he been so up on the night.

Jenny: Counting Eight

Mid-morning and the old man kept watch over the movements of those with whom he shared the underpass. It was a good spot he occupied. Dry, protected from the wind and on the route of every food and shelter agency in the city. It meant the place would be crowded at the start and end of the day.

The pretty woman was back again. He had seen her come by a few times, either here or at one of the other places they gathered and slept. She reminded him of the life he had tried to forget. All the bright and earnest young people who brought questions and conversation to him caused him to remember. She was so beautiful: tall, slim, natural, brown hair past her shoulders. Her skin was smooth and he allowed his mind to wander over the fullness of her body. Something in her face spoke of a life she had lived. A sadness or disappointment, of the kind that brought him and all of those she looked at to this place.

She would come and walk at the edge of his world, looking carefully, deliberately, laying eyes on everyone. Not everyone liked it. They must know, he thought, that bitterness and resentment bubbled in the minds of some homeless people who had been spilled from institutions, or toppled from a conventional life. Most feared some new policy forcing them out of the dry noisy comfort and into less protected doorways. Some sought to recover their foothold in the world and saw the clean, well-groomed visitors as a sign of hope. Others simply resented outsiders, save for the opportunity they presented. She was getting closer. Even his fog would not obscure the connection she brought to his past.

What do you want?

Jenny jumped in surprise at the voice emerging from the dark heap of clothing propped up against a concrete pillar. *Sorry. I didn't mean to disturb you.*

What are you doing?

I'm counting. It's my work. I'm counting the number of people without places to stay.

Why?

I work for a social policy agency. We do action research. She scrambled in her bag for her ID and realised what a stupid thing she had said.

Don't bother. I've lost my reading glasses. Jenny looked blankly at him. *I would offer you a cup of something, but I'm out of milk.* She stared awkwardly until he smiled at her. She smiled too and felt her embarrassment show. *Is it my turn to say sorry?* he asked.

No. You got me. It was a good one. I am sorry to have bothered you. She started to move away.

What's your name?

Jenny, she said, stopping. *What's yours?* It was too familiar and she knew it immediately.

I'm known as 'Prof' down here. You haven't said why you're counting.

Well, said Jenny, *we look at social issues, like homelessness, and write advice to governments and policymakers. We want to give them evidence of a problem and advice on how to solve it. I'm collecting the evidence. Counting.* She shrugged and smiled helplessly at him.

I suppose it's easier than asking us how we got here. She shrugged again in reply. *How many have you counted today?* he asked.

She could see no harm in telling him. *At this situation, I've counted eight people. All men, as far as I can tell.*

I think there are seven, he said quickly.

Why do you say that?

He lifted his arm and pointed. *There's one over there, who is probably dead.*

What! Jenny said, turning to look. *How do you know?*

There was a fight last night. He hasn't moved since.

Have you called the police or ambulance?

Sorry, said Prof. *I mislaid my phone.*

Jenny strained to see what she could from a distance. *He doesn't have shoes on.*

I think that was what the fight was about.

Shoes!

Important, if you don't have them. Anyway, that one was waiting to die. It would have been a relief to him.

Jenny stared at the body and again at the man. *Aren't you concerned that someone has been killed, nearby, while you watched?*

Not as much as you, which is the odd thing.

What do you mean? asked Jenny.

He's been dying of cancer for a few years, and you didn't call the police or ambulance while he was alive and suffering. Why phone them now when he's dead and not suffering? The only reason to get the police involved now would be to find someone to blame for neglecting him. The guy who has the shoes didn't neglect him. He just won the fight.

Jenny's head was spinning. *Why didn't you try to stop it?*

They weren't my size.

How can you say that? Jenny's indignation surprised her. *Look, I'll have to phone the police and report this.* She started the search in her bag for the phone she hardly used.

Please, he began. *Don't call anyone just yet.* It stopped her search. *The food truck comes in about half an hour and if the police come now it will skip this stop. All of us will have to walk miles into town to get something to eat. I promise to tell the truck people about it when they come. One of them is bound to have a phone.*

Jenny shook her head. *I can't just pretend that nothing has happened.*

Of course you can. We all do it, all the time.

That's not true, she said.

I think it is.

Well, that's why you... She stopped.

That's why I live down here. Is that what you were going to say? We are all entitled to have an opinion.

No, I don't have that opinion. It's not what I think and I shouldn't have said it. I'm sorry.

Would you like me to pretend you didn't say it? Jenny wilted still further. He relented. *That was uncalled for. Apology accepted.* There was silence between them.

It's ridiculous, she said. *How can someone dying be unimportant?*

All I am asking for is thirty minutes. Remember, I'm just telling you I 'think' someone has died. I don't know, and you don't know they have died. You can't tell from here, can you?

You want me to behave as if what I believe is true, is not true. Is that it? she asked.

Just count eight and not seven. That's all. Then we can eat. Imagine if someone in your family was down here. You would want them to eat today.

She thought of her brother for the first time in a while. There had been times when one of the small shuffling figures among the homeless men caused her to look twice. She had feared encountering him in a dishevelled state and terrible situation. The reminder caught her off guard. Standing on the edge of the homeless world, Jenny listened to the noise of the cars on the road above them. She had always known that none of those travelling by were concerned about the homeless or the events of last night. If it was Tad lying over there, no one would mind if the body lay another hour or two, but there was something terrible in what Prof had said. It had revealed her indignation to be nothing but show. She wondered if she could watch someone die and do nothing. What was important and valuable was suddenly unclear to her. After all the things she had pretended were true or not true, it was possible that she could stand and watch.

Okay. I'll walk past him and look. If I see any sign that he is breathing, or might be alive, I'll call the police.

And if you don't see signs of life? asked Prof.

It will be eight.

Tad: Stealth

The light was nearly gone. Tad had waited in his room long enough, anticipating the evening. Bounding down the hostel steps, he hoped to escape without notice into another night of the adventure that had become his purpose. Tracking up and down the alleyways, looking at windows, testing fences and climbing trees; but tonight he had a place to go. His heart thumped with the prospect of finding something that others had not known, watching people in their homes. He relished peering into bright rooms from the dark hiding places outside, sometimes getting close enough to hear the noise they made.

He longed to know what it felt like to be in their space, lying on their bed or wrapping their robe around him and stroking his face with their towel. They would put fingers in jars and only in rubbing the ointment on his skin would he feel close enough to what he wanted to know. They folded clothes into drawers and only sinking his arms into their clothes and sliding his hands between the layers was satisfying. The risk of being inside a house exhausted and thrilled him. Learning how to get in, navigate in the dark and leave without anyone knowing had changed him. He was larger in the world, gaining ground on others.

Outside a house, he waited and watched for the lights to go out. He had stood in the garden, getting close to the windows, knowing their movements. He was familiar with inside and craved the chance to open the fridge and drink from the milk bottle as the man had done, and sit at the kitchen table turning the pages of the woman's magazine. He would wait for sleep to come to the house. Entrance to this house would be easy. They would not know he had been and gone. There was pride in getting better at his work.

Jenny: The Appointment

Obediently, she attended the specialist appointment and sat with the other hopeful women in the quiet room, reflecting on all of this. Several hours had passed by the time her name was called and she stood up and walked towards the smiling nurse. She entered the room, undressed, robed herself as instructed and waited for the specialist on the hard bed with the steel foot stirrups. She did not like being vulnerable like this, exposed for someone else's convenience, but she could do it. She looked at the contraption and thought that her feet were already cold. Twice the nurse looked in on her, smiled and asked if she was *all right*. She did not respond. Could she say 'no' if she was not all right, she thought? Another friendly face appeared from behind the curtain.

Dr Jay will be here in a few minutes. She has another doctor with her, who has just joined the team. Do you mind if he attends the examination?

I suppose not, said Jenny. There was not a choice.

Finally, the specialist arrived. She was 40 and businesslike, with a hospital coat flapping. The examination started abruptly. *Right, Jenny. I'm Dr Jay and this is Dr Han, who has just joined our team. It's good of you to allow one of our junior doctors to shadow me. Today I'm going to learn about you and help if I can.* Jenny clocked the familiar use of her name and formal introduction of the doctor. It was always like that. *Your doctor sent on your medical notes, which will save both of us some time.*

Jenny looked at Dr Han, who seemed to twitch unconsciously, unable to look back at her. Jenny watched Dr Jay looking at the notes. The doctor, she could see, was not reading; she was thinking. Jenny wondered if Dr Jay disliked performing for her colleague, and needed help to get through the first awkward stages of the examination. Perhaps there was something about examining a nearly naked patient on a bed with someone watching that was difficult for every normal person, even doctors. That was a good sign, thought Jenny, smiling encouragement.

Turning to Jenny, Dr Jay said, *Dr Han has just qualified and has joined the training rotation. There is really is no better way to learn about our work than from seeing patients with someone more experienced. Thank you for being helpful.*

No problem, said Jenny, trying not to sound too flat.

Dr Han, we know our patient is Caucasian, in her mid-twenties and having difficulty conceiving. What shall we do about it?

Jenny realised that she was probably older than Dr Han.

He said, *We have to take a full history and then do a physical examination, with samples and blood work.*

Why would we want a blood work-up? asked Dr Jay.

To check thyroid hormones, prolactin and male hormones. Dr Jay waited. *Look for obvious signs of damage, as well as for HIV and hepatitis, indications of genital infections, chlamydia, gonorrhoea, syphilis.* Dr Han stole an uncomfortable look at the patient and shuffled.

Jenny waited for it to be over. Dr Jay brought it to a close. *Good. Perhaps you could write up the tests that are needed and leave me to do the physical exam.* She turned away from Dr Han, who moved through the curtains and away.

Looking at Jenny and seeing her relax, Dr Jay said, *You didn't look comfortable and I didn't feel comfortable, so I was not going to put you through a physical with Dr Han looking on.* Jenny smiled, knowing that Dr Jay had been uncomfortable from the start.

Jenny thought that, in all probability, Dr Jay had received word from her family doctor that there was something difficult about her, and was trying to avoid making it harder. It was a teaching hospital after all and there was little choice but to expose new doctors to patients. It was a kindness that she had sent Dr Han away, but it troubled her to think that Dr Jay might know things about her. Unknown things her doctor had said in the notes. Jenny knew this to be unusual; it could only mean that she was being given special attention.

So, you have been having trouble getting pregnant, Dr Jay said with the smile of a friend over a glass of wine.

Yes, that's right. She smiled back lamely. The intimate questions would start in a moment. They would come with dispassionate brutality. When did her periods start; when did she start having sex; how many partners had there been; what gender were they; what had she been using for contraception; what were her sexual practices; had she been pregnant before, had an abortion or experienced discharges. Jenny waited for Dr Jay to ask if she was in a stable relationship, as if that was anything to do with the medical problem she presented. Almost certainly Dr Jay already knew the answers to most of the questions, but it was part of the solemnity of the medical profession that they had to ask again and it was the obligation of patients to tolerate it. It was like a television police drama involving the 'good cop' and 'bad cop'. Each playing a role and each wanting to extract the morsel of information that revealed the real truth behind the lies and enhanced their own reputation for masterful diagnostic skills. In this case, it was hard to deny someone the answers when they were trying as hard as Dr Jay to make it easy. Jenny knew that the good cop never got the whole story. She would get her answers, but no more than what was already in her precious notes. There would be no extras for the kindly Dr Jay. In any case, it was all a prelude to the physical examination that was coming, in which Jenny allowed her body to participate. It was a good strategy to be nice to the patient before asking them to surrender their dignity. The other way round was worse. She was reminded of her mother suddenly and recalled being taken to the doctor for her first examination. Her mother had seemed more nervous than she was. It had seemed very odd to be left out of the discussion afterwards, and to have to sit in the waiting room on her own.

Jenny. Jenny! Are you all right up there? Dr Jay asked. Lifting her head from the mechanical device expanding Jenny's vagina, she peeked over the sheet that covered Jenny's thighs and saw a flaccid, masked expression as if Jenny was unconscious. The doctor was alarmed for a moment until Jenny became aware of her name being called. Returning to the moment, she answered.

Fine. I'm okay.

I was worried for a moment. This doesn't usually put people to sleep. Dr Jay had seen that expression before, in African women, after the militias had come and gone. *Sweet dreams, I hope. Anyway, all done now. Let's get you sitting up. Do get your clothes on if you'd like.* Dr Jay turned away to the sink, stretched her gloves off and started washing her hands. It was always good to turn away as the patient dressed and she liked to give herself time to work out what she would say to the patient. What she saw was no worse than when she examined many other young people. It was like the inside of most young and sexually active women. No active infection she could see. There was a little reddening and unevenness here and there, but nothing obvious to suggest why Jenny was struggling to conceive.

The noise of Jenny rearranging herself and getting into clothes behind her had stopped. She could feel Jenny waiting patiently for her to finish washing. Eventually, she turned and they faced each other.

Well, there's nothing obvious I can tell you about. It seems pretty normal so far, but there are always more tests we can do. Try to remember that this is the start of understanding the problem and we have some way to go yet. Let's make another time for you to come back and we can talk about what we've found. Let the receptionist know that you need to come back in two weeks when the first lot of results come back from today. I expect that we'll need to do a few more then. Did you have any questions? Jenny shook her head. *Thanks for being patient earlier.*

That's all right, said Jenny.

The two women smiled at each other and Dr Jay left suddenly. Jenny found herself recalling the occasional man who had left in a hurry, sometimes without even spending the night. She had never been bothered by this, but had always wondered why they, like Dr Jay, had felt so awkward about leaving.

Tad: TV Room

The residents would be half an hour into another DVD and the cadgers would be marauding on the upper floors of the hostel. He had eaten so there was no need to go scavenging for food. He went to his room, dumped his jacket and scampered downstairs to the TV room, glowing with the success of another reconnoitre of a new neighbourhood. The houses were bigger and the streets were quiet. It was best when the house was chosen randomly, like when he had walked by a house just as a car full of people pulled out of the drive. All he needed to do was watch the house for a while, throw a rock at the window or ring the doorbell to see if he attracted the attention of anyone. Where there was no response he would search for a way in. A window unlocked, a garage door, a key hidden under a pot on the step. You just had to be smart, know where to look and keep looking. Tad was getting smarter and it pleased him to out-smart the normals. The prospect of knowing so much about these places made him feel life was good enough to watch a film with the others.

He took the noise out of the doorknob and slipped into the darkened room. No one noticed but Benny, who looked up through the gloom and signalled a chair being available beside him. Tad settled in. On the screen a blonde woman ran through a forest at night. The image of her body flickered between the trees. Tad squinted to make her out clearly, but it was not possible to see what he wanted to see. She was naked, running and screaming. A naked man pursued her. He carried a long kitchen knife. *Trouble?* asked Benny in a whisper.

No trouble. Tad smiled to himself.

I saved you some food, offered Benny. *In my room.* Benny thumbed the direction.

Thanks... What's the film?

Dunno really. 10 to Midnight *or somethin'. Charles Bronson, they said.* The door of the room opened again and the night staff edged into the darkness.

Fuckin' shut up, would ya! From the front row, a menacing voice spoke without whispering. It was Darryl, the 'top dog' of this hostel. The chase in the forest continued. The naked man was getting closer and a hush fell over the audience. The woman tried to hide, but he had her now, against a tree. She cried and cried, but he held her fast. Their naked bodies must have been touching. The screen showed her recoil from a thump to the body. Unseen, the knife plunged into her stomach. An unlikely scream came from her and she sank out of shot. There was blood on the knife and satisfaction on his face. The audience's attention was suddenly locked on the screen and Tad's heart pounded as if he had been chasing the woman in the woods. He recalled Mrs Legs through the window and the fat drunken slag with her legs open. His cock was hard again and he squeezed it in the darkness.

Where ya goin'? Benny asked in surprise as Tad got to the door. Tad pointed to his mouth and patted his stomach. *Wait!* Benny fumbled with his trousers and then held out the key to his room. Only Benny would trust someone in this place with his key, thought Tad, but he took the key, squeezed past the night staff and out the door. He would grab the food after he had been to the shower.

It was quiet as he came down the stairs, clean and relaxed. Just the sounds of the DVD, still on in the TV room, could be heard through the door. Everyone was out or in the TV room. The night staff were drinking tea in the office. The tension of the day had gone for now. What a day it had been. Tad walked around the quiet hallway and saw it as never before. He normally flew up the stairs and spent as little time as possible in any area where the predators and prey circulated. There was a painting on the wall of the hallway outside the TV room. He had not noticed it before. The hallway was brightly lit and the cheap glass of the reproduction reflected it. He shifted back and forth to get the best view, the bright lights causing him to squint. It was old and did not make sense to him.

Tad opened the door of the TV room and the familiar smell of young and poor men emerged. It was too dark to see if there was somewhere to sit. He stood at the door and turned to the TV. A woman arrived home, walked into her bedroom, dismissed her clothes and headed for the kitchen wearing just her purple underwear. The audience of young men watched intently and without sound or question. She walked back and forth, making toast and putting the kettle on. This was normal in the world of those with money to spend on fitted kitchens, hairdressing, living in clean, bright houses. It was an unobtainable world in which people did these things. After a few days of filling time on damp streets, it was a transportation to something that might be more. Tad thought of the new neighbourhood he had discovered and wondered if the inside of the houses would be like this.

From a closet off the kitchen, a man watched through louvre doors. His features chiselled, hair sculpted, body taut. The music collected the attention of everyone and heralded an impending horror. As the toast popped and the kettle sang, blood spurted across the wall. Wide eyes looked with disbelief from the screen. The man from the cupboard was naked, as he had been in the forest, and as before had shoved a long kitchen knife into her stomach. She sank helplessly to the floor as the girl in the woods had slipped down the tree with a gentle cry. He was calm, relentless and mechanical. His destruction of this woman was inevitable. His place in the world carved out by the impact. The room was full of fascination and envy. To be so close to such a beautiful woman in such a glamorous place; to experience that intensity and to have such influence within that world was intoxicating. As the scene ended Tad felt the tension in his body ease. The sudden loss of purpose on the screen brought awareness of others in the room. It made him feel vigilant, like the hunted.

Tad turned away, his eyes quickly adjusting from the bright screen to the dim light surrounding him. From where he and Benny had been there were shuffling sounds. Tad looked to see Darryl leaning back, almost horizontal in the armchair where he had been sitting. There looked to be a mound of coats or blankets on his lap. Darryl looked at Tad with eyes that said, *what are you going to do about it*, and, *fuck off*, in equal measure. It was only then that Tad understood the strange configuration of bodies and movement. It was Benny, leaning over the arm of the chair, head plunged into Darryl's lap, hidden with a coat over his head. Tad could only think that it must be stinking hot under there. Perhaps he should not have left Benny alone in the room – and then he realised it might have been him under the coat, had he stayed. Then it came to him that it might still be him under the coat. The exhilaration and empowerment of the video left him. Tad decided not to see the ending. He did not want to be around when the cadging started again. Neither did he want to see Benny. His only friend would want to be alone anyway.

Jenny: Regret

She was lovely, said Jenny, smiling at the recollection of Dr Jay. *There was a new doctor with her, and she just sent him away and was really nice to me. I thought it was going to be a nightmare.* Mark listened to her bubbling away with more enthusiasm than was usual, while he cleared away breakfast.

That's good, said Mark. *I was not looking forward to sharing your vagina with 25 others, even if they were spotty nerds in white coats.*

There was only one, but that's very sweet of you, to be jealous.

Not jealous really. I just don't like the idea of someone else knowing more about us than I do. Jenny noted something frail in his voice.

I don't tell them about 'us', I just let them look at 'me'. They are just looking at and examining me.

Your fanny isn't a magazine in a dentist's waiting room. It does matter who flips through the pages. He was not angry, but there was something else.

It only matters how I feel about them looking. If it doesn't matter to me then they can do what they want. Jenny knew that was not quite right. *It doesn't mean anything. Don't let it matter to you. Please.* The appeal was too much and the lightness of mood darkened. *Anyway, it's still sweet of you to be jealous.* She hoped the tease would recover the moment.

Mark smiled. *Okay, I confess. I am jealous... I hate it when someone beats me to those magazines.*

Don't be mean, said Jenny.

I just hate the dog-eared pages, torn covers and someone always messes up the Sudoku.

Oh stop! She paused. *I like that you might be a little jealous.*

Maybe I should be more jealous and follow your every movement, said Mark.

I said, 'a little jealous'.

Quiet and then Mark started. *That's fair. I'll be a little jealous of you, if you're a little jealous of me.* There was something hopeful in his voice.

What do you mean? Jenny struggled with the idea of being jealous.

Mark asked, *Are you a little jealous of me, sometimes?* Jenny heard the danger.

I've never had to be jealous of you, so I've never thought of it. She thought it was too lame. *I would be if you fell in love with someone else. I guess I don't think about you having sex with someone else. Maybe I am not a jealous person. That didn't sound like I meant it to mean. I mean it only matters that you're with me.* Jenny's mind raced to rescue herself from this death spiral. Outside a car's horn honked. Another scenario came to mind.

Are you saying I need to be jealous? Are you seeing someone? Jenny asked. There was nothing to be done but be resigned to whatever was now said. She knew this scene well; there was no point in asking, pleading or demanding. It was likely done.

No. I'm not seeing someone.

It was too precise. Jenny could see the furtive movements of his eyes, shifting his gaze away from hers. *You are thinking about seeing someone else.* The only way to do this was to make it easy for him.

Not really.

'Not really'?

Mark shuffled. *I met an old flame the other day. I've told you about her. Irish, smart, she's the social worker at the case conference I went to. We had a drink in the pub after. That's all.*

But it got you thinking.

No, I told her I couldn't see her again.

It sounds like you got an invitation into her bed.

I said 'no', because I'm with you. He found her gaze and turned away with the understanding he had confirmed her assumption. *It was nice to be invited.*

I can understand that, and thinking it would be nice with her.

But I only really think of you.

She smiled at him and contemplated another kind of ending. Was it possible?

Mark started again slowly. *Sometimes I think you're not really thinking about me, in bed.* Mark regretted his words escaping as they sailed between them, landing heavily and cracking the ice on which they fell. Both felt themselves sinking. Jenny recovered first.

It's not like that. It's complicated for me and I find it hard to understand it myself, but it's not you. Promise. It isn't you. The horn sounded again, more insistent this time. *I better go. Dee offered me a ride today. Can we talk tonight?* Mark nodded. She headed for the door.

Jenny. He stopped her. *I wish I hadn't said that.*

I know. Maybe it's been coming. She could not go to him. The same regret prevented it. She headed for the door, thinking he had opened her private space and knew more than she wanted him to. It had been easy to pretend that he did not know something of her private place until it was said. It was now known to be true and would wait in the bedroom to be seen. Something would need to be done to heal this.

She was gone. The morning sporting bulletin from BBC Radio 5 could not mask the disquiet. The kitchen clatter was louder than normal as he tidied up breakfast. He wondered if they would get past this. It had seemed so small and quiet before it had been said, and then it emerged like a barking dog. He had opened his trap and out it came. He offered a long sigh and wondered what to do. Go to work. There was nothing else.

Tad: Stealing Secrets

Mrs Myerson had spent the evening with old friends, playing bridge and sharing food. It was not like her to be out past 8.30pm, but she received fewer and fewer invitations to go out these days. The occasion had been a little awkward because of the uneven numbers of men and women around the table, but she did her best to be less on transmit and more on receive during dinner, rather than allowing her loneliness to be revealed in gushing enthusiasm for conversation. The irony of the invitation was that it dragged into her consciousness a recurring disappointment with friends. Sitting in the back of the taxi on the way home gave her a few minutes to reflect on the novelty of the event and rehearse the frustration of being abandoned.

She had often thought that sympathy for her left as the undertaker took her husband away. Not that she had wanted sympathy from others when her husband died; she had long since got over him going. His departure had relieved her of his interminable company. He had been such an interesting man in his prime, handsome and vibrant, but after his retirement he stopped being interested in the world and stopped being interesting. Neither would she feel guilty about her lack of charity. It was possible that their friendship group was fading even before his death. She could hardly blame them for disappearing when he was alive, and perhaps it would be surprising if they came back in abundance when he departed. *Glad the old fart is gone. Want to come to a party?* No, not very likely. A smile came to her lips; she must not be too hard on the old friends. Anyway, it was not really sympathy she wanted. It was a little understanding. Being included in gatherings of friends did not seem too much to ask.

If only they knew the girl she still was underneath and could see the parties of her youth. Her mind flooded with memories of dancing, uniformed young men, big band music and the desperate, urgent times of war. Those moments burned brightly and even now kindled wanting like nothing else. Mrs Myerson calculated that she had many more recollections that made her smile or sigh with pleasure than memories that made her sag with age. Sometimes she wanted to remind people of this and that not only was she not dead yet; pleasure of all kinds was still possible for her. Thankfully, her son had done everything he could to stay in touch and tonight was the night he was likely to have rung. She would have missed him of course, but she was desperate to get to the phone and check for a message he may have left. There might even be time to phone him back.

The taxi came to a stop outside her home. She paid the driver, gave him the usual tip and stepped onto the kerb, being careful to straighten her stiffening hips slowly. It was dark, but there was enough street light to see the path to her door.

The house was detached from the house on each side. It was imposing, sitting squat and square in near darkness on the comfortable, leafy street. A dim light under the porch and over the front door had illuminated her blue-grey frame, an elderly woman searching for her keys, as she walked up the path, peering into the bag, pushing the contents north and south and then east and west. She arrived at the door, opened the bag's jaws and lifted it towards the lamp as if allowing it to gulp light before her head plunged into the mouth. Inside the house the telephone rang and the search became vital. It was hopeless. The phone continued to ring. She abandoned looking and shoved one arm deep into the bag's gullet, but still the keys could not be found. Mrs Myerson wondered why telephones seemed to get louder and more insistent the longer you took to answer them. She took a step to the small window beside the door. Her arm reached behind the plant pot to where her husband had hidden the spare set of keys 30 years previously and where they had always been kept for emergency use. A large key was selected from two, inserted into the deadlock.

Tad was not close enough to see the large key but he did watch her retrieve it, insert it in the door and turn it all the way round with an exaggerated movement of her arm like a quarter-turn of a propeller. Then she twisted a smaller key in the lock just above it and the door opened. Mrs Myerson replaced the keys and went inside. There was suddenly light in the hallway as she stepped in. The door closed and more lights went on.

The locks turned and clicked shut, but it did not matter: the secret of the door was his.

Tad congratulated himself for being quiet and watchful from the darkness. He would give her time, wait for all the lights to go out and then go for a walk. When he returned she would be in bed and fast asleep. He expected that she would be deaf and unable to hear him even if he crashed through the window, but the door would be an easy one, and he could stay as long as he wanted. Already he had an idea of making himself comfortable in the living room or at the kitchen table. With that thought in his mind, he set off for a long walk until it was time. He could not help but think of the things he had done in the last few months. Sometimes he would alter things in a house so that there would be an uneasy feeling that something had changed, without there being apparent evidence of him having been there. There was a satisfaction in having felt the cloth that someone would wear or sleep on, or flipping the pages of the books they read. He would look under beds, use the toilet, plunge his hands into boxes of cereal and through drawers of clothing. Occasionally he had tried to create secrets. He would hide an object from the house with the thought of gaining entry weeks later to see if they had found it. He often thought that he knew more about a house than the person who lived there. Perhaps he would eat a little of something in the fridge. A wave of derision washed over these memories. These other houses with flimsy doors, flaking paint and cold walls. Their secrets were sparse and the kitchens barren. None compared to this solid building, cared for on the outside and surely cared for on the inside too. There would be no stench of fried food and the floors would not stick to the soles of his shoes. It was old and cared for. There would be things people had not seen for years. He would find everything he could inside. He could hardly wait. Now it was time to let the house settle.

Tad walked past the house on the opposite side of the road. He had watched each house nearby and saw that they had all gradually put themselves to bed without concern or suspicion. It was going to be tricky only because of the dim light over the front door. There was no point in putting it out, as it would take more time than simply opening and closing the door. There could be a dog, but he had checked around the back and there was no sign of one; neither had there been a commotion on her return. There could be an alarm, but there was not one visible outside. In any case, if someone went to bed without locking the front door, it was a fair bet that they did not use the alarm, even if they had one. Finally, it was just possible that someone would pass by, even at this late hour, or look out from a house and see him going in. He had thought of this and set aside the original plan of getting as close as he could in the foliage and making a dash for it, sweeping through the door and then dealing with whatever happened. It was unlikely to be that bad, but still it was a risk to avoid. A plan reached completion. He would make one final check and begin walking at a normal pace along the pavement; turn without hurrying up the path to the house. Once under the dim light at the front door he would reach into his pocket for a fictitious key. When he could not find it, he would reach to the window for the hidden spare. He imagined being watched by someone from a window or passing car. What would they see? If he got this right, there would be nothing of note.

He set off, walking too quickly at first. Where the path met the pavement he swivelled on the ball of his foot. *Idiot, why are you walking like a robot?* Tad stood at the front door and put his hands in his pockets, momentarily forgetting what was next. It came to him and he started the six-pocket search known to all men. First the front jacket pockets, then the front trouser pockets and then the back of his jeans. It was likely that no one was watching him, but if they were, he would just look like someone who should be there.

After 'failing' to find his keys, he stepped and reached behind the flowerpot on the windowsill and retrieved the spares. There was no rush to do this. His breathing and heart remained just under control. The door opened as he twisted the Yale key. Inside he twisted the steel knob on the mechanism to retract the latch, closed the door softly and gently released the latch into the door catch. He switched the hall light on as she had done, and waited in exquisite terror.

The energy of the moment coursed through him. No alarm rang; no dog barked. There was silence and he waited for his heart to return to normal. There was no need to panic just because the light was on. It would draw more attention from anyone watching if there was no light as he went in. It was all part of the plan. He closed his eyes and tried to listen to the house through the pulse of his heartbeat in his ears and his heaving breath. Thirty seconds passed by. Breath was gradually coming under control and while the light was on, he took stock of all he could see from the hallway. Three doors and a staircase leading from the hallway could be seen from his position behind the front door. Painted portraits of people in old-fashioned clothes, in tarnished gold frames, a small desk in dark wood with a closed lid, and a chest of drawers built of knotted wood with brass handles. The hallway had more secrets and stories than all the other houses he had been in, all put together. The intense arousal he had been feeling changed from anxiety to excitement at the moment he realised he had hit the jackpot. He flicked the light switch off and waited for his eyes to acclimatise to the darkness.

In other houses, he was never quite certain that the place would be empty. That nagging doubt had become something to live with and Tad felt pleased with his growing courage in dealing with the anxiety. In this house, it was so much better to know the woman was in, upstairs, while he stalked the ground floor. Knowing was better than not being sure.

Enough time had ticked away. It was quiet and Tad's squinting eyes could just make out the shape of doorways and furniture. It was time to start exploring. He made for the desk, sank to his knees before it and opened the first of three drawers. Papers and envelopes stacked up neatly in the first. In the second drawer photo albums and notebooks lay in orderly fashion. Tad picked up the top notebook. There were lots of them, each slightly different in size, colour or binding. He flipped through the first and could tell that every page was full of small, tight writing that he could not make out. The people in this house must have written everything down. He took a handful of notebooks to the hall window to get as much light as he could on the page. The first two he opened and flipped through with his thumb. He stopped in the middle to feel the quality of the paper. There were more pages of writing that could not be read, dates and thin lines that could hardly be seen. Finally, it dawned on him that these were diaries. He had never seen one before. This someone had kept diaries forever. He could feel the pages that this person had written on all those days, years ago. Things that no one would have seen for all that time until he discovered them. They were not secrets for him anymore.

The third notebook came to the top of his little pile and he put the others down. This one was small, plain and embossed with the number '1944'. He allowed his hand to touch the cover before holding the spine in his palm. It fell open and gave access to a page. It was a sign telling him where the most important secret lay. Perhaps it was a book that someone returned to time after time and was used to falling open at that page. There must be something especially good there for someone to keep going back to it. Tad wondered if there would ever be something of his that was so good, he would return to it time and time again. The words still could not be made out. The writing was too tight, like that of the social workers who ignored you when you answered their questions and started writing. He squinted harder and manoeuvred the page to catch more light at the window.

> June 4th: Jack and his friends came in to the hospital to see Cpl Armstrong. I can't take my eyes from him. Sister scolded me. Jack said that he won't be visiting next week

as usual, but will come again as soon as he can. He said he
has something important to ask me. Heart stopped dead.

Tad managed a few more words from the page, but it was not that
interesting. It was old and a secret, which he now had, but that was
all he could get from this. He returned the notebooks to the drawer.

The albums had more promise. He lifted the top one out and
opened it over the others. There was enough blue-grey light to
make out the photographs. Black pages, three or four white-bor-
dered, black-and-white prints held in by paper corners. Someone
had written in white scrawl about each one, but it could not be read.
Pictures of men in uniform, sometimes two or three men, all easy
in each other's company, showed a man's life in wartime. Their hats
were tilted on their heads and they smiled broadly. Some had rifles
and others sat on military vehicles. Most had their sleeves rolled up.
Each album was lifted gently from the drawer, opened, touched.
One man's image recurred. Glasses; thin, beaming grin; sometimes
in a headset or a box on his back with wires trailing. From the films
he had seen, Tad knew the man was a radio operator. The faces
could not be made out in the half-light but they had to be looked at.
He squeezed his eyes to take in all that he could. It was the kit, the
equipment, the guns that drew him. All those men, with all those
things. Tad imagined having all of those mechanical things. A clock
pinged and reminded him that he had been in the house for nearly
an hour. There was still so much to find out about this place.

The last album was returned, the old drawer pushed quietly in
and Tad moved to the door on the left. Taking the rattle out of the
doorknob was easy. He grasped the knob carefully and gradually
applied pressure, pulling it towards him. It was an old house and the
spindle had a quarter-inch of travel before stopping. It was important to move slowly and steadily. He released the pressure towards
him, lifted the knob enough to keep strain on the latch and slowly
twisted it clockwise. When it could not twist further he pushed
gently. The door opened a few inches and he released the handle
gradually, making sure that gravity or the tired spring did not bring

metal to metal loudly. There was pleasure in the skill and he relished the opportunity to show it again. Behind the door was a sitting room. The curtains draped slightly open and enough light floated in from the street to see the room. A heavy carpet defined the layout and there were comfortable chairs, a long sofa with small tables at the ends defining the space. He walked to the sofa and sat down, allowing himself to recline heavily, as if it was his room to recline in.

Tad listened to the noises and whispers of the old house and thought that he was probably the only one to hear them in years. The old woman would not have noticed them and very likely there was no one else. As with most of the houses he entered, in just a few minutes he knew more about the place than did the occupants. A car moved along the street and for a moment the room brightened. There was a bookcase in the corner with four drawers beneath it. Oddly shaped bottles stood half-filled with alcohol on a cabinet. A paperback book lay on the sofa beside him. Tad reached for it and flipped through the pages casually. There was a bookmark. He had discovered the exact page that she was last reading. Not as interesting as the notebooks, but even so it was worth something. It was thin and folded limply over his hand. He pressed the leather strip to his nose and shaped it over his lips. Tad turned a few pages before returning the bookmark next to the crease of the book, licked his fingers, wiped them on the page and placed the book where he had found it. She would never know. He imagined her licking her own fingers without realising he had been there.

Tad noticed that the carpet was thick and soft. The pile moved with the shifting weight under his feet. Quickly he pulled off his trainers and socks. The aroma of his old trainers reached his nose. His toes dug into the wool and his feet shuffled, generating a little warmth. It was strangely sensuous. First he rolled forward off the sofa and put his cheek to the carpet between his hands. He could feel and smell the quality. Standing and stepping forward, he dragged his foot behind him and felt the heat build to near burning. He pushed a foot forward and felt the delicious tingling of the deep pile, and set off across the carpet like a skater on ice, gliding carelessly. Each slide warmed the pad of his foot. It was luxurious, liberating. No one would have taken the pleasure this carpet could give as he did. All the years this carpet must have lain on that floor and only he extracted that pleasure from it. A sliding foot ventured off the carpet and squeaked briefly and loudly against the wooden floor before his little toe rolled under his foot. The crunching sound of the little knuckle popping was unmistakable. The pain shot up his leg with force enough to snap his head back. Tad managed to stifle all but the groaning effort to resist screaming anguish, before collapsing on the carpet, gripping his foot. *Fuck, Fuck, Fuck!* The words came in a harsh, suppressed whisper. The sharpness of the pain had brought tears to his eyes and ringing to his ears. There was nothing to do but squeeze it fiercely and wait for it to leave him.

The sharp pain ebbed away, leaving the nagging discomfort. He looked up at the shelves of the bookcase, the drawers beneath, and shuffled towards them and pulled open the bottom drawer. Inside there was a collection of boxes. The long thin blue box was lifted out onto his lap. It sprang open with a little pressure. Inside there was a string of dark metal and silver military medals, each beautiful and dangling from ribbons whose colours were lost in the poor light. It was fantastic to see them. He had seen the pictures of the war from where they came. They captivated him, and he lifted them into the meagre light.

Upstairs Mrs Myerson awoke from a shallow sleep when a light thud, reminiscent of one of her children falling out of bed, pulled her into a torpid consciousness. It was difficult to sleep at the best of times, without branches from the tall trees at the edge of the house falling on the roof. It was the obvious explanation, but as she emerged from sleep, it stopped making sense. The trees had been down for years. She was wide awake in an instant, wondering.

The next small box held an old pair of glasses, round and mottled. He took them out and put them on. There was a larger box made of dirty wood. Eighteen inches long and in two halves. It resisted opening. There was no hinge or lock, just the two halves of the box. It had to be pulled apart at the centre, making sure each side moved equally. It began to move, first one side then the other, and then one half lifted from the other. The knife inside was as long as his forearm, shaped like a butcher's knife, but thicker and pitted. The blade was more than six inches long and was separated from the pressed leather handle by a brass plate. The butt was a solid lump of steel shaped to join the handle without a ridge. It was not new or polished, but it was magical.

There was pleasure in watching it move through the air as he picked it up. The handle tucked into his hand neatly and he lifted the blade through the air like a boy flying a model plane, its path slicing the air. It was the combination of watching it in motion and controlling it in his hand. The flat light from the street reflecting from the pitted blade added a gritty authenticity to the flight, but it was the sense of authority and purpose that wielding it offered that he liked. He imagined the blade cutting through cloth and flesh, like in a real war. It was irresistible; nothing could obstruct it. Tissue sprang apart, recoiling with the tension released by plunging steel. It conjured vivid images of slicing through leather garments and splitting ribs. The suddenness of it bursting through hide, and the finality of the hilt coming to a thudding stop at the leather while the blade travelled deep inside the body, ended all arguments and turmoil. He made wide arcs and plunged the knife into imaginary enemies.

A light went on upstairs and changed the ambience just enough to be noticed. Tad's fighting stopped. Quickly, he removed the glasses from his nose and returned them to the case before putting them in the drawer. Footsteps at the staircase were unmistakable. The two halves of the knife box came together and he returned it to the drawer. This was the time to be a soldier. *Stay calm*, he said to himself. *Just execute the plan.* Tad squeezed the drawer closed with all his stealthy skill as the footsteps came closer. A light went on in the hallway and the noise of the creaking stairs changed to the tapping of slippers on tiles. Tad listened from the room across the hallway, standing barefoot behind the door listening to the noises from another room. He could tell all that was happening from behind the door. She was making something. The fridge opened. There was clinking of bottles, a metal pan on a surface and the sound of stirring. She was warming some milk.

He looked down and saw the knife gripped in his hand. He could not bear to put it away in the drawer, and never see it again. He never took things from the houses he entered, but this was different. It had the capacity to change everything in an instant. Tad wondered if he would do it if she came in. He recalled the film of a man hiding in the kitchen, watching a woman in purple underwear before he stabbed her. It stirred him. *You don't have the stones to do it.* A cupboard clacked open in the kitchen; something removed and placed on the counter; cupboard door banged closed. Something else; his breathing was heavy, his heartbeat was thundering near the top of his chest. Tad went to the slightly open door to look through the gap between door and frame. He stood back about six feet to avoid being illuminated, but there was plenty of angle to see the kitchen and the small grey woman in her dressing gown, organising a beverage to help her sleep. He coiled, the knife pointing at the crack in the opening, waiting to pounce as she came through the door. The knife would crash through her chest and slice her heart. He did have the stones to do this. He had seen it done; now he waited for the chance, adrenaline coursing through his body.

Mrs Myerson placed the bottle of milk in the fridge, having dismissed ideas that the noise that had woken her was a branch of a tree falling on the house, or a gang of burglars that had invaded. How silly she could be. In any case, the rich food offered at dinner at her friend's house had brought on the inevitable indigestion and this would prevent her from getting back to sleep without some assistance. A cup of warm milk and some time reading was required. With cup in hand she came out of the kitchen and looked across the hall, and it became clear to her immediately what the noise had been. She had forgotten to close the living room door and the draughts of the old place had caused the door to bang. It had happened often in the life of this house. How many times had she told the children to close the doors, not to slam? She chided herself for being old and forgetful and walked towards to the door.

From inside the darkness of the living room, through the crack of the open door, Tad watched her approach. The door handle rattled and the door closed suddenly. It was a surprise to see the door close and he startled at the noise of it shutting. It was disappointing. Sweat had formed on his forehead and the handle of the knife, but it was not anxiety that caused his shirt to stick to him. He looked around in the darkness for his shoes and decided to wait in the living room for the woman to go to sleep before looking in the kitchen. He was not finished with this house. He might drink from that milk bottle from which she had poured the drink she was sipping at this very minute, upstairs just a few feet away. He had the knife, could do or take whatever he wanted.

Mrs Myerson headed back to bed. She noted a faint smell, reminding her of her son's gym kit years ago and how he and his sister scrambled up these very stairs when they came home from school. If not for the garden and the memories, she mused, she would have left the house years ago. It was really too much for her and now the living room needed to be aired. She tried to force into memory the task of opening the living room windows tomorrow. There was always too much to remember.

Jenny: The Ride

Dee pulled away from the kerb as the car door closed. Jenny struggled to get the seat belt arranged. The fan blew hot air in her face and morning radio chatted to itself. Dee began.

Sorry to rush you. I told Jon that I would be in early to help with the final draft.

That's fine. She snapped the seat belt into place and squared herself in the seat. *What final draft?*

It's looking really good. All the things we have been saying have been shown to be true. The really good news is that we have got the national press interested, and the local MP. Dee's eyes left the road to smile at Jenny.

I thought we were still collecting data. Jenny's surprise was obvious. *I handed in four data sheets yesterday and I've got two weeks of sampling in my diary. How can we finish the report until we have the data in and analysed?*

Don't worry. Jon has been working on writing the report for some time, so that all we need to do is slot the data into it, do some final revisions and write the conclusion. The conclusions are so bloody obvious; I expect he has already written it. She turned again and grinned at Jenny.

Well, at least it has made you happy.

Aren't you happy?

I'm not sure, said Jenny. *Just a few weeks ago Jon was pushing us to collect the data and get our data sheets through processing, and suddenly the report is written. It just seems a bit odd.*

Why is it odd? The question accused Jenny. *We have all been working really hard to collect the data and Jon thinks we have enough to make the arguments we need to make.*

Okay. Jenny wanted to concede the issue and give way to the morning news, but there was still something discomforting about what Dee was excited about.

So which is it?

What?

So which is it? Has Jon completed the report and have we collected all the data we need, or is he waiting for the data we were going to collect? Jenny waited.

I'm not completely sure. Dee seemed deflated. There was a confession in her face. *I know we're also under some pressure with the funding agency. The report has to be with them by some deadline so they will release next year's money. Maybe Jon has decided that we have to go with what we have got.*

Maybe I'll be doing nothing for the next month.

I hadn't thought of that, confessed Dee.

Jenny's attention was grabbed by the radio.

Dee chirped in, *I could ask Jon…*

Shh! I want to listen.

The radio spoke: *…the second in two weeks. A police spokesperson is asking the public to be especially careful not to leave children unattended, even briefly, while in public. Now to the sport…*

What was that? asked Dee.

Jenny wondered if she should say anything. *There have been a couple of attempts to take a child from a shopping centre near our house.*

Goodness. What a frightening thing to do.

Jenny agreed. *Yes, it is.*

Tad: Triumphant Return

It was late to arrive back at the hostel. The night staff might have bolted the door by now and he would have to ring the bell to be let in. The knife was tucked inside his trousers, held up by his belt. Tad's mind raced for something to say to the staff if someone came to the door. Just in case, he pulled his key from his pocket and put it in the door. It opened. Into the hall and straight to the stairs.

Tad! The voice of the night staffer halted him on the first step. *If you are coming back late, let us know so we don't lock you out by accident.*

Sorry. I'll let you know next time. He started up the stairs. Something else he had got away with.

Are you all right? said the staffer. Tad was desperate to get upstairs and look at the knife in good light.

Just stubbed my toe. It's okay. He limped up the stairs holding his side to prevent the treasure from falling out. Down the corridor he hurried. Benny emerged from the shower room, wrapped in a towel. He looked straight at Tad and turned away. *Benny!* Tad said in surprise. Darryl stepped out of the shower room behind Benny, also wrapped in a towel.

I see your boyfriend is back, Benny. Do you think he will be jealous? Benny did not respond or join the mockery. Tad looked at the couple of towelled men walking down the corridor in front of him, each with one arm swinging and the other holding the towel together at the side. Benny turned into Darryl's room and Darryl hesitated at the door, turning to Tad. *Well, you little fucker, are you jealous?* Tad had come to the attention of Darryl just by being associated with Benny. He had always known that he was at risk of his cover being broken. This was a challenge of a kind, not necessarily a threat of violence. It was an invitation to be submissive that only victims like Benny and he understood. To go back down the stairs would identify him as a target of exploitation for as long as he lived there. Others would see the weakness and take their chances with him too. To stand his ground meant a beating was likely at some time, either now or later. Darryl had made an assertion of the order of things and if that assertion was not true Darryl would expose himself to challenges from all sides. He had to make the assertion true at any cost and that meant pounding the square peg into the round hole until it fitted. Tad knew he had become the square peg and could not hide now. Darryl would come and find him. He felt the knife against his side and realised he had a choice this time.

Darryl stood in the hall, blocking Tad's progress, and then stepped towards him. Tad reached under his jacket and gripped the handle of his knife, still in the belt of his trousers. Darryl hesitated. His eyes searched for clues while he calculated the risk of a weapon or being seen to struggle in dealing with this.

Don't be too brave, you little fucker. Not too brave. He let the towel fall, exposing his cock. He smiled, knowing that Tad would do nothing, and turned into his room after Benny.

Tad waited for the door to close before moving. Darryl had walked away from him. It was hardly believable. Sure, there had been a threat but he had stood his ground against Darryl and it was not him who had turned away. Energy surged through him. In the few paces to his room, two things became certain for Tad. He would not sleep tonight until he had milked the excitement out of him, and he would have to carry the knife with him now. Darryl would take any chance he got to put the world into the order of his choosing and no one would protect him. Tad needed to be ready.

In his room, Tad locked his door carefully, laid the knife on his bed and wondered at it. It might have been used to kill people in wartime. His heart was pounding from the encounter with Darryl and now the elation of having such an object. Owning something like this was beyond his thinking. Anyone can have a knife, but having a knife like this was like having grown six inches in the night, having a pretty girl on his arm, driving a sports car, having a big TV on his wall or having a proper job. He was somehow inside the world with this knife in his hand. He was a player, could make things happen and had discovered one very important thing; he did not have to back away anymore.

Jenny: Office Life

Jenny sat at her workstation wondering what she should be doing. There had been no morning meeting with Jon and the other researchers. There had been nothing. She, with all the researchers except Dee, listened to the faint sound of voices coming from Jon's office. The computers waited for emails. Jon's door opened and he walked into the open office with Dee following. Jenny watched her. Dee's arms were folded, face sullen, looking away from Jon and making eye contact with no one. Jon started.

Sorry for the delay in getting going this morning. A few things have happened and I want to keep you all in the loop. Jenny watched Dee's eyes search the floor in front of her. *You all know I like to be as transparent as I can with all that we do here, but I should have told you all why I've put you under so much pressure to get your data collected and analysed.* Jenny recognised her conversation with Dee. Jon continued. *About six weeks ago, I heard from the funding agency that we were likely to lose our funding for next year, because their priorities have changed.* The team of researchers shuffled. *I know I told you that our funding was certain for next year, but as with everything in this life, nothing is completely certain. I was hoping to have solid news before alarming anyone. Obviously, I'm concerned to keep the research group going and keep as many of you as possible so I've been working hard, on your behalf, to generate some pressure on the funders to change their minds.*

What happened? Why have they changed their minds? A voice came from behind Jenny. Even the question suggested where the fault lay.

To be honest, I'm not sure. Jon's sincerity was palpable. *In some ways it does not matter exactly why it changed; all that matters is that we face the problem and deal with it. Let me tell you what I've been doing, because I need you all on board if we are going to keep the project going.*

Jenny became aware of the quiet in the room. He had them all in the grip of his confidence and the courageous effort to save them from unemployment. Jenny looked over her shoulder at their faces and could see they had already forgiven his deception and were already willing to do what he asked, without knowing what it was. *My plan is to write the report now and release it as soon as we can, before the decision to cut our funding is made public, at the end of next week. I've set up the local Member of Parliament, who will support us publicly, and I have a few contacts in the national press who will be doing an article and some follow-up on the reaction, because the findings are important enough. So—*

The same voice from behind said, *But we don't have the data to write the report.*

Jon continued without hesitation. *Thanks to everyone stepping up and increasing the data collection, we have quite a bit of data that we can use, and there are ways of transposing the data to get the most out of it. I've already drafted the body of the report; the background, methodology and so on. It looks really good. My task now is to take the data you have collected and make a public splash with it so that your jobs are safe and we get the problem of homeless men into the public domain so it won't be denied. It's what we've been working towards. All we need from you is a little patience until I finish writing the report, then I'll ask you all to read it before final editing. Of course I'll make sure that you all get credited with the work, and all your names will be on it. It will be a feather in all of our caps.*

What do we do today?

Jon turned to Dee, whose arms tightly squeezed her body. *Dee will help me get it out to you just after lunch. I need you back in the office at two and you'll each have a paper copy to annotate before going home. We are on a tight schedule and need every minute this afternoon, but this morning make use of the time to do whatever housekeeping and emails you need to do.* A smile spread across Jon's face like sunshine warming everyone. *Or go find a coffee shop and do some 'team bonding'.*

The team began settling at their workstations.

Jenny asked, *Can you tell us what you told the MP and the papers?* The rustling stopped.

What do you mean? asked Jon. Dee looked at Jenny, then to Jon before searching the floor again.

Jenny looked up from her seat at Jon standing above her. *Well, you said you have already told them what conclusions are in the report. I know there's data that's not been entered yet, so I just wondered what it was that you told them.* She had not meant it to sound challenging, but it did. *Sorry, I don't mean to imply—* Jon interrupted her.

That's true, I have had a couple of great meetings to rally support for our project, but you'll get the full story at two o'clock. I can tell you that there will be no surprises. You have all been in the field and know what is going on out there. I won't be saying anything outside of what you already know. Jenny – he looked down at her as a parent would stand over a child – *you have to remember that statistical inference is not as simple as you suggest. Adding more data to a clear trend doesn't change the trend, but does increase the confidence with which it can be reported. Now, let me get back to my desk, and get that report done.*

Jon turned, heading out of the room and down the corridor as the rustling of the office settled to a murmur. Dee followed.

Jenny looked around. No one looked back. It was not yet 9am and already it had been an unsettling day. She had no desire to go and bond with these people, sharing their optimism and acceptance. It was obvious that something unusual was happening, but she was alone in thinking this. All the talk of sampling theory, scientific methods and procedural rigour did not stand up beside arriving at conclusions before data had been entered. She was separate from them and could not bring herself to bridge that space. It was time to find a coffee, go for a walk to clear her head. She gathered her things and went for the door. The voice from behind said, *We're heading for Starbucks.* It was an effort to bring her into the fold, a kind gesture, but not enough.

Thanks. I've a few things to do first.

Coffee in hand, she walked into the park. It was mild out and there would be life to watch. It was past nine o'clock and the schools were all in. Mothers wheeled and tugged their infants away from the school gate. A brief diversion to the swings for the tots was a treat not to be missed and it came with the chance of resolving the breakfast fracas and the promise of getting to lunchtime without drama. Jenny settled down on the park bench and watched them pass, imagining their lives. There was crying on the swings and shouting on the slide. Mothers lifted and hoisted their children on and off, up and down. Two others chatted aimlessly at the edge of the playground while their children, jackets flapping, shouted and trundled around. The turmoil of motherhood was never so attractive.

Someone sat beside her. Dee said, *I followed you here. I hope you don't mind.*

No, of course not. They both looked over the playground. Dee pulled a cigarette from a packet, put it in her mouth and lit it in quick little movements. The first drag was held in until the packet and lighter were back in her bag, and only then did she relax and exhale.

Are you hoping to have a family? asked Dee. Jenny acknowledged it was true, with a smile and a nod. *The clock is ticking for both of us,* continued Dee. *I guess I was never suited to motherhood. I don't feel like I would make a good mother.* Jenny smiled and waited. It was not the reason she had followed her to the park. Dee continued, *You don't seem too happy.*

It's complicated right now. I'll get over it. Jenny hoped that would be enough to stem the questions.

I thought you were a little tense when I picked you up this morning. Jenny stayed quiet, then Dee started again. *Jon is a little worried that you're unhappy about finishing the report and getting it out.*

I was just surprised. It just came out before I had thought about it. I seem to be doing that a lot lately.

Dee took another drag on the cigarette and turned her head to exhale. *I think you should speak to Jon and let him know that you are part of the team over this.* Jenny looked at Dee, realising that it was Jon speaking through her.

Did he send you to check me out, to test my loyalty?

Not exactly, said Dee. *He has said to me that he wondered about your commitment, but I am looking out for you. It may be that we do lose some funding and you don't want to be the one that is let go.* Jenny saw it for what it was; as clear a threat as could be made and still be denied.

Should I be worried? said Jenny, knowing it to be true.

He wants you to talk with him before the team meets again at two o'clock. It would be worth the trouble just to let him know that you're supporting what he's trying to do. Jenny watched Dee's face, which looked down and away. Eye contact was momentary. It was not the expression of someone looking out for her. There was something going on. There was a motive unsaid and a shame to be avoided. Jenny wondered how some people believed it could not be seen. Then it was clear.

You're seeing him again, aren't you? Jenny's gaze scorched her.

That's nothing to do with this. I'm trying to help you. Dee's appeal to Jenny seemed lame to both of them.

What have you said to him? Jenny looked away to make it easier for Dee to confess the exaggeration of their conversations and any other fabrication suited to Dee's purpose. It did not really matter what Dee had said, or what she confessed to saying now. The damage to her prospects was done and a decision about her future was almost certainly already made. This was a pattern familiar to her. Jenny said, *You didn't need to say anything. I have a relationship. Jon is of no interest to me in that way.* She needed the job too, but did not want to say.

I don't know what you're talking about now, said Dee. *It's your decision whether to go and talk to Jon or not. I've done what I can for you.* There was righteousness in Dee's voice. The pretence of not knowing what Jenny was referring to distanced her from harm done. The indignation just confirmed her connivance. For all of her life Jenny had watched people shed their misdeeds onto those who had been harmed. It was standard. *I need some cigarettes.* Dee stood and walked away quickly. Jenny looked over at the park at the children playing.

Tad: The Knife

Tad noticed changes. First the content of his rich internal life altered and then leached into the real world. He could soothe his shame with thoughts of vengeance. Previously he could only manage resentment. The thought of physical confrontation had been so closely associated with his denigration that he was only capable of escape, fear or helplessness when the prospect arose. There had been times when he was unable to escape and had accepted a beating, knowing it was coming and resigning himself to it. Offering no resistance was disarming to the assailant. He had discovered as a child that resistance prolonged the abuse. His silence and passivity had the power to limit the punishment, although it never quite compensated for the humiliation. Now, just having the image of the knife in his hand slicing through the flesh of his tormentor was enough to alter the balance. He could recover from descent into dark shame without weeks of turmoil and internal mockery. He would remove the knife from the drawer and practise the physical movement of vengeance until sweat ran from his body.

There was pleasure in removing the object, wrapped up in a grubby towel like the stolen artefact it was. He unfolded the towel with what he had come to think of as ceremony. Several times each day the ritual was performed and it had given him a satisfaction that he had not previously known. It was something to look after and be responsible for. Sensuality was in the touch and discipline in the ritual. He had nurtured this piece for weeks and it was from this care that fascination had transformed the knife into surreal fantasy. Tad imagined his hand bringing the knife to the enemy with brutal force. The hilt stopped at the skin but the blade kept travelling, elongating, cleaving through organs. It was magical. Sometimes he imagined finishing an eviscerated tormentor with a chopping hammer fist, bringing the butt of the knife onto the skull. Bone fragments squelched into the brain. The tension of imagined effort vibrated in grinding teeth and stretched tendons.

The training changed his body. He was getting stronger, leaner and more confident. There was pride in his expertise. The stealing of secrets and the magic of the knife gave him a foothold. He had refined the strike by learning to reach forward with his left hand, grabbing the elbow and pulling it towards him, clearing the way for the blade to enter under the ribs. It was a small addition, which pleased him. It made the strike more certain and did not interfere with the powerful rotation in his thrust.

He became the authority with this object, acting under its magic, and for the most part was untroubled by the doubts and intrusive thoughts that had humiliated him each day. With the knife in his hand he became a player, an influence on the world. He could have time without shame and could repair the damage of outrageous fortune, or casual slight, with just the image of a violent jab, settling the argument, concluding business. They all deserved it. It did not matter if the insult was large or small. Gradually, whether or not there was an insult did not seem to matter. Life with the knife had become preferable to all that had happened to him.

Jenny: Visit

It was still early. Jenny dropped her coffee cup into the park bin and started walking. She wondered what others would do. Some would start crying and wait for comforting attention, some would go home and write lists, others would walk through the shops, looking, touching, fantasising. Jenny wanted to disengage completely. To find that space where no one else mattered, where she was responsible for nothing, and without intrusive thoughts of what she wanted or needed. This was a time to go back there. Normally she resisted going there as long as she could, but today was different. There was too much to contain; she had been drawn a long way into the open.

There was plenty of time for the visit before seeing Jon. It was just a bus ride away and she could be back at the office for the bad news by one o'clock. Already it was starting to feel that it did not matter. The world receded in the strides to the bus stop.

Dee did not know the young man who entered the park just as she was leaving. She was far too occupied with her own thoughts, which flipped from shame to indignation and back again. The young man was intent on something and stretched his neck to see something or someone in the distance. He locked on to Jenny walking across the park to the far exit. He wanted to catch up, but he was intrigued now with where she was going.

Tad: Lara Croft

In the hostel dining room, Tad ventured up to the counter for his evening meal. The tray of grey food altered only marginally each day, but there was plenty of it. He had taken to eating with others in the dining room. It meant that he did not have to hang around the streets every evening and wait for the danger to clear, and his food was even hot sometimes. Benny approached and sat next to Tad for the first time in a week. Nothing was said between them until Benny spoke up.

Don't ask me about it.

Okay, said Tad. There was another long pause as they ate.

I don't like it, but what can I do?

Tad looked at the lumbering hippo and thought that all he needed to have was the knife. That would deal with it. He spoke between shovels of food. *I know. It's not your fault. Bad things can happen to people like you. You have to be more careful.* Until that moment, Tad had not considered that he was all that different from Benny. Both were low order, outsiders, without prospects – but Tad was different now. At the edge of his vision Tad saw that Darryl had entered the dining room. Two more shovels and he would be away. *Gotta go, Benny. See you in the TV room.* He was still forking mouthfuls as he stood up, and then he bounded out of the dining room, upstairs, into his room. Darryl watched him go.

It had been a mistake to go into the dining room without the knife. He could have been confronted, and all the sense of status and the confidence that had grown would have been reduced to the state of Benny.

Tad removed the drawer at the bottom of the rickety wooden chest in his room. On the floor inside the chest it lay wrapped in a grey towel. He removed it, laid it on the bed and returned the drawer to the chest. The ceremony began. There was plenty of time before the film would start.

His whole body warmed to the task. Practice and preparation were new sensual pleasures. Tad thought of it as being like an athlete who would look forward to the gruelling training and the energising high that comes with sustained effort. He lifted a pint glass of water to his lips and drained it. He wiped the sweat off his face with the towel and then wiped his arms and chest. The old shirt was back on and he slid the knife up his sleeve, just in case. All his rehearsal tonight had just the one enemy.

Tad waited for the lights to be turned off in the TV room before venturing downstairs. He walked through the door of the TV lounge without hesitation but was stranded for a moment at the door until his eyes adjusted. Benny sat in his usual spot at the back, where Tad joined him.

Benny bent over and whispered, *I saved it for him.* Tad acknowledged that with a nod but did not move and wondered if this was to be the moment for the strike. He would not get away with it with so many people in the room. Just a moment passed until the door rattled open. Tad stood up in alarm and moved forward through the rows of seats looking for an empty one. He heard Benny say that he had saved Darryl a seat. Finally, Tad found an empty seat near the front, hoping that neither Darryl nor anyone else had seen him get up and scamper away like he was afraid.

The alarm he had felt caused a sudden loss of confidence. His mind raced with every conceivable explanation. *Don't bother, you little chicken shit. Everyone knows why you run.* He ground his teeth and forced his head back into the chair. *I was just startled, that's all. Just didn't expect the door to open.* For a moment Tad was unsure if those words had left his mouth or stayed inside his head. In the darkness, he let the handle of the knife slip into his hand. His breathing settled and he concentrated on letting his shoulders relax.

On the screen an animation of *Lara Croft: Tomb Raider* played to an enthralled audience. A childlike, voluptuous Lara with huge eyes was tied to a post. Her arms pulled by ropes behind her caused her breasts to jut off the screen. From a short distance away a mean-looking man raised his gun and shot her. In a moment she was being held against a wall by a man so large as to be of a different dimension. He held a sword to her throat and pulled it swiftly down. She cried out like a child and the audience giggled. Before the resolution of the scene, a new clip started.

What's this? Tad asked, to anyone who would answer.

From the game, Tomb Raider. *From all the ways she gets done,* came a proud anonymous voice. *Got it from YouTube.*

Cartoon Lara was now being washed through a surreal underground labyrinth with tangled tree roots and splintered timbers. Through a narrow passage and down a gully she went, before stopping with a thud in some ruins as the rapids fell away. A large stake pierced her throat, exiting the back of her head, and for a moment she whimpered and struggled, dangling by her skull before dying, still beautiful, voluptuous and childlike. Another scene started immediately. She waited helplessly with an arrow protruding from her side and another high on her chest. It did not stop. Every 15 or 20 seconds a new scenario started, each ending with the sweet cartoon Lolita tormented by sadists in new and exotic ways until her sudden death by penetration. The audience offered gasps of pleasure and approval. They bulged with the excitement of gorging themselves in horror without sanction. There was no one here to disapprove. Noise in the lounge increased until the most shocking and ghastly endings resulted in spontaneous, hysterical laughter.

Tad stayed glued to the images without story, until the need to relieve the tension in his trousers became more than could be ignored. He got up and made his way to the door just as Lara fell off a cliff onto some long pikes. Impaled, she arched her back in orgasmic pleasure, blinked slowly and expired gently. *Ooh* and *aah*, said the room. Tad got to the last row and could see Darryl's face, lit by the cartoon. Head back, eyes closed, Benny's head in his lap, now so brazen as to not require coats to protect anyone's modesty. The public dominance and humiliation of Benny had become important. It could have been done in a bedroom or shower or even in the park, but it had to be done here, in the company of those who lived together. The scene was disgusting and humiliating to be near.

Anger bubbled up like a geyser, transforming sexual energy to fury. His mind raced and muscles tensed. He imagined the knife slipping into his hand.

Darryl became aware of something else when an arm encircled his neck and the blade entered his mouth. Instinctively, he grabbed Tad's arm and tried to sit up. He felt the point stick in the roof of his mouth and the blade slice his tongue. He recoiled into the chair and froze. Tad had his left arm around Darryl's throat and with the right he slid the blade as deeply into his mouth as it could go before it stopped against the flesh. Darryl's blood ran down his throat and he gulped in desperation. The sharp edges of steel brushed the soft fleshy palate. He heard Tad whisper in his ear. *Suck it.* It was hard to understand what to do, but Tad reinforced the message with a little jab. *Just suck it*, and he twisted the knife against his teeth. *Go on.* The audience turned from Lara's torment to see. Darryl slowly closed his lips around the blade. *Suck, suck, suck*, Tad whispered as he pushed the knife deeper into his mouth. *Blow, blow, blow*, and Tad pulled and pushed the blade into his mouth. *Don't take your lips off it or you'll choke on it.*

Tad could see and smell the terror of the hostel's top dog. As long as he kept the knife in Darryl's mouth he ruled the universe. He could drive the knife hard enough to pin Darryl to the chair – Darryl, who squealed as the knife cut the back of his throat. The room watched him. In the dark, his blood ran black over his chin and dripped on the chair. Other faces were silhouetted against the tormenting of Lara Croft, each agitating to get a better view. Lara was again tied to a post waiting for her body to be penetrated by a samurai sword. She watched to see what Tad would do. He squeezed hard enough to make it impossible for Darryl to breathe or swallow the blood accumulating in his mouth.

Tad's breath was hot against his ear. The words he used arrived easily, as if he was just ready to say them. *Just fuck off and leave Benny alone. If I see you again, I'll cut you.*

Benny began punching Darryl's body. Heavy, thrashing left and right fists landed. Tad pulled the knife from his mouth and Lara screamed. Darryl folded, retching, begging to be left alone. Benny's weight fell on top of him, one knee into his back and the other to his head. The audience recoiled at the thudding crunch.

Light from the hallway recalled Tad to himself, splashing into the room and down the wall with the door opening. It was the night staffer.

Benny. Is Benny here? I need you to come into the office, please. Benny looked up for the first time and saw Tad standing by the door, blocking the view of the staffer. Darryl sat up and adjusted himself in the half-light. The others were too concerned with Lara's peril to be interested in turning.

Tad stepped past the staffer and headed for the stairs, past the police officer standing in the hall. He was still cupping the handle of the knife in his hand, with the blade hidden up his sleeve. Blue light swept into the hall from the police car outside. At the top of the stairs, Tad looked to see Benny and the night staffer enter the hallway from the TV lounge. Some others followed them out to see what there was to see. The door of the office was open and from inside radio crackle could be heard.

The hostel was hushed, as was usual when the police visited. It was obvious that Benny had trouble. Now it was known the police were in the house, some moved quickly to get out the door. Tad went to his room. His heart pounded with the exhilaration of the night's events. The knife had changed everything. He had known it was capable of this from the first time that he held it in the old woman's house, but to see in his mind what it could do – it was magical. The clarity of the image in the TV room confused him for a moment. It only mattered that it showed him the way.

He pulled his shirt off, wrapped the knife and returned it to the hiding place, and started rehearsing what he would say if the police came to talk with him as he prepared for the shower. He would say that he was in his room and knew nothing of Benny. It was what everyone would say.

Tad closed the tap of the shower. With the towel wrapped around him he opened the door and walked to the handrail. Downstairs it was quiet. The question of what Benny had done, or what Darryl had got him to do that had landed him in trouble, had stayed with him. He recalled the image of Benny descending on Darryl as if it was real, but Benny was gone now, to be locked up somewhere. He had made his choices and was lost for a time. The police or the courts or prison would have him, and nothing could be done.

A door opened behind Tad as he walked to his room. Darryl stepped into the corridor. *Hey, little fucker, don't walk off.*

Tad continued to walk, wishing he had taken his knife to the shower with him.

Jenny: Icarus

Jenny rode the bus towards the stop just a few minutes' walk from the office. Two hours had passed since leaving the meeting with Dee in the park. She reflected on how easy it was to get on a bus and escape to familiar ground. It never failed to provide the distance from the world she needed, like the moments of serenity offered to an addict by the hit. It promised so much in trying times. The tension was now spent. She looked out on the grey landscape and began wondering if others could see or smell what she had been doing. She brought her hand up to her face and sniffed her fingers before checking if others were watching. It was never shame causing her sensitivity; it was the disappointment that she could not always resist it.

The bus stopped and Jenny heaved a large breath as she got up from her seat and stepped onto the pavement. There was time to think how she would manage the meeting with her boss. It occurred to her that if a decision had been made there might still be a chance of keeping her job, if she played her cards right. The reassuring words that might be used filtered through her mind. She would have to flatter him and pander to his ego, none of which would be troublesome; it was just what some men needed and she was content to oblige.

The office door was open and she entered the empty corridor, walking past his office and dumping her bag and jacket at her workstation. There was no one there, but he would be in. She looked into her blank computer screen to get some idea of how she looked and was grateful that she could not see clearly what she knew to be true. It was time to face him.

Before she knocked on his door, he said, *Come in, Jenny.* She walked through his door. *Sorry to surprise you. I saw you through the window.*

Dee said you wanted to see me before the others came back.

Jon smiled. *Well, I thought we had better speak.* There was not a hint of awkwardness in his voice. *I was surprised by your reaction to our situation today. You made me think you were disapproving of our plan to finish the report early.*

Sorry, I didn't mean to give that impression. I think it's really good of you to find a way to keep the agency going.

Jon smiled again, but more slowly, without the eyes. He continued, but Jenny knew already that a decision had been made to let her go. She had to stop him from saying the words. It was the only way. *That's good to hear. It has been really hard for me lately, with the finance issue looming, I've had to work hard and make some difficult decisions.* She stopped him.

Is there something I could do to take some of the pressure off you?

Jon hesitated, *Well, I...*

There are plenty of things I could be doing, other than walking the streets, collecting data.

I wouldn't refer to it as 'walking the streets'. It was more important than that. Jon relaxed, took his weight off the desk and watched Jenny being coy, believing he had wrong-footed her.

I didn't mean... Jenny smiled.

I know. I didn't mean to be defensive. So, what did you have in mind?

Jenny looked at the pile of papers by the window. *Is that the report?* He nodded. *Can I look?* She stood up without waiting for an answer and walked to the small table by the window. She walked with the knowledge of him watching. Copies of the report were stacked up. She opened the cover of the top copy, stroked the first page and turned it. It was not easy to do this, at least not as easy as usual. She had to stop thinking of what she was doing and concentrate just on him, and then it would come: the rhythm and control. Jenny wondered if the morning was making it more difficult. He appeared beside her.

Looks good, doesn't it?

It does. Very impressive. You have been busy. Jenny turned the pages and fell upon a table in which her data was reported. It was in a familiar form and it only took her a few seconds to comprehend and detect the inflating of the numbers in the sample. He noticed what she was reading. She said, *It should convince the funders, and a few politicians,* and smiled broadly at him.

So you didn't answer my question. She looked at him. *What did you have in mind, to take the pressure off?* He was standing too close to her for his question to be mistaken. The back of his hand brushed her. It was all she could do not to recoil and then she wished she had. Her stillness was now an invitation; her passivity was acceptance. In any case, the pace was no longer in her control. Maybe she had brought it on too suddenly. He took no time at all to read the signals. Perhaps it did not matter. All she needed to do was wait for it to be over and the job would be hers. *Relax; drift away.* It was starting to work now. She was drifting off, slowly. His hand cupped one buttock and then the other. She leaned over the table and reminded herself to let it go. His hands engulfed her, searching for the fastener of her trousers. In a moment the band was loose. She tried to ignore it, looking down. The report's table looked up and distracted her from drifting away. She closed her eyes.

The hand was inside her underwear now, probing and pushing, gripping her flesh too hard for her to escape the sensation. He leaned forward, bringing his mouth to her ear without losing his grip. *You're soaking wet. You must be desperate for it.* The morning raced through her mind without pleasure.

His thumb pressed deeply inside her and he gripped her pubic bone, lifting and pulling her into position. She felt him fumble with his belt. All the time her pubis was gripped fast.

What would your boyfriend say if he knew about this? The recollection of Mark emerged suddenly, sweeping her back to the world. Anger came with it. It was not enough that he have her in his office, he wanted to undermine everything about her, even Mark. She tried to stand straight but his weight and grip pinned her to the reports.

Get off! Get off! She twisted and fought to stop him, but the hand clamped her in place and his weight allowed only her hands to flap helplessly. *Stop. Just fuck off, would you!* It was too late. She felt him plunge effortlessly into her, sliding through her, taking up all space within her. There had been one previous time when the anguish of penetration escaped from her in a noise that could not be contrived. Tears came along with the guttural sound of air forced from her amid the sobs. Recollections of her mother, of her childhood, of the morning and of Mark buffeted her consciousness. There was no escape to the distant place within her this time. There was only the intrusion, crying and fury. She reached for something to fight with, flailing at everything within reach. Reports slid off the table and the lamp tilted over. Finally, she had something.

What are you doing? Dee's shout from the doorway of the office caused him to stop. Jon struggled to cover himself and turned away from both women. Jenny clenched the cheap plastic pen in her fist and brought it down hard on his back. He yelped as it burst through the shirt and stuck in the muscle next to his neck. The blood started to spread across his shirt. He struggled to pull it out and turned to see Jenny's face reddened, trousers and pants at her knees, and Dee, frozen.

Tad: Planning

From this spot, he could see all the pathways that could be taken through the clearing. The contours of the park funnelled passers-by into a long, shallow basin from three sides, but from the north a steeper slope and dense bush along the ridge had discouraged planners from giving access with trails. No one was ever there, where he was now, looking down at the park, imagining.

He turned to the west and began calculating the speed and distance he would need to travel to the adjoining path at the west side of the park. He would have to pace it out carefully. Once there, he would have to compose himself, control his breathing and start walking into the basin towards her from the opposite direction, as if out for a walk, with nothing on his mind. She would see him coming and must not be scared off by the closing distance between them. How would the blade be concealed? He needed a strap to dangle the blade from his shoulder or a means of disguising it as he approached her. Working out how the blade would get into his hands should not be too difficult. He would have to prepare the route from this place to the west side, so he would not trip while moving at speed through the bush. The right shoes were going to be important. It must be in broad daylight and he must leave no trace. A task list was accumulating. His head was beginning to swim with the number of things to keep track of. Maybe the first thing to do was to establish an escape route.

His thoughts returned to the moment that had been honed to clarity. That moment, despite the energy of cutting and flesh falling open, seemed effortless and controlled. His body stiffened and for a moment his mind was swept clear of clutter. The plan was in every part of him.

Involuntary movements of his head followed imagined foot-steps from the east along the path that stretched out to his left. He closed his eyes and watched her face as he approached her. He knew she was aware of him coming and was wary. She would be wondering if she should turn back or walk quickly by him. The connection between them excited him. His fingers rippled as if closing on a handle and the muscles of his forearm and biceps tensioned. Each breath held momentarily before release. In his mind the moment approached slowly, and when it arrived his body twisted violently. Starting from the ball of his right foot, his pelvis was driven towards her, causing his torso to whip around like a golfer's swing. The tension in his arm harnessed the momentum of his twisting body and drove his fist into the soft flesh between ribs and pelvis. It had been rehearsed so often the coordination was automated; triggered involuntarily with the intense image of that moment. He had read that internal organs did not feel pain so she would not feel the blade, just the impact. She would not know exactly what had happened. He watched her face as she fell, helpless, her understanding growing as life was flowing away. It was always like this. It never failed to arouse him.

The city's honking turmoil intruded from a distance and the crystalline image was lost. Anger bubbled quickly. It was the fucking taxis in this town again. The fucking foreigners who drove them only worried about their business and never minded who they bothered. He promised himself to deal with them but now, having found the perfect observation point, he would start his reconnoitring.

Making his way down the ridge into the basin was easily done for a young man. He slid and scrambled the 20 metres to the clearing. There was a playground to his left about a 100 metres southwest of him as he stood at the edge of the bush. The path from the supermarket passed through the treeline and by a playground. A child sat quiet and helpless in a swing as her father pushed her. He would have to make sure there were no men in the park at the time. The path continued along two-thirds of the basin before dividing into a 'Y'. The southern branch reached the road through a row of trees and a thin strip of bush. The northern branch arched uphill along the edge of the ridge to his right. He would walk down that northern branch, as if there was nothing on his mind, and watch her coming towards him. He could not help but pause again and imagine.

His escape could not be through the supermarket car park from where she would come. Supermarkets have busy car parks and there are so many people coming and going: young men and fathers, arriving to do the shopping, could cause him trouble. He might be remembered, or even spotted on a camera. Maybe even photographed by one of the endless number of texting teenagers in leggings, with headphones in their ears and a willingness to snap anyone's misfortune and post it on Facebook. He hated them. His moments of embarrassment reeled through his head before he shook free of them. The escape had to be into the open street to the south or through the bush on the north side, risking the climb up the slope, where his shoes would again be important. It was late afternoon and he noted the position of the sun. If it were to happen at this time of day, she would have the sun in her eyes.

He scrambled back to the observation point and onto the top of the north ridge. It was not that difficult going up. It pleased him that this was an escape option. As he emerged from the bush he was confronted by a long fence running east to west, behind which were houses. A narrow dirt track ran along the fence. It was perfect. It meant that he could gain access to the park and perhaps escape without being seen. He could smell the remnants of dogs that had been walked on the path. He went east along the fence in the direction of the supermarket. The track curled around the edge of the last of the fence and gardens and met a road. The road continued down the hill to the supermarket.

The supermarket car park was separated from the playground by a dense boundary of foliage, broken by a 6-foot path between them. From his position, he could see someone walking from the supermarket through the car park and into the park. If he was quick enough, he might be able to get to the west pathway and begin his casual approach. But how would he see the rest of the clearing? He would have to get back to the observation post first, to check for men in the park. Maybe he could miss this out and check out the clearing as he entered it. He could always abandon his plan if there was a problem. *Wanker.* It was part of the plan. *Sure it is, cocksucker.* It was the fucking plan! *Tosser! Just do it. Fucking wanker. Get on with it.* The tormenting voice was never far away. It could always make caution feel like a weakness, but he would not be weak this time. Not this time.

He decided to see how quickly he could join the northern branch of the path leading into the basin from this position and started walking west along the ridge path. By the end of the day he would understand the killing ground, the escape routes, the timing, everything.

Jenny: Empty

Jenny stepped out of Dee's car. There was no goodbye. Dee had not stopped talking from the office to home. It was not so easy to listen to her explain, justify, apologise and rage at what she had seen in the office. Sitting quietly in the passenger seat, Jenny understood that everything in Dee's life had been exposed and torn. She had wasted her adult life on that man, forgiving him everything and granting him benefits of all doubts, for only his charm and betrayal. She could not help but ricochet between her loyalty and the wrongs of the day, condemning and then preserving all that she could. Nowhere was there refuge from the dissonance. There was no space to process all that had happened, so she could not wait to be home, away from Dee's blizzard, but already she had decided not to go to the hospital and not to call the police. No one wanted her to make something of the incident in the office. More importantly, she had not wanted it to emerge and be examined.

She was surprised by blood on her hand as she opened her bag, and wiped it on her trousers. It had dried brown and would not come off. The keys were finally in her hand and she was in the front door of the house. It was quiet. She had hoped Mark would be home, but there was no reason for him to be home in the middle of the afternoon. The house did not seem to be the same. It was too cold, too quiet and there was too much light. She thought it odd that all of this crossed her mind at all. It had been an unusual day and yet at this moment, all she could feel was fatigue and disappointment with herself. There was nothing to do but shower, make some coffee and wait for Mark to come home.

Her clothes lay in her tracks from bedroom to shower. The dried brown blood swirled red down the drain. There was no rush to finish in the shower or to get dressed again, except she was getting hungry and coffee was on her mind. All this time was hers and gradually she was gaining some control of it. It was a matter of being responsible for her behaviour. How she had placed herself in that situation at work by being righteous about the data, inviting him to do as he pleased with her, leading him on. He could not possibly have anticipated her turning on him. She tried to think through that again. It was the stabbing of him that was difficult to fathom. Having never before acted that way, why now? The recollection of his odious remarks and his satisfaction with cuckolding Mark had annoyed her, but it was not enough to explain it. Her conversation with Mark that morning came back to her. She gathered up her clothes and pushed them into the laundry basket, placing the lid firmly down on it as if stowing it all away. It would not leave her. She sat on the bed and waited for the conflict within her to come into view. Contemplating her motives was unfamiliar territory, but she tried to form a question. She spoke quietly to herself: *Why was I angry with him; because he reminded me of being unfaithful? I don't think so!* It did not really make sense and could not be resolved easily. Perhaps she could not resolve it and should stop trying. Certainly it was not the first time she would have to live with something she had done that did not make sense to her.

She slipped into jeans and a sweater, headed down the stairs, turning the corner at the bottom of the stairs and into the kitchen. She filled the kettle and switched on the gas burner. Food was the next thing on her mind. She turned from the sink and wondered if there was enough bread. On the table, held upright by the salt and pepper, was a piece of paper. It was plain white paper from the pad of letter-writing paper they had used to write thank-you notes to Mark's family at Christmas and birthdays. It was a note from Mark. No one else could possibly have written it to her. It would say only one thing. Jenny knew without reading it that Mark was not coming home tonight. She had known that since breakfast, but now it was true and the sadness could start.

Tad: Practice

There were problems still to solve. He had to make a final check that no one was behind him when he approached her on the path, but it had to look natural to her, without alerting her or causing her to turn and run. The other problem was getting the knife into his hand at just the right moment. She would be walking towards him as he would be walking towards her. He would make sure he passed her on the right. At the moment they passed he would pull her elbow forward and drive the blade into the soft flesh under her ribs. If the blade came into his hand too early, she would see it and flee. If it was too late, she would pass by and the moment would be lost. He was not going to run after her and get her from the back. It seemed cowardly.

He stood in front of the mirror with the knife tucked behind his back, under his shirt and into his belt. Walking towards the mirror, Tad watched himself. He dipped his body and reached out with his left hand as if grasping the elbow of the oncoming imaginary woman. His right hand reached behind him, gripped the handle of the knife and pulled fiercely. The handle caught in his trousers, loosening his grip and sending the knife cartwheeling into the air. He tried again, but this time he lifted his shirt off the handle to make it more accessible. He watched himself in the mirror and rehearsed verbally, miming the movements slowly. *Reach for the elbow, go for the knife.* It seemed that it would work, so he tried again. He walked towards the mirror and reached for the elbow. The grip on the knife was too far up the handle and he felt his finger squeeze the sharp edge as he pulled. *Fuck!* Tad whipped his hand from behind him and pushed his index finger into his mouth. The blood came. *Fuck, fuck, fuck!*

You idiot. What a tosser you are. The internal commentary caused him to blush in shame and anger. Tad stumbled irritably into the bathroom down the hall from his room and turned on the tap. The stream of water opened the wound, causing him to wince again. He looked closely at the cut, now magnified by the water running over it. It was not very long, but he could see the inside of the index finger of his right hand and make out the flesh underneath the skin with the water forcing the edges apart. He was reminded of what the knife would do when he used it in earnest. The cold water rushed over the finger, making the blood seem like a trickle as it washed into the sink and swirled down the drain. The aching coldness of the water replaced the pain and the furies left him.

At least he had learned that quickly grabbing the knife and drawing it like a cowboy draws a gun was not going to work. That's why he had done the practice session – *No, you didn't* – to learn that sort of thing. The cut was nothing. It had taught him something so it was good. It came to him that the only way he could get the knife into his hand at the right time, without alarming her, was to carry it in something. All that was left was to work out how he would check behind him for the last time, without alarming the woman.

Jenny: Who To Call

Jenny woke from a restless sleep on the living room sofa with the thought that it must be Mark trying to get in after she had fastened the latch, but the memory of the note was quick to remind her that it would not be Mark. The knock on the door was no longer polite. There was another, then the doorbell, followed by a third knock. The knocking stopped when she turned on the light. Jenny looked around the room for her robe before realising she was still dressed and then stumbled on her way to the door, her legs not yet obeying her intentions.

Two police officers stood on the doorstep; a man and a woman, each bundled in kit and protective clothes. *What is it?* she said, suddenly wondering if Mark had been injured. The serious look on their faces was not that of compassion. It was not Mark they were at her door about.

Are you Jennifer Tanner? said the male officer.

Yes, but I don't go by that name now. What's wrong? she asked, knowing already that it was about the stabbing of Jon, earlier in the day. In a moment, it became clear how this had happened. Jon would have gone to the hospital and there must have been questions about the injury. She had no intention of reporting him, but he was not to know that. He must have tried to cover himself by getting his accusation in first. It was like being in the care of the social workers again. Among the children it was always important to be the victim first and first accuser. Now that she could only be the second accuser, she knew it had to be done carefully. A counter-accusation said too quickly is always a defence that proves guilt. The trick was to reveal it slowly, incidentally, as if unrelated to the accusation.

Ms Tanner, the male officer started, *would you accompany us to the station, please?*

What's it about?

I am asking you now to come with us to the station. There are mat-

ters that we need to talk with you about, and the investigating officer will tell you what he can at the station. The young officer held his eye contact. There would be consequences if she refused.

Are you arresting me?

No, Ma'am. We are asking you to come to the station to help us with enquiries.

Jenny calculated the bearing of the young officer. Standing full square to her, eyes locked on, without expression. There was no decision to be made. *May I get my coat?* Jenny asked.

Of course you may, said the officer. Jenny turned from the door to find her coat and bag, with the female officer just behind her.

The police car moved off quietly from the kerb. It was the middle of the night and no one would have seen what had happened. All of the time, from this moment until the questioning started, would be thinking time that had to be used well, but it was hard to concentrate. The radio chatter in the car intruded. The two officers were in a familiar world and she was not.

The female officer spoke from the passenger seat. *Are you all right, Ms Tanner?*

Yes. I think so.

Have you ever been in a police car before? Jenny thought it was a strange topic for small talk.

No, I haven't. Jenny paused. *I feel like I am under arrest.*

You're not, said the officer. *My partner asked if you would come to the station with us and you agreed to come.*

Did I have a choice?

The officer smiled at her. *Well, you could have said 'no', but we still would need to have a conversation with you.*

It doesn't really matter what I want, I guess. It was too small a hook for them to bite. She continued, *The choice for me is already made. Like everything else today.* Her voice trailed off and she looked out of the window at the passing street.

The female officer scanned the enigmatic figure in the back seat. A voice in her head reminded her not to get involved. Just process the problem and get it off the streets. Normally, it was sensible just to pick people up, be polite and take them to the station. Job done. The more you said, the more likely it was that you would complicate your life. The investigating officer did not like the complication of a police car conversation. The prosecution complained that evidence of conversations occurring without a caution made convictions more difficult, and judges would tear the flesh from your bones if you interfered with the evidence. But there was something about Jenny Tanner. *It sounds like you have had a bad day already.*

It doesn't seem real. So much has happened, and then this. She looked down, gently shook her head, and waited. Finally, it arrived.

So, what's been going on?

Jenny held herself back. This was the chance and she must take it carefully. *Well, my partner left me this morning. That was the start.* Without looking at the officer Jenny felt the attention. *Then I discovered a big lie at work, and talked to my boss about it.*

That's always a tricky one, said the officer.

It was a mistake. Jenny paused, closing her eyes and resting her hand on her head and leaning on the window.

What happened? the officer asked. It was an innocent question to which she could respond.

He raped me in his office. The two officers glanced at each other, both knowing that this would alter the rest of their shift.

Jenny, are you saying that you were raped earlier in the day? Jenny nodded. *Are you injured? Do we need to take you to the hospital?*

I don't think so. I'm not injured.

Jenny, the officer began, *this changes things. We have to inform the Command Centre, and they will ask the Sexual Assault Team to stand by. They will take care of you. They have specially trained people to help you make a statement, get the proper medical attention and counselling.* As she talked the male officer began speaking into the radio as he drove. It was monotone and barely more understandable than the crackle that returned. The female officer continued to talk, but

Jenny was not listening. She had achieved what she had wanted to achieve, and the only thing to do now was to let herself be taken on the journey as the victim.

Is there anyone you would like to call? That question got through the fog.

No. There's no one.

Tad: Nearly

Tad completed the final rehearsal in his room. He would walk towards the woman, watching her intently. She would look away and he would use this as they got close to each other to both check behind him and take the knife from the folded newspaper in the few strides before crossing. It was a perfect day for it. There was a chill in the air and uniform grey cloud would not encourage anyone to spend time in the park unless they really did have to be there. He checked that the knife was in the newspaper where he had put it carefully the previous night, after cleaning it and giving it a final sharpening with the steel he had borrowed from the kitchen. He had imagined the reverence with which ceremonial swords were cared for in the military and had tried to emulate that care. It was all done now. Soon he would have achieved what others do not achieve. Terror would wash over the town by him slaughtering a woman in broad daylight and melting into the environment, unseen and unknown. Women would never be so confident again. Their boyfriends would feel helpless. Everyone would know the fear and shame he had known. Nobody would ignore or mock him ever again. There would always be doubt in their minds that someone was out there and might choose them. He imagined the commotion and the newspapers. He would be the only one to know what had happened; his secret. He set off for the park.

At the east end of the ridge path he stood squinting at the car park of the supermarket and waited. It was too bright to make out the details of people in the car park. He squinted, shaded his eyes with his hands and cursed his poor sight. Almost everyone arrived and departed in cars. An hour passed. It looked like rain was coming. A few dark clouds made it easier on his eyes. He could make out figures in the car park. The rain started falling gently. Finally, there was a possibility. A tall, elegant young woman with a bag of shopping came out of the supermarket, waited a moment to lift the hood of her jacket and zipper up, and then headed for the gap in the foliage leading to the playground. He straightened and watched her direction. There was no one in the park and she was heading straight for the gap. It was time. No more excuses. It was time to move.

He set off along the ridge path, newspaper under his arm. He found the junction with the forked pathway on the west of the clearing and turned down towards the woman walking in the opposite direction, reminding himself that he must not draw attention to himself by moving too quickly. Emerging from the trees, he could see her clearly and the walk that he had envisaged for so long began. It was only a rehearsal, but his heart was pounding. The quick walk along the ridge path had started his heart racing and now there was no way of bringing it under control. He tried not to look at her and then realised whatever he did might look suspicious, so he looked right at her.

She looked away quickly, her chin high and still striding. He kept looking at her, now enjoying the tension that had been created by violating that unspoken negotiation of distance and intimacy maintained by strangers. She looked and looked away several times. He realised that she could not help herself. She was anxious and he was suddenly affecting her. There was a surge of something he had not previously felt. He was now in charge of this exchange, like he had never been in any other. The pounding in his chest had changed too. He was exhilarated beyond anything he had imagined and was grinning. It pleased him to be cool enough to be grinning in the middle of this.

He remembered the paper and the knife secreted inside the folds. It was too late; he had been too enthralled with the novel experience of being in control of the situation and in control of her that he had walked past the point when he could drop the newspaper and retrieve the knife. Instead, he looked over his shoulder to check behind him, casually, like anyone would. A number of people remained in the park, occupying the space behind him. He could not have done it anyway. He had got his observation and timing of the walk just right, managed to check if there was anyone behind him, and it did not matter about dropping the paper. *Yes, it does. You little prick. You'll never do it.*

Ten yards past the elegant woman on the path he turned to his left and started running towards the slope and the ridge path. He could not wait to get to the observation post and reflect on how things had gone. The woman heard the sudden acceleration and watched Tad race over the grass and up the slope. Twenty feet up the hill he started scrambling on all fours to cope with the incline, clutching a newspaper, and making ground quickly. *Odd,* she thought, *what a strange young man. Behaves like an animal.* She had taken note of this young man only because she had become wary of him. It did seem odd that he stared at her for so long with that stupid grin; and what was all that suddenly running off about?

Jenny: Interview

She's here, Boss. Interview room three.

Charles Crossley looked up from the file and nodded at the young uniformed officer who was keen to impress the unit's senior investigator.

The young man handed Crossley a thin file. *More reports from SAT, Sir.*

Thank you.

He returned to his file and rehearsed what had been learned of Jenny Tanner since picking her up. She had been collected for questioning, but then revealed an allegation of a serious crime on the trip in. She had spent 24 hours with the Sexual Assault Team, but not all of their reports were in yet. Knowing people everywhere in the system had yielded frequent verbal reports. She had been helpful, given permission to take samples and retrieve her clothing from her house and even speak to her family doctor. She made a statement about the sexual assault and the stabbing, but nothing else. The officers who picked her up said there was nothing unusual about her: she was educated, polite and in a state of shock; compliant if a little detached. She might fit the profile, but she was either just an innocent victim or cunning beyond belief. Now he could find out for himself. It was never clear until he had eyes on. The time she had been with SAT had given her time to prepare. It would be interesting.

Crossley opened the new delivery and pulled the familiar stationery of lab results onto the desk. Not likely to be relevant to his investigation, he thought, but you never could be sure about these things. He tried to orientate himself to the printout. A long list of samples from body and clothing were listed in a column on the left. On the right was another column listing what had been found. He scanned down the results. All the body samples were negative. She had probably showered. Three samples indicated semen to be present, all on clothing discovered from the house. Two positive samples were not unusual. He looked again to make sure he understood it. He turned to the second page of the report, which listed the positive samples on the left and test samples from her partner and the alleged suspect, neither matching a third sample. There was something odd about this. Crossley wondered if he had misunderstood what had happened to her. Perhaps she had been raped by more than one person.

He closed the results inside his file, stood, pulled his jacket from the back of the chair and started walking. The nods and greetings of busy colleagues passed along the corridor and down the stairs reminded him that everyone knew this case was near solving.

Crossley stopped at the one-way window of the interview suite. It was his first sight of Jennifer Tanner. She sat easily on the hard chair, dressed in loose-fitting clothes of the kind SAT made available to every woman reporting being raped. With lank hair and sad eyes, she looked like a waif, but beautiful. He dismissed the thought he should not have had.

Has she said anything since being here?

No, Sir, replied the officer in charge of the interview suite.

Is she fed, watered, rested?

Yes, Sir. SAT advised me that she has been very cooperative, eaten well and slept well.

Is the clock running?

Not yet, Sir.

She hasn't been arrested, charged or questioned?

Correct, Sir. Everything has been about the rape allegation.

Good. There was a pause marking the end of Crossley's questions. He moved towards the door.

Sir. One more thing. Crossley turned to look at the officer. *SAT told me that she apologised.*

For what?

Stabbing the rapist.

How many alleged rapists were there?

One, Sir. Apparently, she stabbed him with a pen, in the neck, shoulder area. The young officer felt Crossley's eyes inspect him. *SAT collected him from hospital as he was being discharged. It turned out not to be very serious, but it was close.*

Front or back?

Sir?

Was he stabbed in the front of his shoulder or the back?

The officer turned the pages of the file and stopped at the front-and-back diagram of a human figure. *It looks like right shoulder, high up on the trap.* He waited a moment and then pointed to a spot behind the collar of his crisp white shirt.

Thank you. I know where the trapezius is. Is there enough for a charge against him?

Possibly, Sir. They are questioning him, and a witness.

Do we know what he has said?

Yes, Sir. He said it was consenting. She attacked him afterwards.

And the witness?

Apparently she interrupted them.

'She?' said Crossley.

Yes, Sir. She was another employee.

Crossley nodded. *Has the quack seen her?*

No need, Sir. I'm told the psychiatrist saw her and a counsellor was offered, but she declined. She has shown no sign of needing one.

That's not the point. Have we got that in writing from SAT?

Not yet, Sir. We are still waiting on the medical and psych reports, but I've talked to their manager, who tells me that the offer is standard and will be covered in their report. She was fine during their interviews of her.

Crossley looked back through the window. *Thank you.* He had thought that she looked helpless, downtrodden and sad, like so many of those he had interviewed in connection with crime, but there was something more to her than what he saw through the one-way glass.

Jenny waited, alone in the interview room. SAT had discouraged any discussion of her stabbing of Jon, despite her efforts, but now it was coming. The last few days had been tolerable, despite the prodding and pestering questions. At least they were kind to her. Neverending coffee, soft furnishings and sympathetic women. Even the physical examination was relatively innocuous. It was the photographs that were difficult. Legs akimbo, bright lights, every mark and bruise documented. It was now information on the file for anyone to look at. Somehow the pictures were something else. Taking pictures was different from just letting people look at her. They called it evidence. In any case, it had given her a full day to get her story straight about stabbing Jon and it was clear in her mind. She had imagined being asked questions and constructed her truth for each one and was ready to hold her ground.

The door opened and Crossley smiled as he entered.

Jennifer Tanner? She nodded. *May I call you Jennifer, or should it be Jenny?*

Either would be fine, she said.

Good. Thank you, Jenny. Smile. Jenny watched him. He could be police, social services, a doctor or the fire brigade. However they might be feeling, however she might be feeling, it would start like this. *Thank you for coming here. I know what you have been through in the last few days.*

Do you? she said without accusation, recalling the swab in her vagina and the camera clicking and whirring next to her. Perhaps Mark had been right and it did matter who was looking. Anyway, the policemen had provided an opportunity to alter the balance, and she had taken it.

Of course I don't, replied Crossley, knowing he had given away the initiative. *But I can imagine it was not easy for you.* It was important not be apologetic. He reminded himself to push through the bad start and take charge again. *Do you know why I have asked you to come to the station?*

I've a good idea. There was no point in being too innocent.

Well, before we talk about that, I must caution you. First, let me advise you that this interview is being recorded. You or your legal representative will be offered a copy of this and any subsequent interviews. You do not have to say anything, but it may harm your defence if you fail to mention when questioned something that you later rely on in court. Anything you do say will be given in evidence. You are entitled to legal representation, and if you are unable to afford legal counsel, one will be appointed for you. He stopped for a moment. *Do you understand?* Jenny nodded. *For the record, the witness has nodded her agreement. Do you want legal counsel or do you decline it?*

I need one if I'm being arrested, but why are you arresting me, when I've been raped? I only stuck the pen in him to make him stop!

Crossley absorbed the strength of emotion in Jenny's response. It was curious to him that it emerged so suddenly. He clasped his hands together, leaned on the table with both forearms and began, *Jenny, I think you misunderstand why you are in this room speaking to me now.* She stared and waited. *The investigation into the sexual assault on you is a separate investigation. You're now being questioned in relation to the attempted abduction of a child or children in your neighbourhood.*

What?

Tad: The Moment

I don't think you will, I don't think you can. The furies continued their malice. Tad shook them from his mind and focused on the operation. From his observation point he kept a squinting eye on the comings and goings in the park and bided his time. He looked up into the afternoon sky; rain seemed unlikely. Checking his watch, he realised there was more than an hour before the schoolchildren overran the park. He might be lucky today. *No, you won't be.*

He had returned to the favoured routine of caring for the knife with ritual fervour and the daily practice of the strike, until every inch of his body dripped. The fantasy that had preoccupied him for months had ebbed away as he approached the moment of it becoming real. It had bubbled into his consciousness several times each day following his failure, as if keeping him constantly soothed with the intensity of the pleasure he derived from it. He got stronger and gradually his confidence returned along with the resolve to bring this to completion. With that growing confidence, his fantasies and furies were at bay. The afternoon wore on and he got himself ready to check the escape route while making his way to the end of the ridge path. It was time.

The car park had become familiar. People moved slowly through it and into the supermarket. Women from cars walked to the store and back again but none ventured towards the playground and into the clearing. Some came from the opposite direction, through the clearing and into the car park. Others might have been suitable, but people in the clearing or the playground distracted him. He wondered if he had chosen the wrong place. *It's always the wrong place for you.*

A woman bundled in clothing swayed out of the supermarket. He could not make out her face but could see her broad frame and guessed that she was middle-aged. Her pace was slow. Shopping bags draped from hands and shoulders bounced against her legs.

He watched her direction of travel and hoped she would head for the playground. Tad scanned the clearing as best he could from his position. He was not going to make the same mistake as last time. He waited for her to walk through the gap in the foliage and into the clearing before he moved. This time he talked to himself as he bounced along the ridge path, about keeping the pace and his heart rate under control, his mind focused. The newspaper was squeezed tightly in his left hand.

He turned the corner onto the path into the clearing and hesitated at its edge. Squinting at the lumbering figure of the woman, he realised she had not made much progress into the clearing. There was no one around. The clearing was empty. He started walking towards her, controlling his speed, breathing as normally as he could, but his heart and breath had transcended control. He had thought after his practice run that excitement would flood through him, but it did not come. There was just the intensity of mind racing, chest heaving and heart pounding. He had to get through the fear and finish this. She was getting closer and he looked behind, not with the confidence he had practised, but with the fearful vigilance of the timid beast he had been most of his life. He thought he had looked too soon and would have to look again.

Idiot. The commentary in his head started up. *You're going to chicken out. Wanker.* He would not quit now.

He remembered to look at her and forced himself to stare. He thought she looked at him and turned away, then looked again. She was uncomfortable with his stare and suddenly he was in control of himself again. Tad knew he had connected with this woman, dominating the exchange, causing her to doubt her ability to cope with this. She was no longer in a state to humiliate him. It was that easy. At 30 feet apart he casually glanced over his shoulder to check for new people entering the clearing. There were none. He tried to penetrate her face with his stare. She glanced at him again and then away. She was flustered and unable to decide what to do but look away, walk straight by and hope. At 20 feet from passing her he moved to the right side of the pathway, forcing her to the other. He looked past her to the children's playground and saw that it was clear. His heart still pounded, but there was a confidence in his movement.

Ten feet from her, the knife slipped into his hand from the folded newspaper. She looked away. He jumped towards her with three quick steps, reaching out with his left hand, grabbing her elbow. He pulled hard to move the weight she carried, exposing her flank. His right arm stretched out behind him with the knife firmly in his fist. The moment had come. The spring that had been coiling in his body unleashed the knife towards the soft flesh under her ribs. He anticipated the thudding stop of the hilt concluding business.

The baby on her back gawped at him without any understanding. Tad leapt backwards as the woman's groceries flew into the air. Enraged, she swung her bags at him, screaming. *I knew you were up to something, you little bastard. Is this what you wanted?* she yelled at him, waving her handbag. *You can have it.* The assortment of bags she had been carrying became an unwieldy two-handed club, swinging from one side to the other and then back again. With each swing tins of beans, cereal, dog food and kitchen soap sprayed through the air like shrapnel. Tad stumbled back under the assault and fell heavily just off the path, and brought his legs up to protect himself. She picked up a tin of pineapple and flung it at him, and then it was a box of something, followed by three bananas. Something hard and metallic struck him on the shin and he howled.

She stopped and looked at the frightened young man, curled up and wailing, and then she advanced on him. He rolled to the side and tried to get up. She pushed him down again. He scrabbled to get far enough away from her to stand up, but she stood over him. Again she shoved him and he spilled onto the path. This time, she did not follow. Her baby's cry found its way into her consciousness and she watched him get up and limp off before gradually breaking into a run.

In front of her, the groceries were spread in all directions. She was tired, her baby was upset and there was a long walk home, now this. She looked around to find a place to begin. *What was that lit-*

tle bastard doing? If he wanted my handbag he could have grabbed it, so why pull the other arm? Uncomfortably she bent and squatted low enough to pick up a bag to begin assembling the strewn supplies. Her baby was still muttering in the secure papoose on her back. She started picking up her groceries in no particular order; beginning where she stood and working towards the epicentre, where it had started, occasionally looking in the direction of the limping boy's departure, cursing with every stoop. The boy had gone up the slope towards the houses on the ridge; she knew there to be a path along the ridge and it seemed that he would avoid going towards the supermarket by turning left on the path. She would have to report it to the police, but not until she had recovered her groceries.

The knife lay in the grass, just off the path where the young man had gone down. She could not quite make out what she was looking at, or understand the implications of finding it as she stooped again and picked it up. It fitted in her hand comfortably. She touched the blade in awe of it, reckoning the sharpness of the edge by dragging her thumb across it and turning the blade in the light. It was old and cared for; a coveted heirloom. The realisation that the boy might have dropped it came before the realisation of what he was intending to do with it. A hand came to her face, covering her mouth and nose as if holding back the teenager's squeal that was desperate to break out. She ran to her handbag and rummaged for her mobile phone.

Jenny: Interview II

Crossley said, *You are being detained. Your cooperation has been duly noted and will count in your favour, but we will be arresting you and what happens next depends on the outcome of this interview and several other inquiries that are taking place.*

Why do you want to arrest me? I haven't done anything.

Arresting you is a formality, the question is whether we charge you with attempting to abduct one or more children. We would prefer to help you and stop this happening again. The assumption of guilt was so clear in his voice. It was convincing before he explained anything. Crossley continued slowly, patiently, moving carefully, like a train nudging forward. *You have come to our attention on the basis of information received from the public, which we followed up and this led us to think you might know something about these incidents. We think you may need help, Jenny.*

Who said this? Jenny was tumbling with confusion. All the preparation had been misplaced and she was lost in this. *I want a baby. I don't want to steal one!*

Crossley waited for the energy to disperse. *We have had lots of leads from the public. When two or three leads point in the same direction, we look more deeply. What do you know about these events, Jenny?*

Nothing! What are these 'leads'? The scoff in her voice was convincing, she thought.

Do you not read the newspapers or watch the television?

Well, of course I do, said Jenny, nearly mocking his question.

Then you know something. Now, tell me what you know.

Jenny tried to gather her thoughts. *Just that some desperate woman has tried to take several children near the supermarket. That's all.*

How many children, Jenny? He looked impassively at her.

I don't know, there have been several reports, so probably three or four.

Crossley looked through her. It was a cheap trick, but it had worked. There was advantage to be taken. *Three or four is a pretty good answer. We know that there are three occasions and possibly a fourth, but we have only released information to the public about two of them. Can you tell me how you knew there were three or four?*

I don't know. It was just a guess, because you asked. Please, I don't know anything about these children. Nothing of this was in her control. She was helpless to him.

You need to be aware, Jenny, that we have statements from several unrelated people, each of whom say that you have said or done something that suggests you are desperate to have a child, and possibly willing to take a child.

Who? Tell me who. What could possibly have been said?

Crossley wondered if this was the time. If so, it had come earlier than expected. She was overwhelmed and vulnerable; desperate to make sense of a misunderstanding, or desperate to evade a truth. Either way, he decided, it was time to play some of his cards. *Okay, Jenny. We have statements from several mothers at the school just a few blocks from your house, telling us that you have been watching children in the playground and saying how much you wanted one of them.* Jenny looked even more intently at Crossley. *One such statement is to the effect that you said, there are 'so many children, surely there were enough for you to have just one'.* Crossley looked up from his file and tilted his head to one side. Jenny recalled the wistful friendly conversation with the mother outside the school.

That was nothing. There was a woman I was talking to and I said that I envied her. I said that I wanted to have a baby, that's all. I was envious of her. There's nothing wrong in that. Jenny knew immediately that it confirmed Crossley's story.

It's very helpful that you accept that you have been at the school. We have some security camera images of you or someone looking very much like you, on several days, just watching the children. There is also a report of someone, matching your description, approaching children not far from that school.

He pressed on, *We also have a statement from a woman who says she prevented you from walking out of your doctor's surgery with her child.*

I've no idea what you're talking… Jenny stopped herself, recalling the incident. *I bumped into the little boy as I was leaving and tried to comfort him. His mother was angry with me. What's she said?*

Crossley had the momentum he needed. The pounding continued. *It's not simply what she has said, Jenny. There were two other witnesses in reception who saw everything. They say that you seemed reluctant to let the child go. Does that help you recall it?*

Jenny wrapped her body tightly with her arms and tried to think how to explain the unexplainable to someone already certain of what they believed. *How did you get to know what happened at my doctor's?*

He looked down at the file and turned back a small sheaf of papers before looking up. *You gave us permission to speak to your doctor. I have the consent form here.* Crossley looked up without expression and waited. *We went to your doctor with this, and the receptionist thought your encounter with the boy was suspicious. Your doctor said you were insistent about seeing a specialist, when you couldn't conceive. Then we talked to the mother of the little boy, who also saw you at the school. Then there were other mothers, and CCTV.*

Jenny felt the energy leave her and weight compress her body into the chair. She was falling into that private space without intending to.

He said, *Jenny. We have also been talking to Mark.* She surfaced for a moment. *He told us he moved out a couple of days ago. Is that true? Has it been difficult between you?*

Well, not really. But he did leave the other day.

She stared at him. *Tell me about that conversation you had with Mark,* he said, *when reading the newspaper, the story of a child being very nearly taken from the supermarket, just ten minutes' walk from where you live.*

She could say nothing.

Apparently you felt sorry for the woman who was trying to take the child. You tried to convince him that it was that woman who was deserving of sympathy. You also said something to the effect that the child wouldn't be harmed. Is that true, Jenny?

Crossley watched the complexion of his suspect change to another shade of grey. She was helpless and he waited for her to start explaining herself. It would come in fragments. All he needed to do was wait, allow her to disclose inconsistencies with which he would wrap her in tightening knots, only then relieving her suffering with a plausible thread, linking the pieces, mitigating her blame and understanding her motive. She would accede to this and then it would be over.

They were both still, her skin like wax. He knew she would be scrambling to find a connection to the ground. Any anchor point would do – but there was something wrong. The tension in her body changed, her face sagged. Crossley felt alarm in his chest and sat upright at the table's edge before understanding what was happening. She was tipping gently forward, as a tree cut free of the tension holding it upright, building momentum. Crossley lunged towards her, grabbing her head as it hit the table.

Get in here! he shouted to his colleagues. Her body fell from the chair and dangled limply from his grip. He cursed himself for pushing too quickly and then the realisation came to him as officers swarmed in to take the weight of her to the floor. If the SAT report did not say the doctor had cleared her to be interviewed, he was in the shit. Crossley swept the thought away. There was blood on the floor.

Get an ambulance. Do it now.

Where are you taking me? Jenny looked at the uniformed man in the back of the ambulance, where she lay strapped to a gurney.

You're awake, he said in surprise. *You will feel a bit groggy, but that's normal. You fainted and fell over and took a bang to your head. You'll need some stitches over the eye and you've had some medication.*

We are taking you to a hospital. There's nothing to worry about. He smiled. It was enough for her. She closed her eyes and sank again.

Tad: The Chase

Officer Mulroney's shift had been routine until the call came of a knife attack on a woman in the park. The second part of the message locked him into what had to be done without much contemplation. The assailant was reported to be running north, up the hill from the central area of the park. He and his partner had worked for several years in the neighbourhood and both knew that the houses on the ridge had a path behind them. It meant that the assailant would reach the path and turn either east or west. There were no other choices. All he needed to do was drop his partner off at the west end of the path, drive to the east end above the supermarket and they would close on the prey from either side. Mulroney was mobilising before the message was completed. A quick radio message to dispatch told them that he and his partner were responding. *I'll drop you off and come back along the path from the other end.* His partner said nothing, unplugged his seat belt and waited to leap out. Mulroney thought for a moment about the siren. No, not for this one. It wasn't that far, not much traffic to warn; they might avoid spooking the culprit into something desperate. Just be quick and careful.

The scramble up the hill was much more difficult than when he had tested the escape route weeks before. The ground was wet and traction was difficult. As the slope steepened, his foot slipped and he was down on his chest, grabbing the grass with his hands and running on all fours. She would not follow him but, still, speed was everything. He would be away if only he could get up as far as the track. *What are you going to do now, idiot?* the furies mocked. A new pain emerged from the back of his leg and he was reminded of the first time he had experienced it, on the fence. The hamstring had gone again, but the pain could not stop him. He just had to get to the top of the ridge, with his heart pounding and the pain in his shin making his leg feel numb. *What will I say if I'm caught?* The muse followed, *You can't say anything, you're done for now.*

Tad looked back at the scene in the park from his elevated position. His chest heaved. He squinted to make out the detail. The woman stood with groceries and bags all around her. Someone had come to her aid and a man was pointing at him. All the faces turned towards him. There was shouting. He squinted again at the woman. She was holding something in one hand and pointing towards the woman who was helping her. He strained to see. *Oh God, it's the knife, she's got my knife.* Instinctively he moved towards her, and then stopped. The other hand went to her head. *It's a phone! Fuck, fuck. It's a phone.* The terror welled up and only him getting away mattered. He turned towards the ridge top and began scrambling faster towards it, falling, rising to all fours and falling again. An unearthly squeal emerged from the desperate boy.

Finally, at the end of his energy, Tad put his foot on the path. With both hands pressed up against the fence running along the path, he rested for a moment. *Which way?* The realisation came to him that the path was not safe. He had taken longer to get there than he had thought and had been seen running in that direction. The police would make their way along the path to find him, for sure. He had to get off the path. It had not been his intention, nor had he even considered it as an alternate escape route, but he did know one garden along the path, where he could hide or get through to the road.

Quickly Tad found the gate to the house where he had watched through the window. The gate would not open, even with his arm pushed through the slats lifting the handle. There was another latch or lock preventing it from opening. He cursed Legs for going to the trouble of changing it. There was no time to waste. He lifted himself onto the top of the fence and let himself down on the other side. It was, despite his tiredness and pain, so much easier than before and the familiarity of the yard made him feel safe for a moment. Even so, it was daylight, the police would be looking along the path and he could not immediately see a place to hide, so he could not stay. Between this house and the next one was a passageway leading to a gate, through which was access to the front of the house and into the street. Tad calculated that it was his best chance of escape and moved quickly towards it. His hopes were rising.

In the house, the woman stirred from a slumber taken before the children arrived home from school. Even from inside the double-glazed windows she knew the familiar rattle of the back gate and wondered which of the children was trying to come home that way. She walked into the kitchen and opened the back door. The dog followed. The gate was closed and there was no one there. She recalled that her husband had fixed the gate with another lock, so perhaps one of the children had forgotten and was making her way around the block. It was a little early for them to be home, but in any case it was time to get ready for them arriving.

Mulroney had discharged his partner and was making his way along the road towards the supermarket. It would only take a minute to get to the end of the road, dismount and start the pincer movement they had planned. He pressed on.

From between the houses, Tad leaned out to see down the street. A few cars came by and he strained to see more of the road, left and right. Across from the house was a long road leading away from the park. It invited him to escape. All he needed to do was cross the road and by the next street his connection with the park and the path would be broken. As far as the police were concerned he could be anywhere. The back door of the house opened and then closed, and he knew that he had to move before being seen. *Get away from here, you idiot. You can't even get that right.* Tad started off and felt the twinge at the back of his leg. He moved as quickly as he could, half-limping and half-running. The front yard was open to the pavement and then he was through the gap between two parked cars, looking right as he approached the open road and then he swung his head left as he stepped into the street. It was already too late to move out of the way of the oncoming car.

Officer Mulroney saw the boy for just long enough to avoid

hitting him. He wrenched the wheel hard to the left, the momentum taking him into the row of vehicles on the left of the road.
Even before impact Mulroney knew the boy met the description
of the suspect they were after, and acknowledged to himself that
there would be an inquiry as to why he did not have his siren on
while rushing to apprehend a suspect on an urban road. *You can't
win.* Then a startling bang of the airbags, before darkness.

Tad was frozen, not quite believing that he was still standing.
The police car had been so close to him that he felt the pressure of it
passing. Then it had buried itself in the row of cars in front of him,
passing through the front of one car and under the tail of another.
Everything stopped for a moment and then people began coming
out of houses and running to the scene. Tad looked up and down
the street at people everywhere moving towards him. He needed
to get away from this without looking as if he was running away
from the incident. The woman from the house ran past him towards
the carnage. He turned and went back towards the house, down the
pathway between the houses and through the gate into the garden
he had just left. Again the familiarity welcomed him. No one looked
in his direction; everyone was focused on the crash site and there
was no one in the house whose garden he occupied. He could relax
for a moment.

Mulroney's partner lumbered along the path, waiting to catch
sight of either Mulroney or the culprit responsible for the attack.
Neither could be seen. A large bang and a commotion coming from
the other side of the houses and some way ahead got his attention.
Instinctively he was on the radio calling Mulroney, without success. Then the radio controller asked for support to attend that street
where a police vehicle had been involved in an accident. It was clear
to him what had happened and he quickened his pace. He heard the
noise and knew where it was. All he could do now was to get there
quickly and let dispatch know that he was not injured. The little
bastard with the knife would have to wait.

The shock of the near miss and crash had not left him, but Tad
saw the opportunity of the crowd of people, which had become

large enough to be lost within. It was time to get out of the garden. The shuffling noise from behind startled him. He had already worked out what he would say to appear innocent, but was frozen. The little dog seemed agitated to see Tad amid all the commotion of the street, but as before there was no sense of him backing down. They stood on the path locked onto each other, one in anger and the other in fear. *It's a little dog, you wanker. What's the matter with you? It's just a little dog. Kick it!* Tad moved forward, and the beast growled and the barking started in earnest. There was no time for this; someone would notice the bloody dog soon. He went for the side gate but the dog leapt forward, snapping at the calf and heel. Tad yanked his foot away and the pain from the newly torn hamstring rippled through him. The dog went for the other leg and in a moment he was down, kicking and struggling against the determined creature, who had jeans and flesh locked in little jaws and was pulling with everything he had to keep Tad in the yard. *Get off! Get off!*

Mulroney's partner heard the shouts above the pounding of his heart and wheezing breath. It sounded just like someone crying for help and he came to a halt and looked through the slats in the fence. It looked like a boy, covered in mud and leaves, crying after an assault. His mind cleared as the scene took shape and the description of the suspect he and Mulroney had been after collected around the features of the prone figure. Same colour shirt, trousers, hair, and could be small in stature. He just had to get over the fence and apprehend him. Now it was Mulroney who would have to wait. This little bugger was going to pay for that too.

The street was full of noise but between the house where Tad sat against the fence, hands cuffed tightly behind him, it was quiet, now that the little dog had been removed to the house.

Mulroney's partner loomed over him and talked into the radio. *You're done now*, said the muse.

Fuck off! Tad tried to shake free of them. Large hands grabbed him at the shoulder and waist, and then he was face down on the path with a heavy knee preventing inhalation.

Behave yourself, said the officer. *It can get worse than this.* Tad could not reply. He could only think of the pain of his wrists and growing urgency for breath. In the street, an ambulance had arrived and two more police cars. An area around the crash scene had been cordoned off and people gawped. Children returning from school gathered with incongruous, shrill noises of excitement.

A police officer walked towards them. Both Tad and the partner watched the approach.

You all right here? asked the approaching officer. The partner ignored it.

How's Mulroney?

He'll be okay. He was knocked out by the airbag but regained consciousness before the ambulance took him. Just being cautious with him now. The partner acknowledged the good news with a nod. *He said that he swerved to avoid your man.* The officer pointed to Tad and the knee pressed more deeply.

The partner said, *He isn't behaving himself very well. I've had to sit on him. Let's get him to the station before someone recognises him from the park.* The two officers picked Tad up, still face down, grabbing him under the shoulder and thigh on each side. Tad was beyond resistance. As he flew over the ground he caught sight of Milky Thighs and her mother at their front door.

Don't laugh at me, he said to himself. *I have your secrets. Both of you.* The defiance failed him and he looked away from their gaze.

The two police officers stood him up beside their car. The back door opened and without thinking Tad followed the guidance of the experienced hand on his head pressing him into the vehicle. It was quiet and there was relief in being able to breathe normally. *Pathetic*, said the muse.

The scream was not deliberate, nor the stretching of all the tendons in his body. *I'm not! I'm not!*

Idiot. Fucking little wanker.

Both officers heard the shout from outside the car, muffled by the metal and glass. There was a momentary locked gaze between the officers. A silent decision was made. This need not trouble them further; the boy was contained. There was no danger to anyone and if the little shit started banging his own head, it would save anyone else the trouble. It was all in a day's work. Just get it off the street, process it. It does not have to be understood or reacted to. With a patient and tired response, Mulroney's partner knocked on the window and mimed the universal gesture for silence. He also made a mental note to advise the booking officer of the odd behaviour. He looked again through the window and the boy's dark eyes looked away.

Book Three

Jenny's Asylum

I had no idea they were bringing me here. Jenny looked out of the clunky window, designed to open enough to allow air to pass but nothing else. *I've never been in a psychiatric ward before.*

Outside there was a long low building creating a triangular courtyard. It reminded her of the 'place of safety' to which she had been whisked one morning all those years ago. The eaves stuck out from the roofline, highlighted by the round-barrel anti-climb mechanism along the full length of it. Spanning the widest end of the courtyard was a tall fence of tight mesh topped with razor wire.

What's that? she asked the young and earnest nurse, who was wearing blue jeans and polo shirt, sitting across the table from her in the dining room. He could hear the edge of alarm in her voice.

Just another ward, but it's our Secure Unit. He watched her straining over her shoulder at the window to get a better view of the chain-link fence. *It has to be closed, because there are a few people with mental illness who can be a danger to themselves or others.* She did not reply. *That's the courtyard for the secure ward.* Still nothing. *Our courtyard is on the other side. It doesn't have a fence.*

So this is an open unit? Jenny asked, looking at him.

We were told that you came here voluntarily. No need for security when you choose to come. Jenny smiled, knowing that there was never a choice about it.

So why did you come here? he asked. Jenny wondered if it was a genuine enquiry. Emphasising the 'you' made it clear he was not really interested in her experience of the world or the suffering. He was searching for that morsel of knowledge about her that would make him significant with his colleagues. It would support his contention that he had established a 'relationship' with her and should be the one who took special care of her. It seemed to be important to these people, but she was tired of pandering to them and looked away.

Through the large serving hatch by the door, there was a clatter of pans lifted from a trolley and slipped into the warming ovens. She could see the day area, through Perspex windows in double doors. Haunted women moved slowly and blankly, senses dulled. Others were vigilant, preoccupied, desperately needing something. Earnest Nurse rose in her consciousness and the thought came to her that she might be the only normal person on the unit. She might even be the youngest and most attractive. Perhaps that was why he was more interested in her than in them. She was being rude. She turned to him.

Sorry. I can't tell you why I'm here. It seems like a mistake of some kind. Jenny sat with arms tightly folded. *One day my boyfriend left me and a few days later I arrived here, having been accused of trying to abduct children.* There was mirth in her voice. *Perhaps I should be psychotic by now. Perhaps I should be over there!* With a nod of the head she directed his attention to the Secure Unit. Being flippant was the last thing people who work in these places want to hear.

Do you need to be in the Secure Unit? said Earnest Nurse.

Jenny looked at the young man and said nothing. She had let her guard down again for a moment, and they were at her, inviting dangerous words. Words to be misunderstood, obliging you to attend to them over and over again. It was the same in foster care.

I don't think that's up to me. I think you will be deciding that.

He smiled, *I'm just your key worker. The clinical team makes the decisions about your care.* Jenny nodded.

Can I ask what happened with your boyfriend?

You can ask, said Jenny, *but I am not sure I know, really.* There was silence. He would be getting nothing and she was tired of this.

He started, *It sounds to me like you need some time out to think through it all. Perhaps you're in the right place for that.* He smiled sincerely. Jenny looked at him without asking. He continued, *Well, you don't seem very sure of things, do you?*

If that's a sign of mental illness, I guess I should be here. Clammy hot streaks appeared on her neck. *Perhaps if you give me tranquillisers I can stay here forever, never understand, and not worry about it.*

Sorry, said the key worker, standing, *I didn't mean to upset you. Lunch is almost ready, so I'll leave you. Perhaps we can talk later. Will you be all right?*

Jenny looked at him blankly and tightened her grip on her ribcage. He turned and she watched him go. Fury raged to escape her. She knew what these people were like and yet she had let them under her skin. It was such a disappointment to expose herself like that. There would be reports written, even before lunch was eaten, speaking of her being difficult, uncooperative and hostile. She knew it. Perhaps she was not herself at the moment.

Tad's Asylum

Six security officers stood, engulfing Tad, all having passed through the glass airlock and into the reception foyer. Shaved heads, overweight, serious faces on. They towered over Tad like tall trees over a child. One in front, each arm held, and three others stood behind, close enough for Tad to feel the heat of their bodies. The leader of the team was in front and put his hand out to greet the casually dressed charge nurse who was admitting Tad to the secure psychiatric unit. A group of three nurses stood in the background.

Tad listened to the deadpan commentary of how he had been talking to himself and responding to unseen stimulus at the time of the arrest. Despite the oddity, there had been no trouble conveying him to the hospital. Concerns about him included being unpredictable, putting up some resistance to arrest and shouting inexplicably. The words faded in and out of his attention until a uniformed young man emphasised that the prisoner had been charged with the attempted murder of a pregnant woman in broad daylight. A machete of some kind was found at the scene and no motive was known. He was being remanded at the hospital for psychiatric reports. They had it all wrong and Tad could not help but smile at their confusion. The charge nurse and security man both saw the grin but did not rise to it.

A large envelope passed between the senior uniform and the charge nurse, who opened it. There was silence for a few minutes while the papers were read to ensure everything was in order. Arrangements for the direct transfer of patients from police cells to secure psychiatric hospital had not been in place very long and staff on both sides were getting used to the protocol. *That looks all okay,* said the charge nurse. *We can take custody of him now. Has he got any property?*

None. Just what he's standing in.

Okay, we can get him some new clothes and clean him up. Will you remove the handcuffs please? The morose men wavered and shuffled awkwardly. Each looked at the bedraggled set of two male and two female nurses who were proposing to take custody of the offender in their charge.

Perhaps you'd like us to escort him to a secure place? said a voice from behind Tad.

No, thank you. We can take him from here. The charge nurse was keen to get the uniforms off the premises before her patient became agitated. She smiled sweetly. From the back stepped a uniformed man, who unlocked the handcuffs. The two on either side stepped back as if evading the steam from a boiling kettle. For a moment, Tad stood between the groups, rubbing his wrists, waiting for guidance on what to do next. *Thank you,* she said.

Timothy… Do you mind if I call you 'Timothy'. There was no question and no answer. She continued: *Would you mind going with my colleagues to the ward where you'll be staying. They will introduce themselves on the way, and I'll be along in a few minutes to talk with you. You must be confused by all of this, but don't worry, we'll help you understand things. First we'll get you something to eat and some clean clothes.*

Tad listened to the voice of the charge nurse and felt the confidence of her years of experience wash over him. She was small, boyish, with short hair, and between the buttons of her shirt there was not enough space to see the white of her bra. He would do whatever she said, and walked towards her companions, who turned and walked with him down a long corridor.

The charge nurse turned to the security men. *Well, thank you for that. Delivered safely and the paperwork all done. Is there anything else?* She was already walking towards the airlock, and the uniforms followed. *I'm sure we'll see you all again the next time.* Smile. Among the men murmurs of agreement and muttered goodbyes emerged. She waited and hoped a final comment would not come. The airlock door opened and the first two went in, followed by a pause and then the second two. The four adjusted themselves to make room for the final two, and in the pause the rider came.

Number Five Uniform began, *One more thing you should know.* He looked down the corridor and hesitated until the prisoner was out of hearing range. Number Five looked directly into her face to emphasise the importance of what was coming. *In the car chase to apprehend him, there was a major RTA...*

There was a car accident when they caught him; yes, I heard.

Yes, a road traffic accident. Anyway, one from our side was hospitalised.

The charge nurse asked, *Was this the policeman involved in the incident a few days ago, reported on the news?* Number Five nodded. *I didn't know that a security guard had been hurt, or did you mean the policeman?*

Well, I... yes.

I thought it was a policeman. I was sorry to hear that. Do you know if our patient was injured in the crash? Does he need any treatment? There was nothing in the papers.

A look of surprise came across the face of Number Five. The others looked at her silently. *No, I don't think so.*

Well, that's something. Let's hope the police officer recovers quickly. Thanks again. The inner door closed and with a click and clack the outer door sprang open. The group of overweight uniformed men filed morosely into the street. The charge nurse watched them go and checked her shirt to make sure her buttons were done up.

Jenny: Rosemary

From the dining room, with her back against the window, Jenny looked through the Plexiglas doors into the dayroom. It was a safe place to be. Large and bright with views out and in. The table in front of her kept some physical barrier between her and others, and the remaining space to the door was unobstructed. A woman shuffled through the doors and approached her. She moved slowly towards Jenny, talking in a continuous stream of syllables, tapping her fingers together at a pace too fast for words to keep up.

Sorry, Rosemary, I don't have any cigarettes for you today. Jenny smiled broadly. It was what she always asked for and what Jenny always said. Rosemary continued to talk. Staccato gibberish spilled from her with an insistence. *Sit with me, Rosemary.* Rosemary sat on the edge of the plastic chair and began tapping her mouth with her forefinger. *Sorry, I just don't have any cigarettes.* Rosemary allowed her hand to fall away from her mouth and the monotone stream of syllables came to an end. For a few moments, she rested. Jenny arranged the dominoes on the dining room table and invited Rosemary to play. It was hopeless, but did not matter.

Why do you spend so much time with Rosemary? asked the primary nurse from the doorway. Rosemary did not notice. Her leg began bouncing, springing off her toe. Both hands rolled an imaginary marble between thumb and forefinger. *No one has the patience to spend time with her, but you do. Why is that?* Jenny had watched the young nurse circling, waiting to swoop in and engage her in some meaningful way. The plan to ward off patients and staff with Rosemary's company had failed her on this occasion.

Because no one has any time for her. I don't see anyone spending time with her, so I thought I would. Jenny smiled at the nurse, who acknowledged the act of generosity with a flash of the eyebrows. *How long has she been here?* asked Jenny.

I'm not supposed to talk about patients to other patients, but it has been some time. Rosemary's hand came to her mouth again and tapped her puckered lips. Plaintive old eyes appealed to the young nurse. He ignored her. *We introduced a no-smoking policy right through the hospital about three years ago but some of our patients have never adjusted to it.*

Three years! said Jenny. *She has been here that long?* She looked at Rosemary and reached across the table to stroke her arm. *Poor thing, it's probably the only pleasure she had.*

The primary nurse nodded. *That's probably true, although I don't smoke so I've never really thought of it like that.* He paused. *Rosemary came to us from the old hospital when they took it down. That was nearly ten years ago. A few of the patients from there couldn't cope with care in the community, so they came back to live in the acute wards. We don't have any long-stay wards, other than the Secure Unit.*

Three years is long stay. Jenny recalled counting the homeless men in the shelters and under the railway arches, and wondered if there were actual people from the hospital whom she had seen and tabulated. The relentless wandering and foraging of large numbers of dispossessed men and women, in and out of hospitals, hostels and prisons, had been a constant topic of conversation at work. It was all wrapped in the contempt and bitterness of a class war, already lost. She had come to understand what care in the community had meant for the people affected, but her face flushed with the embarrassment of realising she had not really known; not in the way that sharing an acute psychiatric ward with them teaches you. *How many people were in the old hospital?*

It was before my time, so I don't exactly know, but it was a huge place, in the thousands of patients, and staff. It was its own little town and some people never left it once they were in.

So where did they all go? Jenny knew.

Her primary nurse replied, *Most of the patients in those places didn't really need to be in hospital, but—*

What about the ones that did? Jenny's gaze fell upon him.

I don't know, said the nurse. *You say it like it was my fault.*

Jenny understood his complaint immediately. She had forced an admission of inexperience and youth. She had spoken to him like he was responsible; gathering up all the suffering of the cold lonely men she had counted, the lost years of Rosemary and the vacant women in the day area, and handed it to him. The shame of all that was wrong with mental health services was embodied in his naive complacency. There was nothing wilful in it and yet she had kicked the dog because it did not know. She shrivelled.

It isn't your fault. Sorry, that was unfair.

Don't apologise, the young man said. *Everyone has a right to an opinion.*

No, I'm not… not like that. I know you're trying to be kind to me. Jenny looked around as if searching for words. *But this place is getting to me.* He looked at her, and Rosemary tapped her feet. *I've been over my story so many times with people in here. The psychologist, social worker, three different trainees and three different nurses. I have only been here five days!*

His eyebrows came together. *Who were the other nurses?* he asked.

Does it matter! They're all the same to me. The contempt for these people came to the surface too easily to resist any longer. Any hope she harboured of allowing this young man to feel significant to her ebbed away each time they spoke. She wanted to turn it off but could not find a way to get back to being herself.

Well, said the nurse, *I came to tell you that the psychiatrist is planning to see you today, if he comes in.*

Doesn't he know if he's coming in? Or does it not matter that I am waiting to have my life back?

The young nurse exhaled heavily. *We have a certain amount of time to decide if you can be interviewed by the police. We are trying to get you through it. I know it's hard. He should be here after lunch.* He waited for another thrust but Jenny was silent. Rosemary began tapping a domino on the table while touching her puckered lips. The young nurse left the dining room and Jenny tried to ignore the tapping.

She had to clear her head and get ready for the afternoon appointment. It would be the important one. All the others meant nothing. Jenny stood and edged around the table of dominoes. Rosemary's hand caught her wrist gently and Jenny looked down on her.

Rosemary said, *He likes you, you know. He does. You could be kinder to him. You really could.* Jenny looked in amazement at the old woman, whose words momentarily caught up with the rhythm of her tapping. *Have you got a cigarette?*

Tad: Welcome

Tad wandered the corridors and day area of the secure unit. Others had seen his arrival, several days before, and noted the security arrangements that had been made. He had already established a reputation as someone to reckon with, but it was only a matter of time before he was tested. Without the knife he feared his status would fall and then it was only a matter of time before he became someone's opportunity and that would become his life in this place.

Tad noted the position of the staff. They congregated in and around the nursing station and seemed preoccupied with computers and the writing of notes. There was always someone nearby to watch, but there were no cameras. For Tad, the important thing was to understand which of the people here were dangerous and how to avoid them. For now, there was a kind of liberty for him on the ward, which he could explore as he wished.

Timothy. A voice came from a room off the day area. Tad waited and a man of about his age emerged. *Timothy, come in for a moment.* Tad obliged him and walked into the room without hesitation and the man followed him. Behind a table sat a large man with thick dark hair swept back to look like someone called Elvis. Tad recalled a foster-parent with posters and records of the man. This Elvis wore a white shirt, grey trousers and Doc Martens. Beside him was a smaller man with narrow features, dressed similarly. Tad noticed all the staff on today's shift were dressed like Elvis. The man who had hailed him asked Tad to take a seat in front of the table while he leaned against the wall between Tad and the door.

How are you settling in? Elvis asked, looking up momentarily.

Okay, said Tad, forcing himself to look directly at him.

Any problems or concerns? Tad saw it was the file that had passed from the security people to the charge nurse on the night of his arrival. It was on the table between them.

I'm all right.

Good. I'm glad. Elvis nodded as if approval was important. *What about the other patients?* There was a pause and no response. *Have you had issues with any of them?*

No. They have left me alone so far.

I'm pleased to hear that. It's not always like that. Elvis looked up. Tad waited. *Some of these patients can be difficult. That's why the doors are locked here and that's what we wanted to talk about, with you.* Elvis paused and lifted a page from the file. *We have been looking at your file. You have quite a reputation. The newspapers are full of what you did. We want to have a chat with you and make sure that our female staff are safe, because this ward has a 'zero tolerance' policy towards violence. Do you understand what,* his voiced slowed, *a zero tolerance policy means, Timothy?*

Tad smiled at being in the newspapers.

Is there something funny? asked Elvis, leaning forward, staring at Tad with incredulity. The room froze until Tad looked down and shook his head. *Why are you laughing then?*

I'm not.

We can see that you are. Why tell us you're not?

I'm not.

Elvis sat back in his chair. *Timothy, this is the first time we have spoken and already you have made us out to be blind and stupid. What are we to think of that?*

It wasn't me.

What? The three nurses looked at each other in confusion. *What wasn't you?*

I didn't do anything.

What do you mean, Timothy? You didn't laugh at us, or you didn't make us out to be blind and stupid?

I didn't do that.

Elvis leaned as far over the table as his gut would allow. *Get something straight, you disrespectful, little prick.* Elvis spoke with the menace of Darryl. Tad pushed his face as far down as he could and tried to remember what he had imagined doing to Darryl. Elvis saw Tad cower. *We are not blind or stupid. We won't be putting up with your cheek or your bullshit. If you want trouble, you can fuckin' have it.*

The narrow-faced man spoke. *Boss, he's smiling!*

Two large hands landed on Tad's hunched shoulders, gripping his shirt and flesh, lifting him over the table and pressing his face into the file. Behind the desk the second nurse pressed his personal alarm and then joined his colleagues in securing Tad's legs and arms, just as the control and restraint training had taught them. Elvis spoke loudly for everyone, inside the room and out, to hear: *Timothy. You're being restrained for you own safety and the safety of others. Just relax and you won't be harmed. Relax, Timothy. RELAX.* Elvis's weight pressed on his skull.

Tad felt only the pressure on his head and could only hear the screaming, whining noise in his ears that he believed heralded the crushing end. Suddenly, the pressure was off and his body was being lifted from table to floor. The room was crowded with nurses. Each limb was being held separately and big hands gripped his head and neck. There was panting, shouts and banging of doors and furniture. Through the noise, Tad heard the voice of Elvis. *Remember the drill. Keep the airway clear, and pressure off the chest. That's it. Good. I've got the head secure.* There was a moment of pause and then he spoke again.

Listen, everyone. We will stay here for a few minutes till we are ready to move, just relax and get your breath. The patient is contained and we have control of this. On my say, we'll be moving as one out the door, left down the corridor to the seclusion suite between the wards. There are two locked doors to get through. Tina, break off from the restraint and ensure the way is clear of objects and the patients are in their side rooms. Be ready with the locked doors when we get there and the secure suite needs to be open. Check to see if there's stat medication written up for him, and we better let the psychiatrist know. We need one more person to start taking notes.

Timothy. How are you doing? Can you breathe? Are you in pain anywhere? There was genuine concern in his voice. Tad knew how this worked. The process of making him to blame for these events had started and there was no point in complaining. The procedure would have been followed, documented appropriately; the professionalism and leadership of Elvis would be noted by others. That was the point of making it so public. It was not that it had to be done that way, but it hardened staff against a complaint later. Tad waited for the drama of being moved to seclusion and injected with something to ensure he would be both docile and responsible for this. It was always like that in the children's home. He thought that he must just relax and let them take him away, but then the strewn papers of the file came into view. There was silence and a calm in the room save for Elvis, who kept asking, *Timothy, answer me. Can you breathe?*

I didn't do it, said Tad.

Don't worry about that right now. We can talk about that later. Do you have any pain anywhere?

I didn't do it, Tad insisted. *The file.* Tad tried to indicate with his eyes the papers spread over the desk and floor. *I didn't do it.*

The five-man team looked at the papers and then at each other, knowing that there was nothing to do but finish the 'take-down' and get the patient into seclusion, whatever the patient said.

Okay, Timothy, said Elvis. *Just relax.*

Jenny: The Psychiatrist

Will you be coming across to the rehab centre today? The friendly voice of the occupational therapist filled the day area. Jenny smiled at the woman, who seemed endlessly enthusiastic and provided relief from the ward to anyone who could be encouraged to attend. It was all that kept the spirits up in a place of few visitors.

I don't think that I can, said Jenny. *The psychiatrist might be coming today, so I had better stay on the ward. Sorry.*

Still hopeful, the therapist suggested, *We can always bring you back to the ward when he comes.*

No, but thanks, I'd better stay. Jenny turned away and wondered what good therapy was and what could be achieved if you just broke off every time a doctor turned up.

The day area and dining rooms were full of people, as they were each afternoon at this time, with nursing shifts changing over. Staff moved quickly among the patients. Jenny understood how it worked. Each patient would be talked about and a note entered into the clinical record, so that the staff arriving were up to speed with all that had happened in the period before. The morning staff were in a rush to get off, and the afternoon staff were not in a rush to be on duty. The transfer of information would be reduced to notifications, problems and risks. Patients hovered to see who was coming in, how the afternoon would feel and what risks had to be managed. Every shift was different and patients cycled through modes of adapting to the quirks and priorities of each group of nurses accordingly. It was sometimes relaxed and sometimes dangerous.

Jenny tried to find the space to prepare herself for the interview with the psychiatrist if it occurred. She had realised that her legal status was unclear, even to her. On one hand, the police had asked her to come to be interviewed, but they had not arrested her. On the other hand, the key nurse had said she was a voluntary patient on an open ward, and something else about having to complete their report within seven days. It did not make sense. There had to be some 'legal' basis for the report they were doing, but who was the report for?

The ward gradually settled down as the morning shift departed and the pattern of the afternoon became clear to patients. The dining room was quiet but for the clearing away of trays in the kitchen. Catering staff loaded up the trolleys and headed out. There were a few minutes to collect her thoughts. Mark was so practical in all kinds of situations; she wondered what he would do. The loss of him began swelling in her chest, but it had to be squeezed out of her thoughts just now.

Sitting across from the doctor in her police-issue track pants and top, Jenny could smell the tobacco on him. It was out of keeping with the sharp creases, collar and tie of a young professional. He might have been a banker.

Do you mind if I call you 'Jenny'? The staff have told me that's what they call you. He smiled with the confidence of someone in command of his space.

That's fine. What else have they told you?

We will get to that. So, how are you finding it here? Dr Flannery offered another smile.

Okay. It's a little boring I suppose.

I think that might be a good sign. It means you need more stimulation than a psychiatric ward can offer you. It would be bad if this place met all your needs. Smile. *Perhaps we could start with why you're here. Why do you think you are here?*

Jenny tried to resist the heavy sigh invited by hearing that question again. *I think I'm here because you want to see me, but I'm not sure why you want to see me.*

Well, of course, that is correct, but I want to ask you about the events leading to you being here for me to see. Dr Flannery was still smiling. He waited for a response.

I was being questioned by the police when I fainted. I woke up in an ambulance, with a cut over my eye, being driven here. Dr Flannery continued to smile as she spoke. *It has been a very difficult time and everything came as a shock to me.*

That seems to me to be a very reasonable summary of what happened, with which I agree completely, from what I know. Do you mind taking another step back and helping me understand what it was that came as a shock to you?

Jenny looked at Dr Flannery and wondered how much of her she should reveal. She would have to be careful with this one. He knew what she was going to say anyway and knew she would be judged by the way she said it. She decided not to play charades with him. *I was brought here from the police station, so you will know I was raped, lost my boyfriend and was accused of stealing babies. It all came as a shock.* She raised the good eyebrow, cocked her head at him and waited for a response.

Indeed. It would be a shock for anyone.

Before we go on, can I ask you a question? Jenny asked.

Of course.

Why are you seeing me? Jenny looked at him intently and continued, *I know why I am here. I certainly needed a few days to get myself together after the trauma of it all, but why are you seeing me?*

I'm your psychiatrist.

I think you know that's not what I mean.

Dr Flannery sat back in his chair and looked at her. *If I understand you correctly, I think you're asking me about the capacity in which I am seeing you.* She nodded. *Well, it's more complicated than it appears, but let me explain. I am first a doctor, with all that entails about professional responsibility for your care and treatment while you are here. It also implies my obligation to keep the best interests of my patients foremost in my mind. I'm also a forensic psychiatrist, which means I advise the courts and other bodies on the best management and care of patients with mental illness who are engaged with the law in some way. There's provision for this in the mental health laws of this and almost every other country.* He looked through his designer glasses and smiled again.

You mean anyone who has been arrested or is in prison might be seen by a psychiatrist? It sounds like Russia before glasnost and the wall coming down.

Exactly so, but don't judge too quickly. We have moved on since then, but I see the parallel you're getting at. In your case, it's unusual because you have not been formally charged, but the police think that there might be a risk of you harming someone… children. The police don't want to prosecute women who seek to abduct children because often it's associated with a mental illness and everyone recognises they need sympathy and treatment, not punishment. Hence, I'm seeing you because you may be suffering from a mental illness, which is mentioned in your notes. I am to find out if that is so.

If I am not suffering, as you say, from a mental illness…?

Your case will proceed through the courts without evidence or recommendation from a psychiatrist, said Dr Flannery.

If I do suffer from a mental illness…?

The court will take a different view and most likely expect you to be detained in a psychiatric hospital for a period until you have received treatment and are not likely to pose a risk to children. Dr Flannery smiled gently at Jenny, who watched him carefully.

I am to be locked up, whatever the outcome of this? asked Jenny.

Possibly, said Dr Flannery.

Jenny paused. *Wasn't there a time when suspected witches were dunked in rivers? If they lived they were witches and burned at the stake and if they drowned they went to heaven, so it didn't matter.*

I think that is true, but what are you saying?

It sounds similar, said Jenny. Dr Flannery's head dropped. Jenny asked, *Aren't you missing something?*

What do you mean?

What if I'm innocent? What if I did not try to take any of those children?

Dr Flannery recovered quickly. *That would render all of this unnecessary, other than if you did have a mental health issue that we could help you with—*

Jenny interrupted, *And if I did have a mental disorder, but was innocent, you could still keep me here?*

Within limits and with certain conditions being met, yes, that's possible. Jenny thought that at least he was being honest with her. He continued, *But I think we should talk further about why the police think that you may have been involved in these incidents. If we can agree what happened, it's so much easier to talk about why it happened and that's where I can help you.*

I'm not sure who you're helping.

It was frozen between them. Dr Flannery looked over his glasses. The benevolent smile was gone. *I'm sorry you're unable to trust me, Jenny. I'll try not to take it personally, but see it as you distrusting the 'system' I am part of. Having said that, you appear to have struggled to establish relationships with any of our staff here. That's true, isn't it?*

What have they said?

Well, Dr Flannery softened his voice, *you must already know that you have been as uncooperative with my nursing colleagues as you have been with me.* Jenny shrugged. *Shall I say more?* He stopped for a moment but she gestured him to continue. *They think you are unpredictable and a little manipulative.*

That's what patients say about the staff! Don't you have a word for that?

Dr Flannery smiled and nodded. *Ah, yes. We call it 'projection' when a person attributes a thought or characteristic they possess to someone else. Is that what you believe staff are doing with you?* Jenny looked blankly at Dr Flannery until the complexity of his question was shared between them. *Ah, yes, of course. I suppose,* he said wistfully, *in any exchange either or both could be 'projecting'. Whoever identifies it first, or has the authority, determines who is said to be projecting. I can see my question being unhelpful.*

Jenny relented. *These places find what they look for and are not very willing to look at themselves.*

I can certainly agree with that, but I believe it's what we all do, as part of the human condition. He smiled at her. *But I don't believe 'these places', as you put it, mean to do harm, not usually anyway.*

Jenny broke the eye contact for a moment. *It's not unreasonable of me to be suspicious, is it?*

No, I don't think it's unreasonable. Tell me, Jenny, you seem to have some knowledge of places like this, but there is nothing in your notes, other than you suffering from depression, about being admitted anywhere. Do you have a history with psychiatry that we don't know of?

No, I don't. I just have an education. She noted the second reference to her 'notes'. *What notes are you talking about?*

Dr Flannery saw the rushing red marks emerge on Jenny's neck and cursed himself for letting the progress he had made with her slip. *The notes came with you from the police station. They already had the notes from your family doctor and they provided a summary of the events in their custody.*

Who gave you permission to see my doctor's notes?

As your doctor while you're in here, I'm not sure I needed the kind of permission you suggest. The notes were provided to us on your admission. Of course you would expect me to read them, wouldn't you? Dr Flannery appealed to Jenny.

Jenny felt anger spread over her skin. *You haven't answered my question. Who gave you permission?*

Dr Flannery paused before answering. *I am anxious not to confuse you with a complicated answer, but the simple truth is that you gave permission, although I can see now you may not have known this at the time.*

I didn't give you permission to see my health records, Jenny insisted. *I recently had a pelvic examination, what's that got to do with you?*

I agree it may have nothing to do with you being here, but you did give the police permission to see your family doctor's notes when you were being interviewed.

Jenny was lost for a moment, realising she had been duped. She had given her permission when interviewed as a victim of being raped, which they used in their investigation of her as a suspect. Her chest pounded. *I didn't give you permission.*

That's where it gets complicated, said Dr Flannery. *Let me explain. We have a partnership between this health authority and the police. When the police are involved in an investigation or make an arrest of someone and there's a mental health component, I or one of my colleagues may become involved. It's how we try to provide a seamless service, so those who would not do well in prison or police custody come to hospital instead.*

Is that drowning or being burned at the stake? Jenny instantly regretted the cheap shot, but Dr Flannery did not respond. She continued, *So, it's true to say, you're working for the police rather than me?*

Dr Flannery's shoulders sagged. *In a manner of speaking, yes, but also for—*

Isn't that a conflict of interest? Jenny asked.

I don't believe so, Dr Flannery replied quickly.

But you do get paid for working with the police?

The doctor struggled to keep his eye on the objective of this exchange. He needed to examine Jenny and the prospect of establishing sufficient trust with her was receding. *Not directly. It isn't payment for service, but it is true that psychiatrists' remuneration is calculated with the work we do for the police taken into account. So 'yes'. But before you condemn me for that, ask how else the service could be provided? The criminal justice system needs forensic psychiatry, and they won't get it for free, will they?*

Jenny had always known of the deals and connections between agencies represented by the people in those rooms where decisions were made, but Dr Flannery's candour exposed it more clearly than she had heard it before. If proof was needed, there it was. All the suspicions she had ever had of the contrivance of systems working to stitch everything together in a way that suited them. Nothing here could be trusted. She became aware that several moments had passed in silence.

Thank you, Dr Flannery, she said, standing, *for being honest with me.*

He asked after her as she moved to the door, *Where are you going?*

Out.

Tad: Seclusion

The thirst tore at his throat, even before his eyes opened. The sedation lingered like a heavy blanket, obstructing sound and senses. There were voices above him. Tad tried to speak but his throat would not allow it.

He's still quite sedated, said a man's voice.

A woman asked, *Timothy, can you hear me? The doctor is here to examine you.* It was the charge nurse speaking to him but he received it through confused senses.

Can I have some water, please? Tad's rasping voice was the first reassurance for the doctor and nurse.

She bent down. *I'm sure we can get you some water in a moment, just try to sit up for us, Timothy. The doctor needs to look at you.* She grabbed his arm and helped him to sit. His senses were coming back to him and he looked around.

He was sitting on a mattress covered in thick blue vinyl, strapped to a heavy grey plastic bed. There were matching toilet and vanity units. He looked at the point of connection between floor and wall and saw they joined in a curve. Looking around, he saw that there were no corners. Everything had rounded, forgiving edges. Inside the oversized door with a small observation window stood two men and two women – he thought they must be nurses – just watching over the situation. It was the two from the night he had arrived. The doctor and nurse squatted beside the bed and watched Tad intently.

The doctor began, *Timothy, I'm going to listen to your chest and take your blood pressure. I would like to look at a few other things. too, if you don't mind. Let's get your shirt off.* Tad fumbled with the buttons on his shirt. The doctor and nurse pitched in to help him. *Are you hurting anywhere?*

I need a drink, said Tad.

The charge nurse turned to the group of four and said, *We'll be all right. He seems very cooperative. Would one of you get a cup of water for him, please?* The charge nurse pulled Tad's shirt off his shoulders and saw the line of four finger marks with broken blood vessels and slightly abraded skin. She had seen pinch marks like this before; they were unmistakable. The other shoulder was the same. The doctor and charge nurse exchanged glances. *He will need a full physical I think*, she said.

Okay, we can do that, but let's get the quick check done first, and we'll come back for the physical. Stethoscope plugged into his ears, the doctor set about his familiar business of listening to chest and back, waving his finger in front of Tad's eyes asking him to follow it, and asking a few questions. His hands cupped each side of Tad's neck and he rotated the head first one way then the other, each time asking Tad if there was pain. Next, he pulled from his pocket a small light. *Timothy, I'm just going to shine a light in your eyes.* With one hand he covered Tad's left eye and moved the beam in front of the right, then away. He stopped for a moment. *Let's just try that again.* He then examined the left eye. *And again.*

Timothy, said the doctor, *have you ever worn glasses?*

No. Can I have some water, please? The water came forward from the door and was handed to Tad, who gulped it down.

The doctor looked at Tad sitting on the seclusion bed. The small wiry body with bruised shoulders sat, slouched and spent. He thought his patient must be almost blind in sunlight. His dark, nearly black eyes had hidden, irregular irises, hardly closing to the light. He said quietly to the charge nurse, *There's something going on with young Timothy, and we need to find out what it is.*

Jenny: Seclusion

With her handbag on her shoulder, Jenny moved quickly from the corridor of her room, into the day area and past the nursing station towards the door. Jenny noticed that in the short time she had spent collecting her bag, Dr Flannery had made his way to the nursing station.

Jenny! Several nurses flew out of the station in pursuit of her. *Jenny, please stop, we need you to sign yourself out. Please, Jenny.* She stopped a few strides from the door, which was always locked to those trying to get in, but open to those wanting to leave. *Thank you. Could you come back to the office where the forms are?*

I'll stand by the door, thank you. You can bring them here. A tall male nurse stood beside her as his colleague returned to the office. He moved awkwardly towards the wall and smiled at her. He was closer to the door than she was. She stretched her neck to see if the nurse was coming. Through the window to the nursing station, Jenny saw the nurse speaking into the telephone with Dr Flannery looking on. From the connecting corridor to the secure ward, staff were arriving and there seemed to be a sudden assembly of staff in the day area.

Jenny moved to the door and announced, *I'm leaving.* The young nurse grabbed her biceps, just firmly enough to stop her progress. *Let go of me!* she insisted, as he tried to explain it would just be a moment or two. *Let go!* she demanded, and lifted her arm up and away from him, and went for the door. The young nurse reached for the arm again, but she threw it off with a swing of her arm, catching his nose with her forearm. The soft squelch of the nose breaking and the yelp of the nurse stopped everything. *Oh, I'm sorry,* said Jenny. Blood began dripping from under the hand clamped to his face and onto his shirt. The gathering of nurses moved as one from the day area towards the door. She looked up and, seeing them, wondered why they were running at all until the first to arrive hugged her arms against her body and brought her to the floor. *Get off me. What are you doing?* She struggled against loss of dignity and the tightening grip. As more staff arrived, each limb was gripped separately until a team held each part of her. The constriction was painful and she struggled to loosen it.

A woman spoke. *Jenny, stop struggling, just relax, Jenny. Jenny! Just relax and you'll be okay. You're being restrained for your safety…*

Get off me!

…and the safety of others. Just relax and you'll be all right. She was shouting. *We are holding you tightly because you're struggling. Stop fighting us, just relax.*

Jenny stopped. The nurses held their grip while everyone heaved breath in and out.

Spit and outrage escaped Jenny. *You can't do this. You have no right!*

We do have the right, Jenny.

You're breaking my arm!

The nurse in charge looked at the two staff securing the left arm and they eased the angle. She began: *Jenny, we do have the right to detain you. The law allows us to detain you for a short period before review, if they believe you have a mental illness and think others may be at risk.*

But I'm not a risk to anyone!

A male voice from her left arm said, *That includes breaking a nurse's nose.* The contempt in his voice was obvious.

The nurse in charge looked at him with horror. *Okay, Jenny, we'll talk about it later. Just let us do our job and we'll sort it out when we're done. Just relax.*

The team settled into the drill. Jenny's limbs were clamped close to someone's body, her head cradled in the strong hands of the nurse in charge and weight spread across her torso. Quickly the concrete set around her and movement of any kind became impossible. The pain in her arm subsided. *Okay.* Someone moved quickly in the background. *Who is taking notes?* The nurse in charge looked and saw a hand rise behind a clipboard. *Is someone looking after the casualty?* Thumbs up signalled from the clipboard. *Okay.*

On my instruction, we'll be moving the patient to the seclusion suite.

What? Jenny heard with horror the muffled comments of the nurse in charge, who held her head with hands pressed against her ears. She shouted, *Just let me go!* The grip of every limb tightened while Jenny struggled again. *Just let me go and I won't struggle. You're hurting me.* Nobody answered.

Nurse in charge spoke again. *Listen, everyone.* The woman with the clipboard moved in to capture the commentary. *On the count of three we'll lift Jenny and move her feet first to the seclusion suite.* The team steadied themselves. *Ready, one… two… three. Go slowly, carefully. There's no rush.* As one they shifted her up and then along.

Jenny felt herself being lifted face down into the air. She could see the legs of those carrying her and hospital carpet move below her. She tried to let herself drift off, but it would not happen. The outrage of being mauled and restrained could not be shaken off. Suddenly she became aware of the police-issue tracksuit bottoms being dragged off. Each shuffling movement of the carriers caused a little more exposure of her bottom. The grip of the left-leg team was slipping towards her ankles, taking the pants with them.

Wait! she shouted, but there was no response. Her bottom was nearly fully exposed. *Wait!* Jenny bucked, bringing her knees up, yanking the leg teams to a stop. She could only feel the anger of being exposed to the world and held there for all to see. The pain was irrelevant now the real struggle had started.

Nurse in charge felt the relief of separation from other patients as the group moved into the seclusion suite corridor and the locked door cut off the rest of the ward. She knew it was not over until she was in the seclusion room, and her team was tiring.

The clamour of urgent voices and grunting in the corridor outside Tad's room was the first interesting thing to have happened in the two days he had been in seclusion. He leapt to the door to see through the small observation window. Standing in just his boxer shorts, he stood on his toes and, pulling up on the tiny ledge around the window, he looked out.

Across the corridor, a female nurse opened the seclusion door. It swung wide into the corridor before a woman with a clipboard joined her. They waited for the commotion to reach them. Tad pushed his face hard against the inside of his door to get a view of what was happening. He could tell by the noise that a struggle was going on and gradually the knot of men and women came into view.

Through the scrum, the naked flank of someone's body could be seen. The young woman's body was lean and exposed, with loose-fitting top riding up and track pants pulled to the thighs. He saw her bottom through small white panties. It excited him to be so close to the fighting. One hand found his penis and squeezed. He watched her resisting the nurses, writhing, pulling and pushing, her legs open and jerking against the holds. Through the secure door he heard her shout, *No, no, don't put me in there!*

The young woman twisted her hips and kicked one leg free. Nurses adjusted their grip to stop her arms from breaking as she turned face up. The free leg thrashed back and forth. Tad could see her naked torso and strained to see pubic hair. A nurse fell back holding his chest and another took a heel to the temple. Others gripped their limb as close to their own body as possible and burrowed their heads into her body. The full length of her body could be seen for a few moments. It was the best of secrets to see her exposed and fighting like Lara Croft. He pressed himself against the door.

A large nurse overwhelmed the woman by falling on her, pinning his body to hers. The air was forced out of her. Jenny knew that she was spent. The adrenaline of combat had carried her for a few minutes, but the intensity of it could not continue. Her anger was turning to tears. If only she could catch her breath under the weight of the giant that lay over her. It was over for all of them.

Tad could see the anguish and desperation of the woman under the weight of him and the charge nurse holding her head. He could see that she was done. There was nothing but shouting left of her efforts to resist. She was so pretty, now that he could see her. Her struggling ebbed to nothing but hopeless flapping against the restraint. The skin on his head tingled as each hair stood. It rippled along the back of his neck and down each arm. The weight of his bowels threatened to descend against his will or leap from his throat with the squeal that escaped from him.

In the corridor a banging could be heard from the door she lay before. Dark and desperate eyes looked out directly at her from the small observation window. They were of a young man, pounding and shouting from inside the locked room. He was trying to say something through the reinforced door.

Jenny, Jenny, fight them, Jenny, don't let them, don't let them. She lay pinned under the big nurse and the banging started again. The eyes seemed desperate to make contact with her. Concussions reverberated in the corridor. Jenny wondered who he was and how he knew her name. Exhausted nurses looked up to the rectangular window on the door to see staring eyes, protruding tongue, and then more banging.

A nurse asked, *Who is that?*

Another voice from the leg team replied, *That's Timothy from the forensic unit.*

Look, the little pervert is sticking his tongue out at her.

Cover that window, said nurse in charge and the clipboard was held over it.

No, Jenny pleaded. *Let me see him. Please let me see him*, but the clipboard remained. It did not seem possible. She had thought he was lost to her forever.

They lifted her again and shuffled into the seclusion room. There was no resistance but for Jenny's twisting to look at the little window from across the corridor. Nurse in charge rehearsed the release process and made herself ready to prepare the team. The last thing she needed now was a further injury to staff at the second-most dangerous time of restraining a patient. The most dangerous time is when you get hold of the patient, and the second is when you let them go. She was already mulling over the consequences of this occasion. There would be an incident report and she would have to account for why there had been a seclusion, why there had been staff injuries, why this person was allocated to that task. Every decision and action would need to be justified. Where there was no justification, something would be created. It was the only way to survive these days.

Then all the work schedules would have to be changed to backfill the lost staff, for an unknown duration, and Health and Safety would be demanding changes in process, whether they were at fault or not. The union would be complaining about staffing and training levels. There was no end to the administration and questions to be answered. She wondered how quickly it could be designated a patient safety event. Once it was designated in this way, all that occurred was covered by privacy legislation and could be withheld from public scrutiny. It had saved their bacon any number of times.

Jenny heard none of the instruction when nurse in charge began. She was lost in thought about another time. The pulling, grunting, chatter and discomfort did not matter anymore. Even the indignation of her humiliation had drifted away. The injection of quick-acting tranquilliser found its mark at the top of her buttock. She thought of Timmy Tadpole wondering if they would let her see him, what he remembered, and hoping she had not found him in this place. The recollection of her little brother and a different time smudged as the drug relaxed everything until sleep came upon her.

Tad: Awakening

Tad paced to and from the seclusion room window, impatient for Jenny to come round from the medication and show herself at the window. By the time the nursing staff had turned their attention to Tad's disruption during the restraint, he had controlled himself enough to avoid further medication, but he was not settled. He had allowed himself to be 'counselled' for his behaviour and then 'taken direction' from nursing staff. Just as in the children's homes, these were the criteria care staff used to assess the stability of residents. The residents knew this and used it to convey their distress and their wellness.

Each room of the seclusion suite was designed to allow the doors to open into the wide corridor, so they might not be barricaded from within. They were offset so that no window looked directly into another. It offered some privacy but, in truth, the position and thickness of the doors ensured there could be no planning between those occupying the rooms. Tad heard footsteps and keys in the corridor and leapt to the window.

Only by pushing his face against the inside of the door could Tad see if someone across and along the corridor was trying to look back. He knew she would eventually show herself, but now three young men and a woman looked through Jenny's observation window before unlocking the door. He strained himself to catch a glimpse of her.

Jenny heard the entrance but could not respond. Her first experience of intramuscular tranquilliser laid waste volition, disconnecting her from movement, memories and intention. Even dreaming was a drab landscape, without intensity or satisfaction. She did not mind being pulled upright to sitting on the edge of the bed. Gradually the voices began penetrating the opaque consciousness. They were asking her to wake up. Someone was rubbing her back. The woman's voice was close and loud, almost shouting at her, but it was hard to care about it.

You must be thirsty, Jenny. I have some cold water for you, said the voice and for the first time Jenny realised how thirsty she was. The voice lifted Jenny's head and brought the plastic cup to her lips. Iced water in her mouth awakened her senses. Jenny let consciousness return to her as the cup drained into her.

Thank you, said Jenny, opening her eyes and gazing at the smiling, angelic face just inches from her. *How long have I been sleeping?* The stiffness from the struggle caused her to wince.

Well, you have had a very long night's sleep, said the angel. *It's just gone seven in the morning. How are you feeling?*

Sore. Jenny looked up to see the three male nurses looming, impassive, near the door. She had seen none of them before, but there was something in their expressions. Disdain, or was it contempt? What was that about? Angel saw the doubt in Jenny's face.

Don't worry about them. They're chaperones, said the angel, smiling. *We have procedures to follow. They have to be here when we unlock you. Just in case things get excitable. Where do you hurt?*

Jenny tried to scan her body. *Everywhere.* She pulled down her track pants, gently peeling them from the red and weeping carpet burn on her hipbone. She looked up to see the chaperones look away. Angel moved between them and Jenny.

That looks painful. We can get a dressing on it. I want the duty doctor to come and examine you this morning, if you don't mind. We want to be sure you're okay. Would you like some breakfast?

Yes, please. A cardboard tray arrived from outside the door and was laid on the floor by her feet. Orange juice in a paper cup, buttered toast on the tray, a polystyrene bowl with cornflakes and milk added. No cutlery.

Will you be all right having your breakfast while I get the doctor? The team moved towards the door.

I'll be fine, said Jenny, wondering how it would be otherwise. *Thanks.*

The angel looked intently at her and moved the chaperones out of the door. *I'll take your pulse before I go.* She stepped away from her colleagues and picked up Jenny's hand and moved close to her as if taking her pulse and whispered, *Jenny, Jenny, look at me.* Jenny looked directly at the angel, obliging a last examination. Angel continued, *Three nurses were injured from yesterday. One of them is still in hospital. They have friends and colleagues here. Do you understand what I'm saying?* Jenny struggled to make sense of the whispering and caution but offered a micro nod of acknowledgement before Angel spoke up. *That's fine. Vitals are good. Let's leave her to her breakfast.* She stood up and was the last out of the door.

The door closed and the lock clacked loudly. Jenny felt anxious not knowing what to make of Angel's warning. She had looked concerned, but what did she think could harm her in a seclusion room? Jenny looked at the tray and lifted it to her knees. It looked normal as she lowered her face towards the cornflakes. Her stomach heaved with the aroma and the breakfast spilled in front of her.

Tad watched the crew of four leave Jenny's door. Almost immediately one returned and, standing back from the observation window, stood on his toes to see what was happening in Jenny's room. After a few moments, he left.

Dr Flannery

Dr Flannery looked in the mirror and made the final touches to his appearance, sweeping the shoulders of his jacket, before setting off for work. He checked his phone and scanned the packed calendar. There were two prisoners to see at the local lock-up and another on remand. Hopefully, he could finish in time to get back for lunch with that drug company rep sponsoring the academic presentation today. He wondered if he had imagined her interest in him. There might still be time to look over the new legal case that had arrived this week in two large boxes of papers and which was likely take him to the crown court for several weeks. The reminders on his phone indicated four reports that had to be done in the next four days. He remembered that he had not yet sent an invoice for the case that had finished a few weeks before. It represented three months' worth of mortgage payments, so he must not forget. Providing the hospital did not throw up any real challenges, his juniors and the nursing staff could manage and he could get through it all.

Outside it looked as if it might rain. He selected his raincoat, picked up his briefcase from the hallway and keys from the side table by the door. His phone rang to Vivaldi and he put his briefcase down, draped his raincoat over it and answered.

Dr Flannery.

Anxiety grew with every word he heard.

Yes, I'm just on my way to the prison. Right. Okay. Where is she now? Tell her straight away and get her breakfast. I'm coming in now to discharge her. No, no. There's no basis to detain her. We must get her out as soon as possible, providing she's well enough to go. Right. Okay. G'bye.

He thought first of the incident leading to Jenny's seclusion and then he thought of contacting his medical defence insurance. A woman he had never heard of had been arrested for the attempted abduction of several children. She had walked into a police station with her husband and confessed. The implications for the hospital became ordered in his mind. He would have to advise the medical director and the chief executive. There would be a statement prepared by the hospital, so he would be going through the clinical notes and preparing a briefing note for the communications team. He would have to be careful. Everything they said would be used again in court or influence the settlement. There would be another bloody root cause analysis to waste everyone's time. The first job was to ensure nothing, from this point on, compounded the complaint. They had to be seen to have acted quickly to put things right, and learned from their mistakes. That was always the patter these days. *Shit*, he said out loud. His day was in ruins, and there would be no flirtatious lunch.

He wondered, with fluttering in his gut, if the paperwork for her admission had been exactly right, or if her outburst of a few days ago was enough evidence of mental disorder to detain her. Had she been formally detained, in the normal way, the violence would have secured her detention for several more years, and in increasingly secure conditions. He scanned his knowledge of the case. She was not psychotic, no real evidence of depression, she might fulfil the classification of personality disorder. It was an unworthy thought, never to be spoken out loud, but it remained true, that if she was mentally disordered, her grievance against him and the hospital was weakened. How could it be said that holding a mentally disordered and potentially violent person in a psychiatric hospital was unreasonable? But then, a mental health tribunal might not be convinced, and trying that one might make it worse.

No, Dr Flannery thought as he made his way to the car, a mistake had been made, and he had allowed himself to be part of the mistake by admitting the woman in the first place. She had been suspected of a crime but was innocent, and the mental health component had been a stretch. The right thing to do was to discharge her without delay and take what came. He reflected that the pressure to keep the beds full might have influenced him more than it should have. It was something else that could not be said out loud, and he hoped it was not true.

Tad: Police Interview

A uniformed policeman walked into the room with a box under one arm and held the door for Inspector Bina Malik, who walked directly to the chair opposite Tad and sat down. Tad looked at his solicitor for reassurance.

Malik began. *Give us a moment to get the tape recorder going again. Did you get your copy of the previous interview?*

Yes, thank you.

The uniformed officer nodded to Malik; the tape was ready.

Okay, turn it on. A uniformed officer began the formal patter. *This is a continuation of the interview with Timothy Tanner on…*

Malik took stock. Tad sat with his back to the window facing her from across the table. On his right side sat a woman wearing black. She had a briefcase open on the floor and had been introduced to him as his legal representative. On his left side sat a male nurse. There was another in the far corner. They had been at this for the whole day. Each hour they would break and offer water, food or tea. Tad looked exhausted.

It was not going well. In fact, Malik thought, it was nearly pointless. If she managed to extract a full confession from the young man, it would be contested in court. After all, even though they had the green light from the psychiatrist to interview him, he was in a mental hospital; a vulnerable person under duress. It would appear they had been overbearing and might have extracted a false confession, whatever they did. There would be no trouble getting some clever psychologist to suggest he had falsely confessed, unless she did everything just right. It was a big ask without much in her hand, but she had one more card to play.

The standard caution ended and Malik spoke. *Timothy. Do you understand? Timothy?*

Yes. Tad looked into his lap.

Malik continued. *Have you had something to eat and drink during the break?* Tad nodded. *Timothy, can I remind you to speak up for the tape.*

Yes.

Have you been given any medication during the break?

No.

During the break, did you talk with anyone or did anyone talk to you? Malik went through her internal checklist.

Tad turned towards the woman in black beside him. *Just her.*

For the recording, the witness is indicating he spoke only with his solicitor. So do you feel able to continue?

Sorry. Yes, I think so.

I want to go over your statement one more time.

Inspector, said the woman in black, *we have been over these issues on three or four occasions already and each time my client has given the same response. How many more times will we need to deal with the same matters?*

Your client, replied Malik, *is reluctant to give full answers to very reasonable questions being asked of him. A court may think, as I do, that an innocent person would have more to say for himself in such a serious matter.*

The solicitor studied Malik for a moment. *Inspector, I have to conclude that you have no evidence to detain my client. He has been very cooperative, to the extent that he's able. It's obvious that he is a vulnerable person, but he has endured arrest, incarceration in a mental hospital and a series of interviews lasting almost four hours. All you're doing is going over the same ground, or introducing unrelated lines of questioning in the hope that he will become confused or say something incriminating.*

Malik reached into the evidence box by her feet and said, *Well, let's move on.* She lifted a clear plastic bag from the box and placed it on the table. Inside was a knife. Tad could see it was his knife. It drew the attention of everyone. Looking at Tad, she asked, *Is this your knife, Timothy?* Tad looked down. *Is this your knife?* There was silence. Tad looked at his solicitor in hope, but she simply looked at him. There was nothing to do but what he had always done.

It's not mine. It was his knife and he wanted it in his hands. It was his knife.

Malik stared intently. *I want you to take a close look at the knife in the bag.*

It's not mine.

Malik pressed, *Tad, let me explain that this knife was found at the scene of the robbery. It's why you have been charged with armed robbery.* Tad continued to look down and shake his head.

It's not mine.

Are you sure, Tad? Someone has cared for this knife. It's an old knife, but someone has cleaned it, sharpened it and polished it, making it ready for something. All recently. These are things we can tell by examining it with modern science. Malik let the silence do its work. *What else do you think we might find on it?* Tad looked up at Malik and waited for the question to be answered. *If we find your fingerprints on it, after you deny taking it to the park, it will be much worse than if you tell me now. We will have to conclude that you took it to the park to hurt someone. Won't we?*

Tad swayed on his chair. *It's not mine. I didn't do anything.*

The woman in black began, *Inspector Malik, I think we are at the end, aren't we? If you had found my client's fingerprints on the knife you would already have made use of that knowledge in these interviews. It seems to me that you have no evidence to connect my client to the knife that you found at the scene, and which you assert was part of a robbery in which my client was involved. My client has no previous record of violence. You have not established motive or connection to a weapon and you have come to the end of my client's indulgence. I insist that you make arrangements to release him without delay.*

Malik looked at her watch and said abruptly, *This interview is concluded at 2.47pm.* The uniformed officer stopped the recording and removed the cassettes from the machine. There was a moment while the cassettes were labelled and slipped into cases. Both copies were handed to Malik, who placed one on the table for the woman in black. *We will take a break.*

How much longer, Inspector? asked the woman in black. *I expect my client to be released.*

We are not finished yet. Malik stood, knowing the solicitor was right and the end was close now. The charge of armed robbery would never stick without connecting him to the knife, and even robbery was off the table if the young man really did have a sight problem and could argue that he stumbled. There might be a chance of pressing charges of common assault and resisting arrest, but there was nothing to hold him. In a few days the paperwork would be completed and they would be back in court talking about bail conditions before the charges were dropped. It was only the hospital transfer that would delay things and then he would be out.

What about Jenny? Tad said with alarm at the prospect of leaving her behind.

Who's Jenny? asked the woman in black.

A nurse said, *I think she was in the room opposite Timothy when he was in seclusion.* He looked at Tad and asked, *How do you know her?*

She's my sister. The room was again silent.

Malik stared at Tad. *Are we talking about the Jennifer arrested for child kidnappings?*

I think that's her, said the nurse.

We arrested someone else at the weekend, said Malik. *Full confession. I hope Jennifer has been released by now.*

Tad stood up. *I haven't spoken to her. Where has she gone?*

I'll find out for you, Timothy, said the woman in black.

She raised her eyebrows to look at Malik. *Well, Inspector, you've had a mixed week.*

We win some and lose some, said Malik and left the room. Walking to her car, Malik reflected on the unusual connection between the two suspects. It might lead to nothing, but it would do no harm to find out who was leading in the child abduction investigation and let them know their cases had a connection.

Home Again

Jenny lugged her shopping towards her little house. It had been a welcome outing until fatigue set in. There was no choice but to go to the shop and replace everything at home. The fridge had soured enough during her time away to taint everything in it. Bread was solid, fuzzy green circles had grown on the cheese. An open bottle of wine had turned to vinegar. Acrid air hung in the kitchen until every window had been opened and the recycling bin removed. Anger, anxiety and sadness came and went with each discovery of something lost or spoilt. So much had gone in such a short time. Her foothold in the world seemed more tenuous than ever before. Her frailty was inescapable.

Closing in on her front door, she recalled the perpetrators who could change her life, collecting notes, making decisions and coming to their conclusions, causing such loss. There was no one to account for what they had done. Everyone was just *doing their fucking jobs*. The words escaped her and she looked up to see if anyone on the street might have noticed. It was maddening, and made worse by the swift, insincere apology of the police, being stuffed in a taxi that she had to pay for and sent home. As if home would be the same. As if the neighbours would not talk. As if she would be the same. There was no apology from the hospital, but she would deal with that later. At least they took her stitches out before discharging her.

Only a few hours had passed since arriving home and already she was exhausted and conscious of how depleted she had become after three days with the police and a week in hospital. Doing nothing but being on guard had made her good for nothing else. It would not have been long in that place before she became one of the shuffling and anxious women seeking relief in deals, medication or masturbation. Even so, it was a relief to be outside and nearly home with the shopping. The kettle would soon be on and she could settle down to sifting through her mail.

She moved the bags to the grip of one hand to open the door. Warm air and the smell of coffee greeted her. There were flowers in the hall and a coat hanging. She had not allowed herself to think of him, but now the hope was uncontainable.

Mark appeared at the edge of the hall. *How are you?*

It did not matter what he said. It was his voice. Just his voice was needed to open her, and out it came. Standing in the doorway, shopping bags stretching from her fingers, everything came.

The tears and shuddering had stopped. What remained was the soreness in the chest and the flaccid limbs that come with giant catharsis. Jenny had felt his arms take the strain of her weight and hold her together, until she was capable of movement. He had nursed her into the living room, prised the shopping from clenched fingers and sat with her on the sofa, stroking her back for long minutes, until she calmed.

He had known enough to stay quiet and for the first time it had not mattered that she allowed him to be responsible for her. The relief of giving herself to his care had made her more exposed and been more intimate than all that had gone before. He had held her up and would not allow her to fall into that safe place, deep within her, where she was alone and untouchable. It was as comforting as mother's milk but also humbling. Only his gentle kindness allowed her usual humiliation at real intimacy not to matter.

They wouldn't let me see you, said Mark. *I really did try.*

How did you find out where I was?

The police didn't tell me where you were when they questioned me about you. They just said that you were helping them with their enquiries and I couldn't see you. I thought you were with them. There was nothing I could do. They even said that you had been offered a solicitor, so I thought you had someone with you. When they arrested the other woman, I went back to the station. That's when they told me you were in the hospital. I couldn't believe it. Anyway, I found the ward you were on, but then they wouldn't let me in! It was crazy. All a bit surreal. Apparently you were being 'violent and unsettled', and were in seclusion.

All of that's true, I'm afraid, said Jenny. *They wouldn't let me go, and wouldn't tell me why not. I fought them.* The memory returned with an unfamiliar pleasure. *When I was in seclusion, there was a nurse who was kind to me. She brought me tea in a real cup and sat with me for a while when the tranquilliser wore off. She said that my family doctor had given the police my notes and somewhere in them, from a long time ago, it said I'd been depressed. Apparently most women who try to steal children are depressed, so when they thought I might be the person, it was an easy connection to make.*

They would not tell me anything, said Mark. *Eventually a nurse said you had some kind of breakdown under questioning with the police.*

Actually, I fainted when they accused me of stealing children. It came out of the blue. Apparently I fell and banged my head and was out for a while. She looked up to him, turning her head to show the red line above her eyebrow. *Does it look very bad?*

Mark squinted to examine the scar at close range. *No, it will fade. Anyway, a blemish or two adds character.* They smiled. *I am sorry, Jenny. Really sorry.* She knew he meant it. He had not intended to leave her to that fate. She let her head fall more heavily against him. *So, what did you do to be labelled 'violent and unsettled'?* Mark asked. *You haven't been violent in your whole life.*

He waited for the reply while Jenny thought for a moment. She said, *You don't really know much about me. It's not your fault. I haven't told you. It's me who should be sorry.* It seemed important, like never before, that he know her. *There's so much to tell you, but if you knew it all, what would you think?*

I may know a few things already, Mark said. *Anyway, I have it on good authority that you're a child–stealing, antisocial psycho. How much worse can it get?*

Okay, she said, with a sigh that hurt every rib. She thought he had left her, but here he was nursing her through one of the great ugly moments of her life. *Let's drink the coffee. I need fortifying before we talk.* Stiffly she levered herself to the edge of the sofa. He got to his feet and pulled her up. She lifted the shopping from the floor and padded into the kitchen.

The coffee seemed drinkable.

Did I say that I think I saw Tad, in the hospital?

Your brother? What was he doing there? Mark asked.

She pulled mugs from the cupboard, placed them on the table and poured. *I really don't know, but I think he was looking at me through a little window, while they were putting me in seclusion. It was a bit confusing at the time, but I am sure it was him. I should have asked about him before I left, but I didn't think.* It reminded her of another time and another failure. *I should have tried to find him.*

Maybe you should go back and see him.

I think I'll give it a few days before going back to that place, she said, and wondered if she would let that slip too.

The note Mark had left before departing was still folded and tucked under the salt and pepper. She picked it up and read it again. Their words on that morning had not seemed like much but, she had reflected, her relationships had never ended with fury. She had thought it ended as the others had ended. The note gave nothing but the outcome. It said they needed some time apart and he needed time to think. It was the ubiquitous ending without acrimony, but no less an ending for that. But this time it had been different. For whatever reason, Mark had returned. She sighed again with relief.

Mark sat down at the table. He spoke evenly. *If we are going to talk, and get things out, can I ask you about something first?*

I think that would be fair. We have to start somewhere, she said.

Maybe we should start with you telling me who you were visiting and whose house you went to.

Her hand came to her mouth and she sat heavily in the nearest chair before her weakened legs gave way. He knew. She had never contemplated that he would ever know, but now his departure made sense. It had not been the accumulation of her distant moments that separated them, as it had with others. Mark had seen something of her other world.

He continued. *That morning, after we had words, I got to work and realised I had made something important that was not important. I might lose you over something stupid if I did nothing. I went to your work and saw you walking towards the park. You didn't see me when I honked the horn. It took me a few minutes to park the car and then I came after you. You were sitting on a bench talking to a woman, who got up and left as I got there. Then you got up and walked off.* Jenny's eyes were closed, hands to her mouth. *I should have shouted after you, but I didn't. I wanted to see where you were going. I always suspected something, so I followed. Then you got on a bus. I know where that bus goes so I ran back to the car and followed it. It felt ridiculous, chasing after a bus, stopping every time it stopped, checking to see who had got off. I did think that I was following the wrong bus, and then, I saw you get off.* Jenny's eyes closed again, knowing what was coming.

I parked the car and watched you. You had a key to a house and you let yourself in. That was a surprise. I didn't know what to think. And then, after a few minutes, a man came to the window upstairs and closed the curtains. Then, I did know what to think. What you have to tell me won't be so bad as what I've already thought. Don't worry about how it looks, it already looks terrible and I'm still here. Hoping it isn't what it seems, or if it is, we can find a way through this. Just tell me.

Mark, I'm sorry. I…

You're not to say 'sorry', Jenny. There's no place for 'sorry'. His pace was even and his voice was calm. *The only thing you should apologise for is for what you do not tell me now. Tell me everything and there's no need for 'sorry'.* Jenny looked at him, confused. He tried to help her in that sincere, almost plaintive voice, appealing to her, *I will always love you, Jenny. That's what I've come to know in the last week, but I can only stay with you if you tell me what's been going on. Now, just say it. Right now, and it will be okay. Well, I think it will be okay. Whatever you say, I'll still love you and I hope we can be together, but I guess it depends on what you want too.* She was frozen. A question was needed to help her start. *So, how long have you known this man?*

She was out of tears and out of resistance. The first reaction to escape his gaze had gone and she allowed the distance between them to close. *For years. Quite a few years.* Jenny registered the flicker of recoil in Mark's face before he recovered.

Do you love him?

It's more complicated… No.

Is it sexual?

Yes. Jenny felt Mark closing in and braced herself for the reveal.

Who is he? Mark asked.

Jenny could see several ways out of this. It was not, for someone like her, the most difficult of questions to evade, but she did not want to evade him or manage his emotions anymore. With all that had happened, she was tired of it. At this moment she resented having to keep him happy by teasing and appeasing. Why should she have to? Neither did she want him to be the object around which she manoeuvred. Every moment of manipulation, every secret visit, every contrivance, the pandering and drifting away at her convenience, she regretted. Perhaps being truthful now was the only way to stop the visits and having to hide them. Maybe, she thought, she would not miss it if she could tell Mark this truth. There was not, as she always feared, something about her that stopped her being loved. It was this last truth that had stopped her loving any of the men who had come and gone. She had never risked love like this before and now, if she did not risk everything, it would be lost. The words came more easily than she thought they would.

His name is Richard. He lives with my mother.

Connected

Jenny surfaced from sleep and heard the shower running next door and a phone ringing downstairs. The clock said it was ten thirty in the morning. The endless talking, the coffee and stirred emotions had disrupted both sleep and being awake. Now the working week was pursuing one of them. On the stairs Jenny remembered that work would not be trying to contact her, but the ringtone was from her phone.

Hello?

Hello, are you Jennifer Tanner?

Well, yes, but I don't go by that name anymore.

The voice continued, *I am the legal representative of your brother, Timothy. We are waiting to go into court where I'll be making an application for bail. But he does not have an address at the moment and the judge is unlikely to allow bail unless there's an address at which he can stay. I'm phoning to ask if we can use your address for the bail application?*

I haven't seen Tad in a long time. Jenny immediately knew it was not an answer to the question.

The solicitor detected the hesitation. *He did explain that to me. Our problem is that he has no one else. Tad tells me you nearly met again in the hospital, in rather difficult circumstances. It raises a difficult question I must ask you. Do you mind?*

What is it? Jenny asked.

The phone voice asked, *May I assume, with you having been discharged, you have no mental health problems, and you do not have a criminal record? You see, I have to tell the court that the placement at your address is suitable.*

Yes, you can assume that, said Jenny.

That's good. It must have been very hard for you to be in those circumstances.

Yes, it must be hard in any circumstances, said Jenny. *How did you get this number?*

The hospital gave it to me when they found you were related. He's very keen to see you again. Silence. *Jenny, if you want me to tell him that you do not want to see him, I will. You're under no obligation to keep him out of prison until the charges are heard.*

Jenny asked, *What's he been charged with?*

He was initially charged with armed robbery, but he may now only be charged with resisting arrest. And, there may also be an assault charge, but the prosecution can prove nothing of what they assert and Tad denies it. In fact, there's a good chance that all the charges will be dropped, and he hasn't been cooperative with the hospital, so they don't want him taking up a bed. He will be returned to the remand prison if he hasn't a suitable address to which he can be bailed. The solicitor had sold the plan as best as she was able, using a carefully judged balance of pressure and sincerity. Now she waited on the line.

Well, I don't want him to be in prison. What happens if I say yes? What do we have to do?

Would you come to the court buildings at about two today? Bring some ID and something, a letter or bill with your address on it, and a court officer will confirm who you say you are and you will have to declare your willingness to have Tad at your address. The charges are minor so it should go as expected. Then, he will be handed over to you.

I'd better ask my partner, said Jenny.

I am sorry, Miss Tanner, I am going to have to go into court now. I'll expect to see you at 2pm. If you're not there, well, I'll assume you have had a change of heart and explain that to Timothy... I mean Tad. Will that be all right?

Yes, I suppose it will. It was impossible timing, thought Jenny, but could not be helped.

That is wonderful news. Your brother will be so happy that you have come to his rescue. I'm sure it will work out fine. Thanks again. Goodbye.

The phone went dead before Jenny returned the goodbye.

Mark stepped out of the shower, feeling momentarily lifted by the magic of hot running water. The towel scoured his head and then dragged heavily across his chest, making his flesh livid. He wondered if he would ever reconcile himself to all that he had heard from Jenny. His preparation had done exactly what he had hoped. She had accepted his invitation to exchange honesty for his commitment. She had been candid, sorry, but strangely disembodied. The sticky threads drawn from her childhood brought regret, concern for him, yet no shame, and little sense of betrayal.

Mark tried to order his thoughts but could not hold it all in view. There was Angela, who could not resist bad men and could not be alone. Richard, the last of a string of these men, who abused Jenny until she and her brother were taken into care. Yet he managed to form some kind of bond with her, from which she could not escape; she would return to the house time after time, wherever they placed her, even when she changed her name.

With Richard, she had been unfaithful to every boyfriend. He corrected his thoughts. She had been unfaithful to Richard with every boyfriend but neither was that quite right. It was not a moral thing about being faithful or loyal, apparently. How could she be raped, and then accommodating of the same man over years, without ever loving or even liking him? The towel scraped across his back, then swept over his head, and with both hands pulled and pushed up and down his legs like a dirty shirt over a washboard. She had said it was separate from her 'normal life', whatever that meant. But what did she mean by saying it was like a 'parallel universe'? It seemed hard to fathom that, despite everything, she never thought of herself as being abused. It was bizarre but he tried to reason through it.

The hospital time was not her fault, nor was the incident with her boss. Neither was in another universe. Fighting the hospital staff or stabbing the bastard who raped her was surreal. Nothing of this she deserved, but whatever she could be held accountable for, right now she needed him to get her through this. He needed to get through this. Decisions would be for later. For now, he would be with her. It would be so much easier if that one thought would leave him. What was he to her; a convenient floating object to keep her from drowning, or something more, something important? He had to be more.

The door of the bathroom opened and Jenny entered the fog. *That call was from the courts*, she said. *They have asked if we could have Tad living with us while he's on bail. What do you think?*

Evidence

The police collator listened to the elderly woman on the end of the phone reporting a break-in, noting that she did not know when it had occurred and she could see no signs of forced entry. It was similar to the spate of reports of possible break-ins and intrusions into gardens that the community had suffered. Things moved, no damage, nothing stolen. It might have been part of this series that had been monitored for several months, or it might have been the elderly woman's imagination. He thought about how to record and code the report.

Mrs Myerson, the collator said, *was anything stolen?... A 'wartime knife'. Could you describe it?... Thank you, I am just typing the information into the database. Was there anything else taken? What makes you believe it has been stolen, Mrs Myerson?* He detected the change of temperature on the line. *I am sorry, Mrs Myerson,* said the collator, *but I have to ask these questions. It helps decide what priority your report has over others.* He listened patiently to her explain that the knife lived in the same box, in the same drawer, in the same room, in the same house for 40 years, and now it was gone. How much more were the police expecting?

I see, said the collator. *I will pass on your report for allocation today. Someone will come out as soon as an officer becomes available. I have an incident number if want to note it down. Yes, I will give it to the officer who comes out. Thank you very much for reporting it. Goodbye, Mrs Myerson.* He wondered how close he had come to adding to the complaint statistics of his department, and then thought that he had probably recovered the situation, and started typing.

After five minutes of scrolling and tapping through the fields, he was happy with the completeness of his entry and moved the cursor over the 'Submit' icon and clicked. He waited for the next blank template to appear and the phone to ring with another crime to be processed. There was something about this call that tugged at

a memory. It was the 'wartime knife'. There was already an investigation featuring a special knife of some kind, *what was it coded
under?* The collator sat at the console and tapped again until the
screen listed investigations where knives had been identified. Most
were closed or dead. A handful remained open. A few minutes
searching found one described as an 'antique' knife, now in police
possession. It was connected to one of Bina Malik's cases. She might
be interested. It could not hurt to pass the knowledge on to her.

Meeting

In the vast lobby of the Court building, Jenny and Mark waited for Tad to appear with his solicitor. Jenny watched the hesitant, disorganised trickle of nervous people hoping to catch hold of the black legals flowing by, carrying papers, lugging cases and looking past them. It was a place suspended between innocence and guilt. Dread appeared on the faces she could see but none of them was Tad.

Looking up from the lobby to the landings, Jenny could see animated groups exchanging whispered secrets. Her mind filled with questions. How many decisions had already been made, the die already having been cast and only the theatre needing to play out? She wondered what had happened to Tad in the years that had separated them. Guilt was never far away from thoughts of her younger brother; the most guilt reserved for not thinking about him at all. He was so young when she was taken. What would he think of her now, and how would they greet each other? She had not tried to find him but always knew she should have. He might have tried to find her, but changing her name would not have helped him.

Mark stood with her, waiting quietly. Jenny was grateful to him for being there and letting Tad stay with them, but dreaded Mark meeting him now. It was a different place, a different time, and why did he need to know everything about her? She chided herself for still trying to keep her worlds apart. Nothing of this was comfortable for any of them. All that had happened to her in recent weeks returned to her consciousness. Of course he deserved to know something.

Jenny? a woman's voice asked from behind her.

Yes. Jenny turned to see the woman in black smiling at her.

Here's your brother. The small young man stepped from behind the solicitor, with two short steps. Looking up, he launched himself into Jenny. She felt his desperate, two-fisted embrace, his face hard into her chest. Tight, moist, incoherent words squeezed from him.

It was all she could do to keep herself standing under the pressure of his hold on her. The strength of his embrace began to capture her. She gave in to his affection, wrapped her arms around him like a big sister does and laid her cheek on his head.

I'm sorry. I am really sorry. I should have come for you, Timmy Tadpole. I should have come for you. She felt him grip her more fiercely and reply in lost whimpers. He had rushed the barrier of uncertainty between them. Jenny felt the relief of their meeting and the unburdening of the apology. It would never be enough, but it would do for now.

Tad felt her whole body squeeze against him and the stiffening against his trousers, and he pulled away from Jenny, wiping his eyes. *She felt it. Little pervert.* The voice accused him. *Fucking little pervert.*

Sorry, said Tad, *I didn't mean it.*

What are you talking about? Jenny looked at Tad with puzzlement. *There's nothing to be sorry for.* She went to him, draping her arm over his shoulders. *None of this is your fault. Let's get you home.*

The Conversation

Jenny and Tad sat in the living room of her house. The awkward conversation over dinner made it obvious that sitting at the table with friends, drinking wine and eating salad and pasta, was alien to Tad. He ate with a fear that his food would be taken. In some ways, Jenny thought, he had been in suspended animation and not really changed from the little boy she had known. Mark shuffled them off to the living room, promising coffee and privacy for the next few hours. Jenny began helping Tad tell the story of what had happened to him.

The words were simple but her understanding was drawn with the crisp lines of someone who shared that time and the experience of going into care. She searched for something good after a marathon of talk.

What did you do for schooling? Jenny asked.

Tad looked down at his lap. *Didn't go very much. Never really got on with school.* He hid the disappointment of new starts at so many new schools with a smile. *You went to school, didn't you?*

I was lucky. I went to a new school and stayed there – even when I changed foster–parents I managed to go to the same school, said Jenny.

Did you like it?

It was okay. I went to university too. Jenny regretted saying it.

Tad did not seem to mind, and said, *You were always smart. I bet you had lots of boyfriends.* Jenny raised her eyebrows. *I didn't mean…*

Jenny laughed and Tad joined her. *The truth is, Tad, I've had my share of boyfriends. What about you?*

No. He shook his head.

No girlfriends, ever? she teased.

Not really, said Tad. *When I was in hospital I heard about you. They said you tried to take some children. Is that true?*

Well, Jenny started, *I was accused of trying to take some children, but it was not true. I didn't. When someone else was arrested for it, then I could go.*

Me too, said Tad, pleased with himself, knowing this to be true. *I didn't try to rob that woman.*

Jenny smiled at her brother. *Why were you in the hospital, if they thought you tried to rob someone?*

Dunno. I tried to run away, and there was a car crash. I was upset and shouting at them. They said I had to go to the psychiatrist before they could interview me. But there's nothing wrong with me. He smiled. Jenny remembered her conversation with the psychiatrist, and nodded in understanding. *I had some tests*, Tad said.

Jenny allowed the diversion. *I'm having some tests with the doctor too. What kind of tests did you have?*

My eyes don't work very well.

Did they tell you about what the problem was? Jenny asked.

I have an infection. I don't see well in the light. The doctor said I was nearly blind in the daylight. It isn't that bad really. I can see if it's not in the sun.

Jenny asked, *Do you mean you had an infection in your eyes, or you have an infection now?*

Tad reached into his pocket and retrieved a folded letter. *The hospital gave me this for some treatment. I have to go to a special clinic somewhere.*

Jenny unfolded the letter. A second page of test results was appended. She began scanning to make sense of it. The hospital letterhead was familiar to her. It was from the department of general medicine and spoke of 'bilateral ophthalmic abnormalities', and the irises being 'unresponsive to light'. A blood test called 'RPR' and then a confirmation 'FTA-ABS' test, whatever that was, she thought. It was meaningless to anyone outside medicine. Then there was a comment near the end about deferring treatment until a specialist opinion had been sought. There was no diagnosis. Jenny returned to the beginning. There it was. The letter referred Tad to a sexual health clinic.

Do you know what the problem is? Jenny asked Tad.

They said it was an infection, he said. *A tertiary infection.* Jenny looked again at the letter to get her thoughts together.

Tad, I know you said you haven't had a girlfriend. He looked sheepish and shook his head. *What about men?* she asked.

I'm not a poof!

Jenny looked at her brother and wondered what the truth was. *Sorry, Tad. It was a stupid question. How long have you had it?*

Dunno. They said I must have had it for years. He spoke up again. *What are you having tests for?* he asked.

I'm trying to have a baby. Actually, I have to go to the doctor again this week to get the results. Jenny responded cheerfully to her brother's question and smiled. She started to speak again, but the implications of the letter and what Tad had said grew suddenly. Her shoulders hunched and arms folded tightly, as if holding in the memories would prevent them from connecting. *Oh God. What happened to us?* Nausea bulged within her and churning bowels warned her to move quickly.

In the toilet, only the indignity of diarrhoea and stomach cramps offered distraction from the horror in her mind. Old memories came rushing in as the liquid left her in uncontrolled, unwelcome spasms. It could only be that Tad had tertiary syphilis. He could only have got it all those years ago, and he had gone without treatment since then. It could only mean the unthinkable. Images of the stinking rot, filling her belly, brought another wave of cramps.

Attending the Doctor

Hello, Jenny. How are you? Dr Jay asked.

I'm okay, she said.

Good, Dr Jay replied. *I have the result of the tests we did a few weeks ago.* She looked up and saw Jenny's face for the first time. Jenny clocked her checking the scar above her eye. *I should tell you that several weeks ago, the police contacted us with a request for your clinical information to be released to them. They had your permission and a signature, so we did release it to them.*

I know, said Jenny.

Your results from all the tests were not back, so we have not passed those on. Dr Jay waited. *What happened, Jenny? We only get those requests when someone we are dealing with has been assaulted.*

That's half-right. I was raped and taken to the Sexual Assault Suite for examination and what they called 'care'. That's where I gave them permission to get evidence from my house, talk to my doctors, take pictures of me. She felt the anger rise again and stopped.

You said that it was 'half-right', said Dr Jay.

They used all that evidence to arrest me.

What for? Sorry. It's not my business. Don't feel you must answer.

It doesn't matter. I was arrested on suspicion of attempting to abduct children. You probably read about it in the papers. Because I wanted a baby; because I asked my family doctor about having a baby and was seeing you, and because someone once said of me that I was depressed. I was an obvious candidate.

Didn't they arrest someone for that a few days ago? Dr Jay asked.

...and that, said Jenny, *is why they let me out.*

What a trial you have had, said Dr Jay. *Let me know if I can be of any help to you.* She consulted her file and hesitated. *Well, Jenny, we have found the most likely cause of the difficulties you have had becoming pregnant. It seems that you have had an infection for a very long time.* She paused to allow the message to soak in. *You wouldn't have noticed it for many years, but it has done some damage to your reproductive system.* She paused again. Her patient was calm and relaxed. *Do you know what I'm talking about?*

Yes, I think so. I remember, in my early teens, my mother took me to the doctor and then to a clinic. I was examined, like your examination of me, and there were tests. Then there were pills. My mother gave me some pills.

Do you know what pills they were?

Oh yes, said Jenny. *They were aspirin.*

Dr Jay cocked her head, not understanding.

Jenny looked squarely at Dr Jay. *My mother gave me aspirin.*

Do you mind me asking how you know it was aspirin? Dr Jay asked.

I could taste it. Everyone my age knows what aspirin tastes like. It was when they didn't sugar–coat pills and the powder stuck to your tongue with a bitter taste. If you didn't get it down in the first swallow, it was so bitter you had to spit it out. I knew it was aspirin, even then. She paused. *I didn't know what they were for exactly, but when the infection was gone, I didn't think any more about it. I thought it was gone.*

Why did your mother give you aspirin?

Because she needed the medication. She had the same infection. It was the first time Jenny had said what she had always known. Until that moment, it had not really been true. Another time, even two weeks ago, it would not have been said and remained untrue, but now it brought a crimson rage spreading up her neck.

Dr Jay let breath out. *If it's any comfort to you, you have not been infectious for a very long time, probably since your early to mid-teens.*

I suppose that's something, said Jenny. Some of the boys she had taken to bed raced through her mind. She winced at the thought of infecting them. *I've had difficulties with periods, but no signs of infection.*

That's the way syphilis works, said Dr Jay. *It does damage silently and goes unnoticed for years. We can do something to stop any more harm being done to you, but there's nothing we can do about the harm that has been done.*

It was not the information Jenny wanted, but it was what was expected. Dr Jay continued, *Technically, it may be possible for you to carry a child, but it's very unlikely that you'll ever conceive naturally. You must try not to be hopeful. I cannot be more optimistic than that.*

Will you give the prescription for the infection, or do I need to see someone else?

No, said Dr Jay. *I've dealt with this kind of problem before and I have consulted with our sexual health department. I can give you a prescription.* She smiled at Jenny. *It will save another examination.*

Jenny thought this might be what she deserved. It was just for someone like her, having done the things she had done, to be denied what she most wanted. *Thanks, Doctor. You have been very kind to me.*

Discovery

Malik waited for her colleague outside Mrs Myerson's house. The forensic science officer was collecting his bag and dragging his feet in protest at being tasked with a job that normally would never trouble their service. A standard break and entry with hardly anything taken was just not a priority, but Malik had insisted.

Do we know what the rush is for this one? asked the FSO.

Yes, said Malik.

Perhaps the chief has a new strategy of keeping dear old ladies happy. Is she related to someone special? said the FSO.

If it helps, said Malik, *we are looking for fingerprints belonging to a suspect in the attempted murder of an innocent mother, walking with her baby in a park, using a knife that may have been stolen from this house. We are about to dismiss all charges against him, which means his prints, which we have on file, will have to be disposed of.* The FSO worked the rest out for himself. They would never prove the suspect's connection to the knife if the file records were lost to them.

They arrived at the door and Malik knocked. The door opened and Mrs Myerson looked out at the tall man and short Asian woman on her doorstep.

Mrs Myerson? Malik asked.

Yes.

I'm Inspector Malik. You made a complaint about some stolen property. Do you mind if we come in?

Please do, Inspector. Mrs Myerson opened the door wide and signalled for Malik and her colleague to go into the sitting room. All was ready. She ushered them into the room and invited them to sit down. *Would you like tea or coffee?*

Malik smiled at her. *No, thank you, but that is very kind of you. Perhaps we could see where the knife had been before it went missing.*

It was in this box, she said, pointing to the wooden box on the coffee table.

Is that where it's usually kept?

No, she said. *It is normally in that drawer.*

Is anything else missing?

I don't really know. The two officers looked at her. Mrs Myerson shuffled awkwardly. *The house is too big for me really, so I close this room off most of the time. Haven't been in here for weeks. I do lose track of things sometimes.*

How did you discover it was missing? asked Malik.

I noticed things had been moved around on the anniversary of my husband's death. In the morning I was getting ready for my son to visit. I was going to open up this room for the children to play. That's when I noticed the drawer was open. I checked inside the box and it was gone.

You're sure it was stolen?

Well, it hasn't been outside that box or outside this room for more than 30 years. It isn't very valuable, but it was my husband's keepsake. I've looked at it from time to time. When I get nostalgic.

Malik smiled at her, and reached into the large envelope she carried. *Mrs Myerson*, she said, pulling out a plastic bag, *is this your husband's knife?*

She peered through the plastic bag. *Yes, it is! Where did you find it?*

It has become evidence in another investigation, said Malik. *We can't give it back to you just yet. Would you mind if my colleague examines the box and this room for evidence?*

Of course you may. Are you sure you wouldn't like some tea?

Angela

The key turned and Angela's door opened and then closed, marking the threshold of another world. It had been unnoticed all of these years, but today the smell of rooms without air was only a fug. It reminded her of the rotting compost and sour milk in her own home on her return from the hospital, and made her angry.

Jenny removed her coat and walked into the living room. The television was on; the tiredness of the room registered as never before.

Hello, Jenny luv, said Angela, turning her head from the television.

Hi, Mum, said Jenny without a chirp in her voice.

Angela heard it. *You don't sound very happy. What's the matter?* Jenny walked into the kitchen without replying. Angela lowered her voice. *He's not here if that's what you're after.*

Jenny knew how to control the flow of sweet and sour from her mother. *Shall I put the kettle on?*

Yes, luv. That would be nice.

The tap gushed water into the kettle, which then clattered onto the burner. Jenny shouted from the kitchen into the living room. *You'll be surprised at who's staying at my house.* It was unusual to mention anything about her other life.

Angela waited and then turned to the television. *Would I?* said Angela.

In the kitchen, Jenny calculated how much alcohol had been consumed. There was a bottle of vodka on the counter, with three fingers missing. An empty bottle was in the bin, but there was always an empty bottle of some kind in the bin. It was mid-afternoon, earlier than she normally arrived. Richard was still out. She concluded that not much had been drunk, but it had started, in anticipation of Richard's arrival. Now that Jenny had arrived, it would be oblivion by the time he did.

With two fingers, she lifted the washcloth from the counter and dropped it in the rubbish pail under the sink. A new one was pulled from the packaging and she was off in wide sweeping motions over the table and counter. The cloth was rinsed and hung over the tap. She opened one cupboard and then the next.

Angela raised her voice. *Jenny luv, what are you looking for?*

Nothing, Mum. Waiting for the kettle to boil. Just making sure you have what you need... What about your medication?

Just had a new prescription from the doctor, Angela shouted, *so I'm fine.* Her voice lowered. *You don't have to go through my cupboards... checking up on me.* Jenny would do what she wanted, so she waited.

A clinking of cups signalled the arrival of tea. Jenny put one cup on the table beside Angela's chair and took a seat on the sofa. *Thank you, luv*, said Angela watching the television.

Don't you want to know who is staying with me? Jenny asked.

Angela reached for her tea. *You will tell me when you're ready.* They watched the television.

The commercials began and Angela pointed the remote control at the television and reduced the sound. They sat in silence and watched the smiling, confident figures express themselves in whispers.

Jenny spoke without looking away from the television. *It's Tad. Tad is staying with me.* Her mother's attention was secured. Jenny drank from her cup. *His solicitor called me. He was going to jail, but would be placed on bail if a place to stay could be found, so they called me. I've taken him in.* It was delivered so that Angela heard the disdain. The criticism implied in a sister, rather than the mother, being contacted by the courts, taking him in, offering the comfort that a mother should give.

Angela looked at her daughter. *Don't be cruel, Jenny. Tell me how he is. Please.*

Jenny turned from the television. *He is very happy not to be in jail, but I don't think it has been easy for him.*

Why was he in trouble?

He was arrested for trying to rob a woman in the park, with a knife, but they've let him go. He tells me he didn't do it. They let him out, so perhaps he didn't. Jenny brought the cup to her lips and looked again at the television. The commercials ended and the programme began. A long moment passed.

I know about that, there was something in the papers. Have you talked to him? I mean – Angela hesitated *– have you talked to him properly?*

Oh yes, said Jenny. *He seems quite well.*

What did he say? There was no response. *Jenny luv, you must tell me.*

Jenny looked at her intently. *Really? Do you really want me to tell you?*

Well, yes. Angela reddened with the anger she always contained with Jenny.

I didn't think you'd be interested.

Yes, I'm interested. I am interested. He's my son! I did what I thought was best for him, and who are you to say I'm not interested in him?

Jenny descended heavily on the fantasy, *He went into a series of foster homes and spent time in a group home. I think it was pretty tough for him in care, apparently, and then they put you out on your eighteenth birthday. They go into hostels or become homeless. You must have seen young people sleeping in the streets. That's what happens to them. That or prison.*

Will you tell me what happened to him then? Angela had come to the edge of her seat. There were tears in her eyes and her chin quivered. *I couldn't protect him. The social workers said that. And you knew that. What could I do against him? As long as Richard was here, you couldn't stay. Tad couldn't stay. You had a better chance being looked after by someone else. You know what Richard's like. He does what he wants.*

He isn't the only one, is he? Jenny's voice was flat.

We all make choices, Jenny. You, too. There was defiance in Angela's voice. *I always tried to protect him.*

But you didn't.

What do you mean? Angela asked.

He's nearly blind. Perhaps I should have told you earlier. Jenny turned to the television.

I am sorry, but what has that got to do with me? said her mother.

Jenny turned on her. *Mum! Your son is nearly blind. Are you not concerned about him?*

Angela raised her voice. *Yes, I am concerned about my son, but I didn't make him blind. Why are you accusing me of making him blind?*

Because you are *responsible for Tad going blind.*

Angela was at attention in her chair, raised up with indignation. *Don't be ridiculous, Jenny. You can say some cruel things, but I've never heard such nasty talk from you. What is wrong with you?*

Jenny replied quietly, without movement. *I have the same problem as Tad. That's what is wrong with me. It affects me in a different way, but it's the same problem, Mum.*

Well, what is it?

We both have syphilis. Jenny paused, waiting for the paralysing frost to engulf her mother. *We are both infected. Have been since we lived in this house. It looks like it goes away, but it stays inside you, rotting bits of you slowly and driving you mad. For me, I'll never have children because I've had it for years. Maybe it's a good thing.* She looked away from the television, gripping eye contact with her mother. *Who would want a rotting, infected mother?* Jenny turned away. *Poor Tad, he's going blind for the same reason. Some chance you gave him.*

Angela said quietly, *I didn't know about Tad. I thought Richard was cruel and might hurt him, but never...*

You did know about me, and that didn't stop him, did it? You didn't try to stop him with me. As I remember it, you'd come and get me when he wanted me, and stroke my head while he...

Stop it, Jenny! Please stop it.

Then, said Jenny, *you didn't need to be there at all. Did you?*

Jenny, please, Jenny. This is too much. Tears soaked Angela's face and her words were louder and blurred into howling appeals. *Please stop!*

Is that why you let me be infected, Mum? Because Richard didn't need you there anymore, and only wanted me?

Angela shook her head without looking up. *No. It wasn't like that. Never like that. You decided to start up with him. It was you that got a taste for it.*

Were you jealous of me and wanted me to rot away with syphilis, so you could have him to yourself?

No, no, Jenny, you were always my favourite.

Was I, Mum? Really? So why did you take my medicine? Angela's wailing stopped long enough for her to stare at her daughter. *You took me to the doctor, got medicine for me, but then you took the pills yourself, didn't you? I remember it. And you gave me aspirin instead. Why did you do that? Why did you let me smell and rot when you could have stopped it? Why?*

Angela spoke through a glistening mask. *I thought if you still had it, Richard would leave you alone.*

No! No! No! Jenny stood over her mother. Noises of a lost animal emerged from Angela. *You were rotting like the rest of us and too ashamed to go to the doctor yourself. Even that's an excuse too good for you. You just wanted him for yourself and you destroyed me for it.*

Wet-faced and incoherent, Angela protested the truth before her, shouting. *Stop!* It filled the room for seconds. Through heaving breaths Angela shouted, *I… am… not… a monster!* She folded in the chair, covering her face like a child hiding from the television, and sobbed.

Jenny walked into the kitchen, returning with her mother's medication and the open bottle of spirits from the counter, and placed them next to Angela's tea.

Yes, you are, Mum. You have made monsters of us all. You are responsible for this, all of it. If you had any courage you'd do the right thing. You would put an end to it. Maybe you don't have the courage, but I hope you do. Jenny removed the key from her key ring, picked up the remote control, turning up the volume before replacing it and the key on the arm of the sofa, and left. The air outside was cool and new.

Homecoming

The house had remained quiet and dark since Jenny's departure, save for the television's constant babble and garish reflections from the living room. The front door lock rattled and pushed open. The flicker of the television captured the house in erratic frames. Richard turned on the hall light. Jenny's coat hung in the hallway. Over the noise of the television he shouted.

Angela. Where are you? There was no answer.

He hung his jacket over Jenny's and walked towards the kitchen, stopping at the stairs to look up and shout, *Angela, are you upstairs? Jenny! You up there?*

The impact and crunching sound of a blade finding a way through ribs came first, without pain, but the surprise caused him to twist and arch his back. Then pain erupted through his body, paralysing him in shock. A second pain arrived. This time lower on the body and deeper, like a punch travelling through him. He reached again and found the handle of the knife protruding between pelvis and rib. In a moment he could not breathe. He tried to recall if he should pull the knife out or not. Weakness, fear and warm liquid engulfed him, and he lowered himself to the stairs, unable to resist. Another wave of pain began.

Angela came to view him through the banister. Her bloody hands gripped the bars and her puffed face came close to his. So often she had seen him climb those stairs to do what he wanted to do with Jenny, while she drank in front of the television. He had walked with such authority through her house. It was fitting that he lay there, helpless on the stairs; breathing laboured and eyes bulging. A sucking sound hissed from the wound on his back. She wanted him to know what he had done that had led to this, but could think of nothing to say. Any mother would protect her children with violence. She could not be blamed for killing him. If only she could explain it in the few seconds that remained for him. He could accept the blame for it all, acknowledge what he had done and she could tell people of his dying words, exonerating her. The terror in his eyes was not satisfying enough. He was escaping from blame as his life departed, and she would be left with it.

Through the rails she spat, *You're the monster. You!* No one would know the truth and nothing she said would change what the world would know about this. Richard would be dead and she alone would be blamed for everything. Pulling away from the stairs she wondered if, when they were found, Jenny and Tad might understand and forgive her for what Richard had done. She hoped they would feel sorry that she was gone.

Domestic

Jenny could see Mark was tired, maybe from a day of work, but more likely from the turmoil of recent days. She glanced from kitchen to living room where Tad watched the television, and lowered her voice before speaking. *I went to my mother's today.* Jenny watched him, knowing that her promise had been to never see Richard again. *He wasn't there.* Mark acknowledged her report with a nod.

I won't be seeing her again either.

He nodded again. *Good. How did she take it?*

With vodka. Like everything else. They both smiled.

How did you take it?

I'm fine. Glad it's done.

That's good. Mark began preparing coffee, as he always did when he got home.

Jenny glanced towards the living room. She had tried to think of a way to start explaining that she had come from a family riddled with syphilis. It was too much to come out with. *I've only just told Tad that she still lives in the same house, and I haven't mentioned Richard yet. I really don't know what he remembers.* Mark continued making coffee. *It's Tad. He's going blind. He has had an infection, since childhood. It's only just been found, while he was in hospital.*

Poor man. He hasn't been very lucky. Can something be done about it? Mark asked.

They can stop it getting worse, but there's damage. Jenny shrugged. *His sight won't improve.*

What caused it?

It was not the worst thing she had said or would say to Mark, but something about this emerging into the world was shaming, eroding her foothold in the world of normal people. *He has syphilis. Tertiary syphilis.*

Mark flinched. *As a child! He had syphilis?* He sat down beside her.

Sshh, said Jenny, looking towards the living room. *I'm not sure he knows what it is.*

My God, Jenny, that's the least of the concerns about Tad. No wonder they took you away from that house. Mark stopped and shook his head. A long moment passed.

Did you know? he asked.

Not until yesterday, when Tad told me he had an appointment and showed me the letter. That's when I decided to talk to my mother about it. And why I won't see her again.

Tad entered the kitchen and both Mark and Jenny turned to him, hoping that he had not heard what had been said. *Do you think I should go to see Mum tomorrow?*

Maybe not, Tad. Jenny knew her response was too quick. *She isn't very well. She has only just been told that you're staying here.*

Why are you looking out for her? Mark's irritation stopped the room.

Tad asked, *Will you tell me how to get to her house?*

Sure I will, Tad. I'll put you on the right bus in the morning. Jenny sagged with the realisation of what Tad might be walking in on at his mother's house. If he got into the house, she would be discovered, and there was nothing to do about it. She imagined the scene of Tad knocking on the door and Richard answering, and explaining what had happened. It might be that Tad would not recognise Richard. Richard might not know it was Tad. Mark clattered around the kitchen making his coffee and Tad went into the living room.

I need to get out tonight. Do you mind if I go to the cinema on my own? Mark asked.

Not at all. You need to get away from this. I'll stay with Tad, said Jenny. Why had she not heard that her mother had done it? Richard would have let her know. Perhaps she had not done it.

Don't worry. I'll be coming back, Mark said.

Result

Ma'am.

Inspector Malik stopped and looked at the young officer in uniform extending his hand, holding a bundle of envelopes. She took them. *Thank you*, she said, and continued walking. She laid the pile on the desk, removed her coat and shuffled through it to find something interesting, in real mail, before her email was switched on. Pension reminder, policy on travel expenses, inter-office memo on communications, budget statement, retirement notice, notice of promotion exams, quarterly report on crime reduction strategy, community engagement review, training opportunities, inter-office memo on building works and new car parking arrangements. Here was something. It was from the Forensic Science Office. Malik opened it and began reading.

The sweep of the Myerson home found lots of prints from unidentified people. The list was endless. Reading near the bottom, Malik suddenly stood. Timothy Tanner's prints were found on the box from where the knife had been stolen.

Malik stuck her head out of the office door and shouted, *Have we got an address for the Tanner boy?*

Yes, Boss. He's bailed to his sister's house. We've got that.

We need a warrant and uniform backup there now.

What's the warrant for?

Attempted murder. And let Crossley know that we're going to the sister's house. Let's go. Bloody emails could wait.

Going Home

There was nothing familiar about the bus trip or the street where he finally got off the bus. He followed the directions Jenny had given him to find the house. Only at the door was there the smallest flicker of recollection, but nothing certain. Tad knocked on the door he barely remembered from being a boy, but there was no answer. Again he knocked, feeling nervous of seeing his mother for the first time since he was a child, but nothing. He stepped back to look up at the upstairs windows for signs of life and remembered he could walk around to the back. Through the gate he passed by the little patch of garden under the kitchen window where he had found a dying bird. The summer day was clear to him for a moment. The garden was overgrown and tangled, but there, hidden under the leggy plants where it had always been, was the terracotta flowerpot.

The kitchen had not changed except, in the morning light, it seemed smaller and darker than he remembered. The house was silent. The idea of being alone here for a little while was interesting. He opened the fridge and then the top cupboards. There were no secrets, and no pleasures he wanted. Something was wrong in the disturbing fragments of memory, rummaging through his mother's house.

Sweet, acrid air hung in the hallway by the stairs. He walked into it, stopping to examine his feet, which clung to the floor. The feet of a man lay awkwardly on the bottom step. The body above them slumped heavily. A knife protruded from the man's back. Stairs and carpet were black with blood drying. His feet stuck to the pooled tacky mass at the bottom of the stairs. Tad stopped to listen to the house. It was silent when he was still and gradually his heart rate slowed and he began looking around.

He had never seen a dead body. Death was seen so often in films and in endless fantasy, but this had nothing of the energy or drama of film, or of contemplation. It was a disappointment to him.

There was just a melancholy that comes with stillness and quiet. The knife looked interesting, jutting out. A carving knife from the kitchen; nothing special, but what it had done was horrifying and exciting in equal measure. It had significance; the power to give authority to action. Edging onto the stairs to avoid standing on the body and the pool of blood at the bottom, Tad straddled the feet on the last step and reached for the handle. A gentle tug suggested the flesh held it fast. Bracing himself, he yanked firmly at the knife. It dislodged suddenly, unbalancing and causing him to lurch forward on the body, colliding cheek to cheek with the corpse. Tad recoiled at the touch of a dead man's face and rubbed the cold moisture from his face. There was something familiar in the smell of lotion from the dead man. *Fucking idiot.* The voice in his head distracted him as the body slid, crumpling and turning down one more stair. The face could now be seen. It too was familiar. The scent on his hand lingered.

Tad clamped himself fiercely against the wall. He was eight years old and waiting in fear of Richard rising up from slumber, to threaten, to pinch his arms, to force his silence by holding his tongue against the floor of his mouth, choking Tad with a large bitter thumb, or a fork from his plate, a coffee-flavoured spoon, or threatening to cut his tongue with whatever knife could be seen. All he could do was to stay upright against the wall, on the edge of terror, incapable of moving forward or back. He cried out. The house was silent except for his breath and pounding heartbeat.

Gradually some ability to think returned. Pinned against the wall, Tad tried to make sense of Richard still being in the house after all this time. He recalled his mother's boyfriends never staying long, but Richard stayed. *It's true, it's true. Even a fucking little monkey like you should get it. Don't you get it? Idiot.* A surge of anger and defiance lifted him off the wall. He leaned over Richard's body and jabbed the knife into the corpse. It felt defiant and powerful. Again he struck with the knife, then one strike followed the other, growing in venom, until his body burned. The clothing tore and the flesh opened. Sweat had formed over Tad's body by the time he acknowledged his burning fatigue. Richard's insides spilled off the stairs. He thought the sight and smell would stay with him. It was something hardly anyone else would know, unless they had been to war.

Tad stepped off the stairs and looked at the helpless Richard through the banister. His skin was pale yellow and grey. The head lay on a step, one eye just open, and the face distorted by the edge of the stair pressing a lax jaw sideways. There was no agony expressing the ending that had been inflicted on him. Bloody prints of hands could be seen on the handrail.

Tad turned away and walked into the living room. It was dishevelled and frozen. Unwashed cups were on the side tables. Papers and magazines spilled from a wooden rack and shoes were scattered under the furniture where they had been kicked off and abandoned. Tad's senses were heightened. Everything was within his range, even the smell of cigarettes, shoes and overcooked vegetables that clung to the walls.

A woman sat in the chair placed squarely in front of the television. She was large, motionless and slumped over the armrest with her head resting on a flabby arm. Beside her, a table with two cups, an empty bottle of vodka and plastic amber pill jars with pharmacy labels. He walked around her chair and confronted her. There was blood on the vodka bottle. Her hands were streaked with blood, poorly wiped. The front of her blouse stained with scarlet prints. Tad recalled the many times he had longed to meet his mother. He had fantasised about the welcome there would be. He had never thought Richard was part of his separation from all that he had known. She had chosen to get rid of him in favour of Richard. The disappointment and contempt seemed to make him stronger. It was good, he thought, that she was dead. Tad's thoughts drifted to images of spilling her insides onto the floor and mixing them with the offal by the stairs.

This was justice, not the exhilarating slaughter he had practised until sweat sprayed from him with every motion. There was no thrill now, and there would be no catharsis to soothe him when it was over. Even so, it waited to be done. He pushed closer, leaning over her with the knife held low and behind him, as if to surprise her. With his free hand, he pulled her upright by the hair. There was no resistance remaining and she fell back into the chair. Gravity took her as far from him as it could. It was not far enough to save her from the ending he intended.

A frothy bubble ballooned from her nostril and disappeared. He waited to see if it happened again. There it was, like a mouse peeking. She was alive. He shook her, shouting, *You're alive! Why are you alive?* Tad saw his mother's lips move and put his ear close to her mouth. *What?*

Angela's words were whispered and slurred. *I am not… not a monster.* He realised suddenly that he was nearly lying on her, face close, pressing her thighs apart with his weight, and recoiled.

Tad looked at his mother and wondered what to do. *Why don't you kill her?* the voice in his head struck up. *You can't, can you?* His mother would probably die if he did nothing. *She's dying anyway, what's the difference?* The choice seemed ridiculous. *Go on, do it. Look, she doesn't want to live.* She was dying from the overdose. *She's taken all the pills and vodka. It's a fucking overdose! What's the matter with you?* The knife was still in his hand. *Stick it in her!* He squeezed the knife firmly. It was true; she wanted to die and deserved nothing else. Over her head, Tad could see the carnage on the stairs. *She deserves it, you said so yourself. Just do it!*

He was suddenly tired. Blood was everywhere. His mother was smeared with it and he had trailed it across the floor from the stairs. It was nothing like the films he had seen, or as glorious as he had imagined. It came to him that someone must have killed Richard. She must have done it. Finally, she had done it. It made sense to him now. She could not let him meet Richard. Now his mum was alive and needing help. He did not want to see his mother's insides on the floor, and could not conjure the image of entrails mixed together, or understand why it had entered his head. He had to find a phone and call for help. *Wanker!* Anyway, he thought, everyone needs help. *Fucking little wanker.*

Arrest

Malik felt impossibly small in front of the house, flanked by uniformed officers. A white car and blue light dominated the street. Radios chattered.

The door opened and a woman emerged.

Malik started. *It's Jennifer, isn't it?*

What do you want?

My name is Inspector Malik. May we come in? Jenny hesitated. Malik stepped into the hallway. *Is there anyone else home?* she asked, looking in.

No, there isn't. What do you want?

We're here with a warrant to arrest your brother. Will we find him here?

Jenny ignored the question. *What has he done?*

We can't tell you anything at the moment. Do you know where your brother is? She hesitated. *Jenny! This is serious. Do you know where your brother is?* The uniforms shuffled and radios crackled.

There was no point in resisting. *He's at our mother's house. At least, I put him on the bus to go there after breakfast.*

Thank you. Do you have an address?

Boss! A shout came from the uniformed officer standing outside the door and all eyes turned and watched her clamp her earpiece to the side of her head. *An emergency call from a 'Tad Tanner' reported on the radio, asking for an ambulance. Is that the same man?*

Malik left the house, striding towards the flashing white cars. *Tell dispatch we're attending. You two*, she said, pointing at two uniforms. *Stay here and search the house.* In a moment, Malik's car pulled away. She looked back at Jenny standing at the door. It was odd, she thought. No alarm, no concern and no surprise.

Triumph

Can we talk? Bina Malik asked Crossley from the doorway.

Of course, come in. I hear that congratulations are in order. He nearly smiled at her but she had papers in her hand and was not looking at him.

What for? We were too late to stop the husband being slaughtered. She laid the newspapers on his desk. *Seen these?*

The first headline read, 'SLAUGHTER HOUSE'. The second began, 'KNIFE HORROR'. Another, 'BUTCHERED!', accompanied by a grey picture of a young man in a police car, subtitled 'Butcher'. Crossley picked up the story in the first paragraph of one of the papers. Bina was the hero, preventing Angela Tanner from slaughter by her son, Timothy, who had already murdered and disembowelled her partner. Crossley scanned down the column and picked out words and phrases: Charles Manson, drug-fuelled, sex orgies, incest, satanic rituals, psychopaths. It went on. All the papers were the same. It was familiar salacious hysteria.

He looked at Bina. She was restless. *I take it this is not quite what happened?*

You could be forgiven for believing some of it. She dropped the crime scene photos in front of him, too quickly for him to decline seeing them. A glimpse was enough to understand, but he did not need to see it for himself. He gathered them into a pile and turned them over. For a moment he was angry with her, but Bina was too young to know that these images would erode the soul and cause her faith and trust in all things to crumble. He hoped she would discover this before it was too late for her.

These tell a convincing story, said Crossley. *Have you got the murder weapon?*

Yep. Tanner had it in his hand when we came through the door.

It does rather put him in the frame. What's bothering you?

It was Timothy Tanner who called the ambulance to save his mother!

What about the man?

We haven't got the pathology report yet, but – Malik hesitated *– he was cold. And the blood on the back of the body was old. It had dried. The blood was wet where the body had been opened up, and it trailed into the living room where Timothy was with his mother.*

He could have killed the man, and gutted him later. He shuddered with the brutality of the image.

That might be possible.

Crossley saw the doubt and released it. *But you don't think so.*

There was no dried blood on Timothy. He was wet with it. But there's something else. He hadn't been there very long.

How do you know that?

He was at Jenny's house until after nine, then she showed him how to get there by bus. It doesn't add up. He couldn't have been there at the time of death.

Is it possible that he went to the house the previous day, and came back in the morning?

Malik replied, *Possible, but why would Jenny show him how to get there in the morning, if he had already been there the previous day? Doesn't seem likely.*

Crossley was quiet. His younger colleague had thought this through. He knew what had to be done, but there was a protocol to follow. *It's your investigation. How do you want to play it?*

One thing more. When we were at Jenny's house and we heard that Timothy had called for an ambulance, she didn't seem surprised. She didn't seem troubled by an ambulance going to her mother's house. There was nothing, just blank. I thought it was odd. There is something going on there.

Is there anything I can do?

I need your help. You know Jenny. She needs to be interviewed and we have to get to the bottom of what she knows. Would you mind stepping in? I'll take Timothy and the mother when we get the all-clear from the hospital. There are a few other things we're waiting on. When I get them I can brief you and we can plan the interviews.

Sounds good.

Malik stood. *Thanks, Charles. I owe you.*

Yes, you do. Oh… and take these pictures with you.

Jenny: Interview III

Crossley stopped outside the door of the interview room. Thinking through the interview plan caused him to doubt everything. The scene at Angela Tanner's house was enough to cause a normal person to question all they believed and it had unsettled him. Only years of experience had disguised his revulsion. Now he wondered if there were things that were beyond him in this case. A few feet from a disembowelled corpse, Tad had sat with his mother, both smeared in blood, talking to her like a hospital visitor. It caused just a moment of unfamiliar doubt. He tried to clear his mind of the image, reminding himself that Jenny might know nothing of this. The last thing he wanted was for her to collapse again.

Inside the room, Jenny waited in silence with the uniformed officer. She tried to order her thoughts, but a strategy had not formed. She had done nothing wrong, so perhaps she did not need a plan to manage this. The door opened. Crossley entered and sat down.

Thank you for coming in, Jenny. Crossley pulled his chair closer to the table and, turning to the uniformed officer, asked, *Has she been cautioned and advised that this interview is being recorded?*

The uniform nodded. *Yes, Sir.*

Do I need a solicitor? asked Jenny.

Do you need a solicitor? asked Crossley.

No. I don't think I do, she said. *What's happened?*

Crossley looked at her carefully. *You already know that earlier today we received an emergency call from your brother, Tad, asking for an ambulance to attend your mother's house.* Jenny nodded. *This happened while our officers were on our way to your house, to where Tad had been bailed, to execute a warrant for his arrest.*

I know. Jenny was subdued. *They were at my door when they got a call to go to my mother's house. Why were you trying to arrest him? What had he done?*

Crossley allowed the deviation, knowing it would unsettle her. *We have suspected Tad of being responsible for breaking in to a number of houses locally. From one of these houses he may have taken an army knife and it seems he used that knife in an armed robbery, or attempted murder, or both.*

Jenny protested, *He told me about this, but he was released from the hospital and the solicitor said there was no evidence to convict him.*

Well, that was certainly true a few days ago, said Crossley, *but evidence has now become available. Tad has been arrested and charged with a number of offences. You don't seem too surprised.*

Well, said Jenny, *I haven't seen him for many years, but I've been learning about his life since we were separated. It hasn't been easy for him. He has been very damaged.*

What do you mean?

It has always been hard for him and now he has some kind of infection in the brain. They found it while he was in hospital, and he's about to start treatment for it. It was enough.

Crossley reeled at the prospect of bringing a case like this to court. A procession of experts in psychiatry, psychology, neurology and God knew what else would troop back and forth to the prison to examine him, and then into the witness stand, for the prosecution and the defence. The effort would take the case over several years, and the cost would be truly fabulous.

You haven't said what's happened, Jenny said.

Crossley collected his thoughts and started, *At your mother's house we found a body.* He looked at Jenny. No surprise. He waited.

I guess it was just a matter of time, said Jenny. *She has been an alcoholic and depressed for years. This is the third or fourth overdose. It was bound to happen sooner or later.*

Your mother is fine. Tad's call was soon enough to save her. She's in hospital now but it seems she's making a recovery. Crossley noted the surprise, or was it relief? Her brow clenched on her forehead.

Whose body did you find? Jenny's hand came to her mouth.

You know your mother's partner, don't you? Crossley could see she had already worked out the identity of the victim. *It was Richard's body. I'm sorry if this has come as a shock to you. Do you need some water, or some time to absorb all this?*

She shook her head. *I'll be fine. It was just a surprise. I'm fine. How did he die?*

Crossley let a moment pass. *Jenny, how did you know your mother had taken an overdose?*

I just assumed it was her, when there was an ambulance involved.

I was surprised that you did not seem shocked or troubled at all. Don't you think it would be normal for a daughter to be concerned if she thought her mother might die of an overdose?

Jenny felt the pressure rising and composed herself. *Inspector, you already have worked out that there's nothing 'normal' about my family.* She looked at Crossley as if she was naked, daring him to allow his glance to slip from eye contact.

It does seem unusual, said Crossley, plainly. *Let me ask – when were you last at your mother's house?*

How did Richard die?

Just answer my question and we can get to that later.

I was there yesterday, in the afternoon.

What time exactly?

I got there about four o'clock and left before five.

Are you sure of that? Crossley asked.

Well, yes. I sat with my mother, made sure she had what she needed, and left before Richard arrived, and in time to get home before Mark.

And when did you get home?

It takes about half an hour by bus and I was home about half past five.

Who was there?

Tad was watching the television and Mark arrived not long after me.

Did anyone leave the house that night? asked Crossley.

No. No one.

What about Tad?

No. I'm sure he didn't. Crossley allowed the pause to grow. *We have talked and talked each night since getting together. He was with us the whole evening. We ate together and watched some TV.*

Could Tad have left the house that night, after you had gone to bed, and visited your mother's house?

Crossley saw the suspicion on Jenny's face. She said, *It would be possible to leave the house, but Tad didn't know where Mum lived or how to get there until I put him on the bus this morning. He doesn't have any money either. He couldn't get there on his own.*

The problem we have is this, Jenny. Her brow furrowed. *Death had occurred, we think, about 18 hours before we were on the scene. That means you may or may not have left the house before it occurred. If what you say is right, first that you did leave the house before Richard came home, and second that Tad did not get to the house until the following morning, which means he arrived too late to be the murderer, it only leaves one person in the house who could have done it.* Crossley waited for the logic to sink in. *How was your mother when you left her?*

She had been drinking before I arrived. I expected her to drink more when I left, as she always does. He stayed quiet and allowed her to continue. *We'd argued. About Tad. I'd always believed Tad had been taken from her, because she couldn't cope, but she gave him up. Gave him up, so that Richard would stay. I was angry with her for it and told her so. I guess I knew something like this might happen, but I never thought it would.*

Crossley acknowledged the candour with the slightest nod. *So, you left in anger, which would explain why you left your coat in the hallway. The other issue, you should know, is Richard was not just dead*, he continued, *he had been stabbed to death but also completely opened up, the entrails were on the floor.*

She flinched at the image and asked, *Has my mother said anything?*

We are waiting. She isn't well enough to be interviewed.

What about Tad? she asked.

Crossley smiled at her. *I can't say anything about that, but he remains suspicious of authority. I expect you would anticipate that. But I think you might help us to understand the background to what's happened. Can you help?*

Crossley looked like a serious man, but she could see something worn and frail about him now that she looked. She imagined he had seen terrible things and listened to terrible stories. The toll was written in his grey eyes and skin. Jenny said, *I'd better tell you about things from the beginning.*

Crossley listened to Jenny's story, moving only to encourage her. Much of it, he knew from the many stories he and every law enforcement officer had encountered. Everyone has a story, they would say. None are innocent because of them. Broken homes, abusive parents, a life in the care of the authorities, more abuse, poverty and disadvantage; none of it mattered at the moment the decision was made to cross a line between right and wrong. Every part of the crossing was accountable to that one, and only that one person. Too many on the front line of justice believed it was the only way sanity could be retained. This dumb clarity was the only way it could work for the righteous holders of keys and enforcers of laws. Not everyone was like that, but even Crossley avoided thinking about the complexity, until someone like Jenny made it inescapable. Still, there was a job to do.

It was the easiest way to deal with being abused. Jenny's voice came through his thoughts. *I just stopped it being 'abuse' and made it something else.* His gaze had never left her. *I became his partner. None of this was clear to me at the time. I was 13, 14 years old, but looking back and remembering how I felt, I was pleased to be the preferred one. It felt good.*

What about Tad? Crossley asked.

We were both used to Mum's boyfriends coming and going, but Richard was different. He really settled in. He took over, really. We had to be quiet when he was in the house and I think he was rough with Tad. I don't think either of us were really welcome. It was like we were living in their house. I found a way, but Tad never did. He was just on his own.

Crossley needed the conversation to flow. *And your mother?*

I blamed her, of course. She was always responsible for what I was doing. I hated her for letting me be raped. She was there sometimes, holding me. Talking to me. Keeping me quiet. Can you see? Letting him just do it, even inviting him to do it, was so much better. She was quiet for a moment. Crossley waited. *She was so afraid that she would be alone if he left her. She couldn't live with being alone, so I kept him in the house. It was pathetic, listening to her begging him to stay. I couldn't stand it, so I made him happy. I knew how to make him happy. But I made her pay for it. I did what I wanted, controlled everything. And I stayed between them all this time. Mum started drinking and never really stopped. It meant she was no competition at all. Then she got depressed and started taking medication and going to therapy. She was finished then.* Jenny smiled ruefully. *Providing she could still cook for him and I kept him happy, he stayed.*

Jenny, Crossley began, *you still haven't told me why you believed your mother had taken an overdose?*

Didn't you say she was in hospital recovering from an overdose? asked Jenny.

No, I didn't. You said that she had taken an overdose. I didn't mention what she was recovering from.

When I left the house, said Jenny, *she was drinking vodka, and her medication was on the table beside her. It was obvious what was going to happen.*

But you said earlier that you didn't think anything would happen. Now you're saying it's obvious that it would. Which is it?

I don't know how to answer you. Jenny knew a trap was shutting and had not seen it being set.

Crossley leaned on the table for the first time, closing the distance between them. *Let me help you, Jenny. Was your mother drinking when you arrived at her house, at around four o'clock?*

Yes. I think she had been drinking, said Jenny. *There was a bottle of vodka open on the kitchen counter.*

How did the vodka arrive at the table beside your mother's chair, if it was on the kitchen counter to start with?

I made her some tea, and then later I brought her the vodka. It sounded ridiculous.

His voice became steady, nearly menacing. *Jenny, you had better tell me now, are we going to find traces of your mother's medication in her tea, or in the vodka she was drinking?*

No! Of course not.

So – Crossley leaned back – *she took the pills herself.*

Yes, she must have.

Did you bring those to her too?

Yes… it was out before she could stop it – *but she asked for them.* Jenny's voice appealed to some mitigation, also ridiculous.

Crossley continued, *Jenny, this is not a good picture. You arrive at your mother's house, already angry with her, and find that she has been drinking. You know she's depressed, alcoholic and capable of suicide. You have an argument with her, give her a piece of your mind and provide her with more alcohol and enough medication to kill her several times over. Then you leave, thinking that the outcome is 'obvious'.*

It wasn't 'obvious'.

That is what you said.

I didn't mean to say that. She felt the panic rising. *It was the obvious thing to think when you mentioned the ambulance. I just knew that it was possible, but I was so angry with her that I left without thinking. I never told her to take the medication, and I didn't see her take any.*

That's a curious thing to say, I hadn't asked if you had seen her take the medication. Why would you say such a thing?

I don't know.

Unless, you had watched your mother take the medication, and did nothing to stop her.

No, I didn't watch her take any medication. I was just trying to be sure you understood properly.

Jenny, what you describe as neglect of your mother's safety, because you were angry with her, sounds very much like you intended that she kill herself.

No, that's not right.

But it is right, isn't it, that you neglected your mother's safety?

No it's not! I'm not responsible for my mother!

Yes, you are Jenny, Crossley said patiently. She looked at him fiercely and Crossley knew the outrage rising within her. She was thinking that she could not be responsible for the mother who neglected her. *We are all responsible for what we do, and what we fail to do, especially when a vulnerable person is put at risk.*

Jenny said, *Richard was coming back from work, so she wouldn't have been alone for long.* It sounded lame, but it was all she had.

Did you know when he would come home?

Not exactly.

In which case, said Crossley, *it's not neglect, it's attempted murder.*

Crossley could see the weight of his words fall upon her. Her shoulders sagged. The colourful rage that had flickered up her neck a moment before ebbed to grey.

When did Richard come back to the house? he asked.

Jenny took a large breath. *I told you that I left before he got home, so I don't know when he actually got back.*

That's what you said, Crossley said deliberately, *but you have said some things that are not completely true, haven't you?*

I've tried to tell you the truth, said Jenny.

No, you haven't, Jenny. You told me that no one left the house that night, but it isn't true, is it? Mark went to the cinema. We know that because we are speaking to him right now, and we are speaking to Tad. Their stories are not like yours, Jenny. It makes me think you're trying to cover up the fact that Mark left the house last night. Did he really go the cinema or did you agree with him to finally take revenge on Richard? He has good reason to be unhappy and want to kill your lover, his rival, hasn't he?

No, it wasn't Mark. He couldn't possibly harm someone. There will be CCTV, or you'll find his ticket for the cinema. Something. It just wasn't him!

Well, said Crossley, we will see. If that's true and Mark did go to the cinema, there's another scenario to be considered. Jenny waited. You had plenty of time to get to your mother's house and then go home, without Mark ever knowing.

Jenny asked, Do you think I am capable of doing that to Richard? Of stabbing him to death and cutting him open?

Here are the facts, Jenny. Crossley sat upright and spoke evenly. I know you're capable of violence. In the hospital, you injured four nurses, two seriously. You got in a fracas with someone at your family doctor's office. We know that you have stabbed a man in the neck with a ball-point pen, and later accused the same man of having raped you. Today you have told me that you were present at or near the time a man, who had raped you when you were a child, was found dead of stab wounds. If that isn't sufficient to raise doubts about you, over a period of nearly twenty two years you have knowingly and deliberately tormented your own mother by carrying on with her partner for the whole of that time. She might have deserved that and no law was being broken, but then you became angry with her, plied her with drugs and alcohol in the expectation that she would take her own life. She did not deserve that, and laws were probably being broken. So, I think you're capable of stabbing and killing a man, Jenny. I think you and Tad went to the house with the intention of causing the death of your mother, then waited for Richard to come home and stabbed him to death. In the morning, Tad had second thoughts about his mother and went back to the house, found his mother still alive and saved her. The only question I have is, why now? What is it about this time that caused you to act now?

Jenny felt the sense of relief that accompanies the end of a long struggle lost; of having staved off the inevitable; of giving up resistance to the mauling beast consuming you. She was at the opening of the safe warm space that insulated her from the world, but could not fall. She could not rest with her insides rotting, and there was something about those words Crossley had used earlier that stopped her descending into the comfort. That Richard had been 'opened up' had stayed with her. All that had been contained was now uncontained. What had been fixed in place was now adrift. He was gone and with it went the bond of knowing and sharing between abuser and abused. Her place with Richard had gone and the righteous anvil on which she held her mother to account had been shattered by Crossley. She had been spilled with the opening of Richard and was without place or purpose.

Jenny, said Crossley, *why now?*

She could do something good, if she was able to gather her wits. There was a chance to pull Tad from the fire and leave Mark out of it. They both deserved that. Angela had been punished enough, maybe too much. She had at least killed the monster and should not be punished for doing what he deserved. All that was needed was for Jenny to finish the story Crossley had started. There is a little goodness in that.

Tad had nothing to do with it. It was me. A small mechanical noise emerged from the recorder. The silence waited for Jenny. *It's because I wanted a baby. I hadn't realised until I went for tests to see why I couldn't conceive that I was infected with syphilis years ago by Richard. It goes away, you know.* Her voice softened. *At least it pretends to go away.* Crossley listened intently. *You don't know you have it, but it rots you away inside. I've been rotting since I was 13. There's no real chance of me having children according to the specialist. You won't have seen those results. I've only just got them myself. My mother knew I had it. She was infected herself. She got treatment and let me rot. Let us both rot.*

Crossley rolled his head from one side to the other. *You said 'both'. Is the infection you have the same the infection Tad has?* Jenny nodded. *You're nodding 'yes'. So he abused both of you.* It never hurt to remind a suspect of the extent to which the victim of their crime had harmed them. Jenny locked her gaze with Crossley, who could see something change. *Jenny? Is that right?*

Jenny spoke quietly. *Yes.* It was not a lie, Jenny thought, but Crossley could not know this truth. She could not face him any more and turned away. There was nothing that would happen to her that was undeserved. She could never be part of the world again. Her head bowed as tears of sadness and relief came.

The confession was clear, thought Crossley. She had motive, opportunity, a history of violence and initially she had lied to disguise her actions. It was a slamdunk. He would have to go over it again and pick up the details, but to keep going now would open the possibility of Jenny offering a confession under duress, or someone arguing that on her behalf when it got to court.

He waited a minute for her to compose herself and allowed her story to sink through the layers of procedures and processes police officers use to insulate themselves from the tragedy of someone like Jenny, whose life would now be wasted. She sat in the chair opposite him looking older. It was a glimpse of what years of prison would do to her.

What happens now? Jenny lifted her head.

Crossley's voice had changed. He spoke to her as if they had shared a great trauma and he was now comforting her. *You need some rest and something to eat. I'm going to terminate the interview now. There are still enquiries for us to make, and reports from the pathologist to gather. If we have not laid charges against you by tomorrow, we'll be applying to the court for an extension of your custody. We will have to take you to court for that.* Jenny nodded but was not listening; it was too much to take in… *and have a solicitor advise you before the next interview.* She wondered who would tell Mark and what he would think of her. *Interview terminated at…*

Angela's Bed

Angela waited for the police to arrive. The overdose had been complicated by all those physical complaints developed from years of being overweight, and the constant flow of alcohol. It had caused her to have a few extra days in hospital, for which she was grateful. It kept at bay the challenges and questions she was about to face. People would know about her and think her to blame for the terrible things that had happened. Sitting up in her bed she could see out of the window and across the town.

She had always thought that she knew about men, but now she was not so certain. The relationships of her life tumbled through the memory. The short, the occasional and the violent were all familiar to her, and then there was Richard. At this moment they lay cold and exposed in her memory. Her skin reddened with every recollection, but she did not care who might see. Men had promised commitment, scoffed at the idea, and sometimes been considerate. She had accepted that sex was often discourteous, sometimes brutal and other times hardly noticeable. It was the medium of exchange, a currency, and had to be used. It had the power to attract, to relieve the agitated and to quiet the turmoil of troubled men. That was all they needed or cared about, it seemed. All that was worthy of fury and rampage was soothed in a moment.

Angela thought her willingness to be generous or kind to the troubled souls who ventured into her life was her contribution to the relationship. It was what she could bring. So many harsh words, final ultimatums and door-slamming departures had been avoided with a few salacious moments. Now she understood that it was all she could bring.

She remembered the angry words with Jenny, and her stinging cruelty. Tad was on her mind. Her little boy, who fought with his sister and played happily on his own for hours and hours. She closed her eyes at the memory of Richard fighting for breath on the stairs

301

and scrambling to find the knife in his back. It had not been fair on her children, or on her. She thought there must be some understanding of her for what had happened.

There were voices in the hallway and footsteps getting louder. The police were coming, but what was she to say?

Acceptance

Jenny let the morning quiet of the police cell comfort her. Outside there were movements but nothing threatened. Breakfast on a cardboard tray offered toast and tea. She had already set her mind to the life inside. Ask for little, expect nothing and never draw attention to yourself, unless there was purpose in that. It would be like that for a long time. There would be no children, so they would not be missed. Her family was gone, one way or another, so there would be no birthdays or anniversaries to celebrate. Mark would be better off with someone who could love him back. There would be times when she would miss a glass of wine or clothes, but she would get used to that and eventually forget. Mostly, she realised, she needed to be inside. It was not safe for her to be out and it felt safe to be in. There was so much shame inside prison that hers would hardly be noticed. It was only Tad that would suffer unfairly from being abandoned again. Whatever he had done, he was not really to blame.

She wondered if she should have told Crossley the truth she held from him. It was a truth that was nearly lost in her memory until she had learned of Tad's infection, and then misleading Crossley made it a truth that could not be evaded. He had seen it but had not known what it meant.

Those times as children, of comforting each other in the same bed, had never intended this. The comfort had transported both of them outside of their life at home, easing Tad's fear and separation from their mother. For Jenny, it was a way of caring, connecting and soothing Tad, but it also gave her something good, something normal. Angela could not provide it with Richard in the house, so there was something important she could do.

That it had gone further than it should have and continued for the years before she was taken away was the last truth. Even now, after all that had happened, it could not be understood, not by her and certainly not by others. She hoped Tad had forgotten the touching and the rubbing or recalled it only as a game they sometimes played. Her eyes closed in the hope the image would leave her. It had not always been a game for her. She had known what she had done. It was why she had never looked for him. It was why she had hesitated to have him in her house or to meet Mark. All that had come from it sickened her. His loss of sight could not have been anticipated, but it was blame that she held. It was only her that could be responsible; she had carried the infection to his bed. There was no one else to be responsible, no matter how complicated the cause.

In a moment, she thought, the uniformed officer would open the cell door and escort her to the interview room. Her solicitor would be waiting. She hoped it would go quickly. The process needed to be over so she could get it out of her consciousness and settle into her time inside. She had learned something from her week in hospital. Footsteps approached the door and the jangle of keys announced the arrival of several people at the cell. The inspection hatch opened and eyes glared in.

Stand back from the door, they commanded.

Jenny stepped back as the lock crashed open and the door swung. Crossley stepped into the cell.

Sit down, Jenny, he said. Jenny sat on the bed. He sat on the stool. Crossley looked at the young uniformed officer and nodded him away. Jenny noticed the door of the cell wide open and looked to Crossley as if asking.

Your mother, he started, *has confessed to the murder of Richard.*

It can't be. It was me.

No, Jenny. He stopped her. *It was not you. Your mother did it. She described what she did and it fits. There was no evidence of blood on you or in your house. We looked everywhere, even on the bus you travelled back on. Nothing. You were not involved in the murder.* Jenny sagged with the idea. *I should be charging you with wasting police time, but I think we might overlook that on this occasion.*

What about the other charge? she asked. *The overdose. Neglecting my mother. You said it was attempted murder.*

It was not for him to understand why Jenny was seeking to be blamed, but it was always remarkable to see the desperation for it to be true. *Your mother wouldn't confirm anything about that. In fact, she said you had nothing to do with her taking the overdose; not even bringing her the alcohol or medication.*

Jenny rallied. *Why would she say that? It isn't true. I told her she should do it!*

Another 'white lie', Jenny? asked Crossley.

There was one last chance. *Will you charge me with assault?* Jenny could see it did not register with Crossley. *The man I stabbed. When I was raped.*

We would not charge you if it was self-defence. Crossley waited long enough for her hope to recede. *Shall we charge him with rape? Would you like us to proceed with that charge? We will if you wish. The case is still open.*

She looked away, understanding that it was hopeless. There would be no escape from living in the world. There would be no hidden repentance in prison. Her mother would disappear while she was left holding everything. *No. Don't do that,* she said.

Crossley explained, *He's said that if the matter is dropped, he doesn't want to proceed with the assault charge against you. He wants the whole thing to go away. I expect you do too.*

Anyway, you need to get your things together. He stood. *Apparently, Mark is coming to collect you.* Jenny had hoped to put off talking to Mark for some time. He could see the prospect worried her. *Look, I made it sound like Mark was giving you up, when we questioned you about the other matter. It's not true. He never believed it was you. I made more of what he said than he ever intended. It's what we do.*

Doesn't it make you feel guilty? asked Jenny.

We are all guilty of something, Jenny, said Crossley. *You have to come to terms with what you do, and make good in the real world, what-*

ever you or others have done. You're not the first to hide away in prison, pretending that you're 'serving a sentence', when really you're avoiding having to live out there. Take the chance, Jenny. Take it.

Jenny watched for Mark through the glass doors of the police station, standing up to the cold blasts of air as they opened and closed. The steady stream of people in uniform and uncertain civilians coming to the counter and then leaving took no notice of her. She recalled her own question to Crossley about why her mother would say that she had nothing to do with the overdose. Why would Angela save her from prison, after all that had happened?

Mark's car arrived on the street outside the police station. She was not looking forward to seeing him, but he had come when needed and the talk about their future might not be necessary for a few days. It would have to be different between them. She would have to be different. There could never be a hidden life again. She would have to find the strength to stay connected. Perhaps that was what Crossley meant when he said, '*Take the chance*'. A fresh blast arrived with a pair of officers marching in. She took a breath of the cold air and stepped out.

Epilogue

Outside the office, on the landing, the noise level had fallen from the morning cacophony of breakfast to the usual hubbub of 50 men finding things to do. On landings above, the noise had also settled. Just the occasional shout or clang of metal emerged from the fog of noise. Soon the line-up outside the office door would grow. The usual customers would hover around until eight o'clock and then move quickly to be first in the queue. Among them were those complaining, wanting their cell-mate to be moved, others would want permission for something, or would make submissions to see the governor, prison visitors, chaplain or doctor. No one who had regular chats with prison officers was trusted on the landing. It was the same in the children's homes. The fact was that no one on the landing was trusted by anyone. Every contact with the officers was an opportunity for them to find out something about you or what was going on in the under-life of the landing. They were sometimes clumsy in this, occasionally obvious in their intention when they would bargain a favour to you for a favour to them. Every contact was a negotiation and every contact you were seen to have added distance between you and fellow inmates, until your isolation was complete, and you became nothing but an opportunity for your peers.

Tad knew to stay away from them, as he knew to keep away from those inmates who dominated life outside the office, but it was not always possible.

What's all this in the fucking paper about you being 'The Butcher'? A London voice from the landing above scoffed at Tad as he made his way to his cell. *Fuckin' good headline, Tanner, but ya' don't look like a fucking 'Butcher' to me.*

More like the butcher's dog, came another voice. Raucous laughter flew up and down the landings through the suicide mesh between the floors. Faces looked over the rails to see what was going on.

The London voice continued, *It says here in my paper that you've been fuckin' your own mum, and she gave you the fuckin' pox. Is that right? Fuck me, no wonder you took a knife to her.* There was chuckling all around. *That's fucking terrible. Mind you, I hope you finished off first. No point in wasting an opportunity, is there?* Laughter erupted.

Don't run, Tad told himself, and he tried to keep walking, but no one moved out of his way. He recalled escaping from the playground with laughter following. There would be no escape here.

Fuckin' butcher's dog. That's a good 'un.

He'll get plenty of bone in here.

Specially down there on the Rule.

All right, said the officer. *You've had your fun.* A huge man in white shirt and black trousers arrived beside Tad, looking up through the mesh. *That's enough.* He looked at Tad. *Let's get you to your pad.*

A few paces on and the large officer turned to Tad. *This is standard. Don't show you're upset and don't respond. In a few days it will go away, but only if you let it go away and don't give them anything to feed on. If you think you're going to get upset, get to your pad straight away and don't let them see it. Otherwise, it'll be miserable. We can protect you on Rule 43, but it's not perfect. Understand?* Tad nodded without understanding anything. His head swam. *Right,* said the officer, looking up and down the landing, *stay in your pad this morning. I'll check on you later.*

Tad turned into his cell and headed for his cot. A voice from the door turned him round.

It is you. Darryl grinned at him from across the landing. *When did you get here?*

Tad could not think but to answer. *This morning.*

You're in the papers. You're famous. Not bad for a little fucker.

From down the landing the large officer shouted, *Get back in your cell.*

I know 'im. We're friends, Sir.

Get away from him.

Darryl moved into the shallow recess of his cell. *See ya later.* Smile.

Tad fell onto the cot and curled into a ball. Eight years; it was a long time. How would he live here for eight years? The laughing outside echoed still. The muse chimed, *You idiot. Fucking little idiot. What did you do to your mum? Fucking little pervert. Should've done her with the knife.* They did not know what really happened. They would never know, even if it meant they believed what they wanted to believe. Only Jenny knew. It would always be their secret.

Acknowledgements

Bowen Island, British Columbia, has been an inspiration and an endless source of support. The people and the place have a magical quality without which I would have relied even more heavily on my wife, Kate. I cannot say enough about the knowledge, wisdom and encouragement she has provided me with in this project, as in so much else. This book is dedicated to her in recognition of that, but also her enduring commitment to the care and protection of children, both professionally and personally. *The Last Truth* is really about children at risk and what has been missed and denied in their care. To work successfully in this arena requires strength, integrity, sensitivity, deep knowledge and a rare quality of judgement. Those who have it, like Kate, should sit at the pinnacle of professional ladders, receive the reverence of everyone working in public service and the respect of the wider community. Instead they endure a precarious professional life, overburdened by case-work, underpaid, frequently unsupported by managers and hung out for public shaming on the rare occasions that things go wrong. People like Kate are infrequently heralded as they deserve to be. I hope it is not always so.

Others have been notable for their support by reading and commenting on all or part of the manuscript in its many stages. At the top of the list is my daughter, Hannah, followed by friends Brean Hammond, Jacqueline Massey, Allard Ockeleon, Judy Gedye, Tina Nielsen, Adam Morton, Manuela Costantino, Anna Hall, Sarah Casorso, Judy Christensen and Sandra James. My gratitude and appreciation barely cover it.

Patrons List

Megs Barnes
Jacqui Barrett
Sue Bethray
Matthew Borghese
Deb Bourne
Roger Campbell
Ray Chapman
Kevin Commerford
Sandy Constable
Manuela Costantino
Carol Cram
V Crawford
Jacqui Crosby
Jessica Cruz
Rupert Davies
Monica Freeman
Tanya Garrett
Lucy Goodbrand
Kris Gustavson
Barbara Hand Clow
Elizabeth Handslip
Heidi Hansen
Dr. Bruce Hardy
Rhian Holland
Marnie Huckvale
Sarah Jay
Tuija Juusti-Butler
Bruce Kanik
Nancy Kilpatrick
Heidi Kuhrt
Catherine Lawrence

Etty Martin
Jacqueline Massey
Kent Matthews
Claire Michelet
Guy Mitchell
Sarah Musgrave
Doug Nickel
Gayle O'Connor
Katherine O'Connor
Sally Rowe
Duane Seibel
Sarah Shanahan
Martin Silk
Susan Thomas-Peter
Tanya Uniacke
John Verver
Yvette Walsh
Jenny West
Bryan Yu